The Bodge Job

Max Alexander

The Bodge Job

Max Alexander

"O God of Cathay! By what death shall these die—these miserable ones who would bind thine Empire, which is boundless!"

—The Insidious Dr. Fu-Manchu

Concerns
The First Part

CHAPTER ONE

Yun Jian felt it was a good day to make an arrest. That morning in the courtyard car park of the police station, Jian's superior at the Ministry of Security, the sub-chief Fang Dazhu, had rearranged a potted papaya tended by his wife in such a way as to align it more perfectly with the main entrance of the station and a public gate leading to the ivory carving workshop across the street. In truth the sub-chief regarded *fēngshui* as pointless and possibly subversive; he was only trying to make room in the courtyard for his new Buick. But Jian understood the realignment of the papaya as holding significance for the day, if not the entire Chinese New Year, which had begun last week with the detonation of so many firecrackers that Jian's ears were still ringing. Jian hated firecrackers, which had scared, and scarred, him since he was a boy and a string with a short fuse went off accidentally in his hands, causing him to black out and get a beating (on general principle) from his father. To this day, sudden noises made him jumpy, and in fact had contributed to the trouble the night before, which he suspected was unfinished and hung over his future like a wet dog.

Jian rolled down the window of his Ford cruiser, which was almost new but already reeked of tobacco and body odor, pushed a finger against the side of his nose and voided a skein of yellow snot along the edge of the road. The gob landed on the back of a small green gecko which (to Jian's surprise) ignored the offensive, as if it were nothing more than a raindrop, and continued sunning on the tarmac. Jian hated taking orders from Fang Dazhu, a dark-skinned ethnic Zhuang who drank too much and could not speak proper Mandarin, and he felt he could someday be the local sub-chief himself if only he resigned himself to a desk job. Police leaders always came from the desk pool because they had the most interaction with the local party leaders. But Jian hated desk work even more than he hated the sub-chief, because it was so pointless. In China the police performed two main functions: maintaining public safety—in that regard much like police in the West—and managing the residency permits called *hùkǒus*, which determined who was allowed to live in cities and who was required to stay in the countryside. Since virtually all Chinese people of working age wanted to move to the cities where they could earn more money in factories and meet more socially mobile spouses, no one in all China was applying for a *hùkǒu* to enter remote Guangxi Autonomous Region, where the main industries were still rice and tea growing, along with certain cottage industries that Jian understood to be vaguely illegal but permissible, such as ivory carving and manufacturing fake-old tea-stained Little Red Books to sell to tourists as Cultural Revolution relics. In fact, the opposite was true: Anyone who could leave Guangxi had already left or was leaving. Certainly no one was sneaking in, not even Vietnamese across the long mountainous border except to smuggle in elephant tusks and then return. As far as law enforcement was concerned, there was nothing to enforce when it came to *hùkǒus* in Guangxi.

If only Jian could arrest ivory smugglers. That would be exciting, he thought, not to mention remunerative as some of the contraband would almost certainly be "lost" and could then be re-sold by the police. But the smugglers were off-limits. The only other people who came to Guangxi Region were tourists, both foreigners and rich Chinese from cities, and they were mostly off limits as well, unless they got too drunk. The tourists came to admire the karst mountain scenery, which (Jian had been told ever since he was a boy) was unique in all the world. Karst is eroded limestone, soft and yielding to water, and over millions of years the swollen rivers in Guangxi cut through and around the limestone, leaving seventy thousand vertiginous forested peaks like jade thumbs, riven with caves hundreds of meters deep. Jian had never been anyplace else and thus had no firsthand experience of a world without karst peaks, but he knew they must be special because they were on the back of the Chinese twenty-yuan note. Tourists from Beijing would come to the exact spot on the Li River with the view on the money, and invariably snap a photo of themselves holding up the twenty-yuan note. If you put the bill up to the sun, the image of Mao on the obverse traced through onto the landscape engraving; two of the tallest karst peaks lined up perfectly with Mao's eyes and made him look like a giant panda. The visual trick always amused Jian and his friends when they were schoolboys, not that they had many twenty-yuan notes. With no personal memory of the Great Famine or the Cultural Revolution, the Mao hagiography had, for their generation, devolved into a form of kitsch or, for those who made the souvenir Little Red Books (in English, Russian, French, Spanish, Japanese and German) with Mao's squinting visage on the cover, a career.

The sun, low in the winter sky, slid behind a peak, casting grey shards of dusk across the naked paddies. A rice farmer in a sedge hat stooped in the muck, transplanting seedlings, ignoring the flies lighting in the corners of his eyes. Planting was the most backbreaking job in the labor-intensive rice cycle. When he was a boy, at planting time Jian would take a lantern and hide from his father in the caves, dodging giant fruit bats and crawling under damp stalactites that oozed luminous blue in the flame of the oil lamp. On the outside the mountains appeared as permanent and immobile as the stone Buddha in the village temple, but inside the caves you could see that they were always changing—dripping, seeping, leaking, swelling. He imagined the karst peaks were festering boils on a giant's back, and he hoped one day they would ripen and explode, coursing rivers of putrid lava on top of his father's rice paddy, and on top of his father. As an adult he felt the mountains simply got in the way—in the way of roads, in the way of rice paddies, in the way of houses, in the way of Mao's eyes, in the way of law enforcement.

Still, the mountains brought occasional excitement. Certainly the most edifying experience in Jian's twenty-nine years was the summer when a small army of Americans descended to make a *Star Trek* movie. He was told that the movie people were filming the karst mountains as an alien planet, so there was no work for locals as extras; this distant planet understandably did not have Chinese peasants in sedge hats, although it was apparently inhabited by voluminously breasted blond women. The Americans all stayed at a very expensive hotel outside of town on the Li River—a Qing Dynasty compound of the type old people in Guangxi used to inhabit until the young people demolished them to build modern concrete-block homes, but which had in this case been restored for tourists, with a website that promoted it as "eco-friendly" even though the flush toilets in the rooms drained into the rice paddies, which guests weren't told. Jian assumed the Americans were doing a lot of drinking, but there could be no arrests.

Jian heard the scooter long before he could see it; sound waves pinged like a shuttlecock against the steep mountain walls, echoing across the paddies, and the scooter was whining at top speed. When it finally emerged around a bend in the road, just as Jian started his car, he guessed it was doing maybe a hundred clicks. It was an older style—two-tone creme and British racing green with a brown horsehide seat and a spare tire on a chrome rack that flashed in the sun. The rider was tall, and as he sped by, Jian tried to see if he was anyone important, but his face was hidden under a helmet and tinted visor. He lurched his cruiser into the road behind the scooter, lights flashing. A hundred meters later both vehicles were parked alongside the road. Jian stepped out of the Ford, adjusted his cap, spat, and approached the scooter.

"May I see your driver's license?" he asked in Mandarin, ending the sentence with the inquisitive *ma?* to indicate it was a polite question, which he instantly regretted; better to be more forceful. Jian hoped the rider did not speak only Zhuang, in which case he would have to communicate with a pen, using the crude *sawndip* characters of the Zhuang alphabet that he had been forced to learn in grade school. The Zhuang were the largest ethnic minority in China and they had certain rights, including (in Guangxi where most of them lived) the right to study in both Zhuang and Mandarin. In practice that meant even Han majority children in Guangxi had to sit through tedious *sawndip* handwriting class.

"As you asked so politely, my answer is yes," said the rider as he pulled his helmet above his head. Jian felt relieved that the man spoke perfect Mandarin, even if his insolence suggested trouble. But as the rider turned to face him Jian lost his breath. The man had dark green eyes and longish dark hair, straight like Chinese, but nothing else about him other than his Mandarin was Asian. He wore a small silver loop in his left ear, which Jian thought probably meant he was homosexual, although his face was rugged and lined from the sun like tough men in Hollywood cowboy movies. Tough yet somehow wholesome, even hygienic, in the way self-assured Westerners and even loathsome Japanese tourists could seem. Jian instinctively felt this man did not spit in public, much less void his nose. The tall man was, in fact, an American. Jian knew he was staring at the man, felt his jaw gape like a child seeing a ghost, but some impish force had lodged in his throat and blocked all speech.

The American grinned and said, in heavily accented but comprehensible Zhuang, "or we can speak local if you prefer."

Chapter Two

Nong Ning shifted in his wooden chair, displacing his considerable weight from one vast butt cheek to the other while discreetly tugging at the wedgie in his undershorts. It was already unbearably hot and humid—a bad portent for the New Year. Ning had lived his whole life under the sultry oppression of Guangxi's climate, generally in a state of physical distress. Like many large men whose hearts beat at open throttle, he seemed genetically predisposed to copious perspiration, which caused his underclothes to stick uncomfortably to the folds of skin that rippled like curtain pleats off his frame. For this reason (he told himself) and not out of laziness, he hated rice farming and was happy to have risen out of the paddies to the position of County Committee Secretary for the Party. He smiled broadly at his guest across the table, feeling certain the esteemed visitor, who was pouring his chrysanthemum tea, had not noticed the indelicate wardrobe adjustment.

His guest Hu Tianhua felt certain that his esteemed host had not noticed him noticing the indelicate wardrobe adjustment. In his undergraduate years at Southern Cal, Tianhua had absorbed all the trite Western aphorisms about how to succeed in business. *Negotiate from strength. Hire slow, fire fast. Prioritize, then delegate. Be authentic.* Blah blah blah. Americans were so earnest, cloaking their selfish greed and social Darwinism behind phony morality, as if clawing to the top in business were something to be ashamed of. Are the rug traders in the *souk* embarrassed? Isn't everything in life a negotiation? After college in California, back in the real world of China, Tianhua learned that transforming a tool-and-die shop in an alley in Guangzhou into a multi-billion-dollar manufacturing empire had boiled down not to "SMART goals" or "finding your personal North Star" or "authenticity" but to one very useful skill: peripheral vision. Over the years, countless business dinners of deer penis hotpot (thought to give men strength) had taught him to focus on the food but look sideways at the man across the table, for it is when men think you aren't looking that their true selves emerge. *A man cannot conceal himself,* Confucius said. Today he could tell Mr. Nong was physically uncomfortable, and probably mentally distressed as well. This knowledge had no specific practical utility in the moment, but Tianhua felt he gained the upper hand in any relationship just by knowing something that he wasn't supposed to know. It could be as trivial as a wedgie, but the point was he knew it, which gave him an advantage even stronger than deer penis. It was a way of being a bully without actually seeming like a bully. How very American, he thought. Irony, like table manners, amused Tianhua.

A Beijing opera stammered from speakers mounted discreetly on columns below the carved wooden *dǒugǒng* corbels, which supported a ceiling of sorghum lattice, like a floating maze above the two men. Giant red paper lanterns hung from the lintels, waiting to be lit a few minutes after twilight. Along the inside wall, in a glass case longer than a coffin, rested a massive whole ivory tusk that had been carved in characters from *Dream of the Red Chamber*, the Qing-Dynasty work of classic literature by Cao Xueqin. Carved in the center of the tusk, surrounded by the Twelve Beauties of the town of Jinling, was the main character Jia Baoyu, born with a magical jade stone in his mouth.

"A beautiful piece," said Tianhua. "Your local carvers are most accomplished."

"That is an antique," said Ning quickly, in the unlikely event his guest frowned on ivory smuggling. It was a lie he often told, and he had repeated it so often that he sometimes believed it.

Tianhua chose not to dignify the absurd claim with any further polite questions about the tusk's age and provenance; he was well aware that Chinese ivory carvers could make a brand new tusk look centuries old. Instead he said: "I recall in the novel that Jia Baoyu was quite the ladies' man. Did you know that his exploits have even been memorialized in outer space? There is a large asteroid called Eros, after the Greek god of love; on this asteroid is a crater named Baoyu."

"I did not know that," said Ning.

"Among other endearing traits, Baoyu despised the obsequious civil servants of Jinling. I have often thought that would be an excellent subject for a carving."

"No doubt," said Ning, who pretended to miss the slur, "but one lacking the soft curves of the female form, which translate so well to the ivory."

In a dusky corner, Ning's wife, Sun Ju, stood silently, hands clasped in front of her narrow waist. "Your home is truly perfect, Mr. Nong," said Tianhua, glancing sideways at Ju as if to deflect the compliment her way, then noticing in his peripheral vision that she bowed slightly and smiled. "What a relief to be out of the steaming metropolis after New Year. I can't tell you how much cooler I feel here."

The mention of temperature caused Ning's wide brow to irrigate stinging beads of sweat, which he quickly daubed with his silk napkin and which Hu Tianhua noted with satisfaction. "The country life has its advantages, Mr. Hu," Ning replied with a wan smile. Around the table were platters and bowls of carp cooked nine ways, a specialty of the region. Every part of the fish was used; even the bones were deep-fried, salted and crunched down like potato chips.

"Fresh air is not to be taken for granted these days," continued Tianhua. "One can scarcely breathe in Guangzhou." Indeed, air quality in the traffic-clogged city of 15 million redlined into the "hazardous" zone on more than half the days of the year, a condition residents mitigated by chain smoking. "And the water! Do you know that the sampans are pulling shit out of the Pearl River that—well, that's my whole point, it's *not* shit. If only it were shit; that we could deal with. But nobody knows what the hell it is! It actually glows." He did not need to add that his own factories were partly responsible for the Pepto-Bismol sky and the fluorescent water of Guangzhou. That was understood and was immaterial to the discussion.

"I gather the officials are cracking down on pollution," said Ning, relishing the opportunity to slide a sharp edge into Tianhua's weak spot. "People are angry."

"It's inevitable," said Tianhua, with a damp sadness in his voice. "But my bigger problem is lazy workers." He immediately regretted using the first-person singular; he tried always to keep himself at a remove from his business dealings. "People move to Guangzhou and they get soft. They go to discos at night. Everywhere are the bar girls. They fuck and get AIDS. Soon they want free doctors, and more money for less work. At the same time, the price of fuel is soaring. Business has become more complicated in China."

"How true," said Ning. "Every day I see the trucks loaded with lotus wood bound for your coat hanger factory on the coast. Would it not make more sense to manufacture the hangers here in Guangxi, where the lotus grows?"

"So now you are thinking like a businessman, Mr. Nong! As you see it, if I moved my factory here I would save on fuel *and* labor costs, eh?"

"I am only a public servant, but it has occurred to me..." Ning passed a plate of stir-fried carp stomach, curled pink flaps skinny dipping in a grotto of soy-vinegar sauce. "Labor is so cheap in Guangxi," he continued, "even the birds work for free. This carp was caught by cormorants in the Li River this morning. The river people train the birds to retrieve the fish, which are then pulled from their throats and cooked. Wild food—not like the fish in cement tanks in your restaurants in Guangzhou. And you can be sure our river does not glow."

"It is truly excellent, thank you. If only I could train birds to make coat hangers! China is running out of peasants."

"Not in Guangxi. And our people are very coachable. In the Zhuang culture, to make a mistake is to bring shame on one's ancestors."

"I am indeed very impressed by your people and have no doubt they would work hard," said Tianhua. "But moving factories is such a complicated business. For one thing, coat hangers are not just made of lotus wood; they have steel, which would need to be brought here. And of course, the finished hangers must be moved from here to a port, perhaps Beihai." Tianhua knew exactly which port, and it was *definitely* Beihai on the Gulf of Tonkin, not *perhaps* Beihai. He also knew precisely what he would need to pay for steel shipments, and labor costs, and bribes to the port authority, but he did not want to sound like he had researched a plan in depth, which would weaken his negotiating stance; it was important to act like moving a factory to Guangxi had barely occurred to him. "Indeed my Vietnamese competitors ship from nearby Haiphong," he continued. "I happen to know they pay less for labor but must pay more for shipping around Hainan Island. In everything is a balance, you see? Most of our customers for these hangers are Western hotel chains. Half of the hangers are stolen by guests, so the hotels are very price sensitive—and as I mentioned, they can buy from Vietnam."

Ning pinched a peanut between his chopsticks and pondered the concept of stealing coat hangers from a hotel. It would never happen in China, he thought—not because Chinese people are more ethical than Americans but because all hotel guests in China are registered with the police; you would be caught. "Americans can't afford their own hangers?" he asked.

"It's a sport," said Tianhua. "Stealing is part of the American culture. Take baseball. In China it's all about the pitcher, but in America baseball games are frequently won by stealing bases."

"Clearly you have deep knowledge of American culture," said Ning, hoping the implication that theft was more than spectator sport for Tianhua was not lost on his guest. But before Tianhua could respond, the Beijing opera sputtered silent in the middle of an improvised aria by the *wénchǒu*, or clown merchant, to the accompaniment of a dozen or more electronic beeps around the house.

"*Ju!*"

Ning's wife stood at attention.

"The motor!"

Ju skittered away like a water bug. Soon came the drone of a diesel engine, followed by the return of the *wénchǒu*'s comical lament.

Tianhua relished his good fortune. The timing could not have been more perfect if divined by geomancy. "Ahh, power failures!" he said. "Another quaint reminder of country life!" He was well aware that poor infrastructure was the main drag on industrial development in Guangxi. Until the region had reliable electricity, few factories would risk moving from the coast unless they could extract huge concessions on labor costs.

Ning felt his wedgie tighten. "Fortunately we have generators," he said weakly.

"Generators!" sniffed Tianhua. "If only I could power a twenty-thousand square meter factory with generators!" He couldn't remember a more enjoyable business lunch in many years.

"I have considered this matter carefully," said Ning. "I have a plan to bring reliable electricity to Guangxi."

"But the government is restricting coal-fired plants in rural economic zones. Will you harness the wing power of the cormorants?"

"I will dam the Li."

Tianhua's chopsticks went flaccid, dropping a carp cheek in his lap. *"Dam the Li?"*

"That's right."

"It's impossible! My good friend—I am a mere *wénchǒu*"—he paused to allow the false modesty of characterizing himself as an opera buffoon to register—"and would not presume to underestimate the influence of an esteemed Party official. But I fear the days when our government could relocate tens of thousands of people by fiat, then drown their villages, are as archaic as your opera. The people will not stand for it. You will have open revolt. When was the last time you were in Beijing?"

"Beijing is too cold for me," he lied; Beijing, with its frozen lakes in winter, in fact represented his ideal climate. "In the past our leaders came to Guangxi. Mao planted rice here for more than an hour. Deng toured a tea plantation. Of course back then they did not wear Western business suits and dye their hair black."

The last comment was vaguely subversive but he felt on firm ground with his southern guest, who in fact chuckled at the thought of his country's septuagenarian leaders and their uniforms of navy suits, red ties and tar-black pomaded hair. In the vast industrial corridor of the Pearl River Delta, home to 120 million people from Hong Kong and Macau to Shenzhen and Guangzhou, ideological purity was like God to Episcopalians: something you do for an hour on Sunday morning. Indeed, the Delta was solidly in the realm of Mammon.

"Even way out here in the countryside," Ning continued, "I am aware of our government's changing priorities. But as I said, Mr. Hu, I have a plan." He crushed a carp bone between his molars. "*Ju!* Dusk is falling; light the lanterns!"

Chapter Three

Theodore Kincaid Dean, better known by his byline T.K. Dean, was *concerned*. In his mind the word was italicized to reflect a level of concern beyond the baseline state of compulsive vigilance that had kept him mostly out of trouble in countries around the world. He had known journalists who died because they dropped their guard and made mistakes. They were not adequately *concerned*. In Fallujah, he and a photographer for Agence France Presse were embedded in a Marine squad that was trapped in a house during Operation Phantom Fury, waiting for reinforcements. The sergeant, a twenty-two-year-old second-generation Mexican-American from Battle Creek, Michigan with the intense, narrow gaze of somebody who had seen things he could never tell his wife, was relating how the purpose of boot camp was to teach recruits not to get killed by their own stupidity. After boot camp, he said, the only way to get killed was being in the wrong place at the wrong time.

"That way if you do get killed," he said, "it's not the fault of the U.S. Marines." His men laughed. "Seriously," he went on, "if any of you die in this shithole, I wanna be able to stand over your grave and say, 'He wasn't a dumb fuck, he just had dumb fucking luck.' "

The sergeant was killed a week later—dumb fucking luck. What remained of his deracinated corpse went home in a few Zip-loc bags. His wife never knew the whole story. The French photographer lasted just two days. He was shooting medium format real film for *Paris-Match* with a Hasselblad H4D-40 (limited red Ferrari edition, for which he had paid twenty-one thousand euros) and a waist-level viewfinder, which he felt gave him better eye contact with his subjects. *"Il faut regarder dans les yeux!"* But his helmet made it so hard to frame a shot in that viewfinder, he took it off. A sniper made eye contact with him, and took off his head. Dumb fuck.

Even under fire (friendly or enemy, the chances were roughly equal), T.K. was never really afraid. Just *concerned*. And right now he had a small list of things to be concerned about, starting with the police officer who had just pulled him over. Chinese cops were all corrupt but not in the same way as, say, cops in Africa, who just wanted a few francs at a roadblock to buy a Fanta or a beer. Chinese cops generally could not be bought with beer money, although alcohol itself defused almost any difficult situation in China—a welcome custom for T.K., who had used alcohol to temper his vigilance about pretty much everything since he was a teenager. For him drink functioned as a form of meditation, without all the bother of thought. Finding an entire country of people for whom strong waters flowed so effortlessly had felt like docking on a rising tide. Since the first day of his junior year abroad at Peking University he felt at home in China, knew that he would always return. He mastered classic Mandarin, starting with all the words for beverages, then learned the local dialects of Wu (spoken in Shanghai) and Xiang (also called Hunanese, the language of Mao), finally gaining conversational ability in the ethnic tongues of Gan and Zhuang.

He learned that you could get around the law against foreigners driving in China by riding scooters, so long as they were small-frames, with an engine under fifty cc. He learned how a machinist could bore out the cylinder of a small-frame scooter, re-gear the transmission and replace the carb with a fuel injector so it could go fast, and far, without anyone knowing where you were—no Buddha-faced ticket agent or conductor or clerk or driver to swipe your passport and feed you into the giant sizzling wok of the state security computer system. Just a throttle and the road and no stares, especially behind a full-face helmet. In Africa he rode motorcycles so cops, bandits and terrorists couldn't tell he was white, but there of course he needed full coverage including gloves. In China, he only had to hide his eyes. *Ne faites pas de contact avec les yeux!*

He was pretty sure at least one cop the night before had seen his eyes, but there was no moon and there were lots of cops. Today, he told himself, he was just another Western businessman in China. True, his business was journalism, and technically speaking he was supposed to have a journalism visa.

But one of the advantages of being a freelancer was that he could slip into country on a business visa and stay out of the giant wok. Not that businessmen weren't monitored, especially if they worked in a business that China wanted to dominate. But it was a matter of degrees. China reporters at the *Times* and the *Guardian* and the *Australian* were tailed, traced, tapped, taped, bugged, hacked and hassled twenty-four-seven. T.K. avoided them and their drinking haunts—the Bookworm in Beijing, Estaminet in Shanghai, the Harp in Chongqing—because if he got caught doing journalism on a business visa he would get thrown out of the country. He preferred to mind his own business, so to speak.

T.K. flipped the kill switch on the scooter, unbuckled his helmet and counted his concerns: There was the whole driving-illegally-in-China concern, the lack-of-a-journalism-visa concern, and most seriously the events of last night. A cluster by default, but no need to panic.

"May I see your driver's license?"

"As you asked so politely, my answer is yes." He pulled off his helmet, turned and saw a slight, light-skinned man with a triangular Han face and small eyes that blinked like a silent movie projector. The cop was clearly not dark enough to be Zhuang, but T.K. couldn't resist adding to his confusion: "Or if you prefer we can speak local."

"Mandarin will be fine," said Yun Jian, recovering and repeating: "Your license please."

T.K. unzipped the map pocket of his bomber jacket and withdrew a battered grey international driving permit, issued by the AAA office near Lincoln Center in Manhattan. It was exactly what Jian had expected; he'd seen these before. "That document is meaningless here," he said, hands on hips. "I need to see your Chinese license," knowing it was virtually impossible that a Westerner had one.

"I don't have one," said T.K. "I'm on a scooter. Small-frame. Fifty cc."

"Fifty cc?" repeated Jian. "You were making a hundred clicks. Are you burning jet fuel?"

T.K. laughed. "Want to give it a spin? We can trade," pointing at the Ford cruiser.

"Your passport, please."

"You're the boss." From his back pocket he fished out his fifty-page passport, which costs more if you need space for lots of visas. It was dog-eared and damp. Jian took it and thumbed delicately through the visas, examining them slowly like a rare stamp collection. Passports were not easy to get for Chinese people, and even cops treated them like medieval manuscript illuminations. T.K. looked out over the paddies. The farmer had finished bending over his plot and was turning the rusty wheel of an irrigation sluice valve. On a trail along the paddy, an old hunchbacked woman walked behind an emaciated ox, whacking his rump with a stick every few seconds.

Jian flipped back to the photo page and pretended he could read the Western letters. "Which is your last name?"

"Dean."

"Your first name?"

"Mister." He said it in English.

"Mister Dean," repeated Jian seriously.

"Bingo. But you can call me T.K. or Teddy. You're the boss."

"Please follow me to the station, Mister Dean."

T.K. laughed. He loved the whole "follow me" thing with cops in the developing world. Sometimes in Africa where the cops rarely had cars, you had to drive the cop and yourself to the station after you were arrested. And buy him a Fanta. "I hope I can get a drink there," he said.

"The sub-chief likely has beer," said Jian.

"Beer doesn't count."

"Possibly *báijiŭ*."

"I'm in. Let's go," said T.K., donning his helmet. *Báijiŭ*—"white liquor"—was China's version of white lightning: a mean, coarse 60-percent grain alcohol distilled from glutinous rice. The Chinese charmingly called it "wine" but they drank it like Russians drink vodka: small shots, uplifted and downed in toast after toast until your brain was toast. T.K.'s blood rose and his head warmed just thinking about it. The sun was now low behind the mountains, and the narrow tarmac had turned as black and formless as the water in the paddies. He switched on his headlight and spun into the road. Happy hour!

Chapter Four

Ju poured her husband's tea and sat in the chair still warm from the recent presence of Mr. Hu. In the glow of the red lanterns, Nong Ning's massive shadow flickered with improbable delicacy across the ochre walls of the courtyard. "That went well," he announced. "Did you see the look on Hu Tianhua's face when I told him I would dam the Li?"

"He was right to express shock," said Ju. "With respect, honorable husband, what sort of crazy plan is this now? So many people live along the river. Imagine the outcry."

"They will not be crying when they have good jobs in the new factories. And families to care for them when they get old. As it stands, the children all leave for the cities as soon as they are able to work."

"So you will turn the town into a city? Where will the rice come from when the paddies are paved?"

"Rice! Is that all you can think about? Rice?"

"For one who eats much rice you are perhaps too quick to dismiss it," said Ju. After thirty-one years of marriage, Ju could speak her mind to Ning—indeed he relied on it—even if custom demanded she remain subservient in public. "Ning, we are old enough to remember the famine years," she said, "but not so old as to be senile. When my parents had fed me all the bark off the trees—"

"—they boiled their shoes! I know the stories by heart! Yes! In our village they dug up corpses for dinner. My parents ate their own house, brick by brick, then took turns jabbing sticks up their asses to unplug the mud! I vowed I would never live with a stick in my rectum." In fact his semi-permanent wedgie served as a constant reminder of his parents' fate, like wearing a hair shirt.

"Besides," said Ning, "they will grow our rice in California, and we will make their coat hangers." Satisfied with the irony of his observation, he ended the discussion by belching with exaggerated drama like a schoolboy.

"What will these new factories bring for you?" pressed Ju.

"At the very least I should expect a position at the district level. A district commissioner can make a lot of money if he is allied with business interests."

"We already have a nice home and a new Audi every three years," said Ju.

"Beloved wife, the next time you are in the temple you may find it instructive to meditate on the recent history of Russia. Come the real Chinese revolution, our comfortable life here will go up in smoke faster than those joss sticks you burn at the Buddha's feet. The Party will fall like dominos, from Beijing to Guangzhou, and once the peasants think they have taken over, the real power will naturally fall to businessmen like our friend Mr. Hu, as indeed it has in Russia and America. Only those of us with business connections, not to mention flats in Hong Kong, will survive the purge."

Ju poured her husband more tea, then filled her own cup. She could never match Ning's facility for strategy; she was not "clever." But she was intuitive, more able to see the implications when her husband hatched a new plan. It was an archaic intelligence, like the knowledge, now lost, that informed her ancestors when to plant rice according to the moon phases. Ning had no conscious way to process Ju's knowledge; his own mind was like the inside of a karst mountain cave, impervious to the transit of the moon. But he instinctively grasped her value in the relationship, and he generally listened to her.

"And what will become of the swine farmers on the riverbank?" Ju asked.

"A very good question. I have given much thought to the pig people and their houseboats. Obviously they must be cleared out to build a dam, but how? Initially I viewed the problem solely from the perspective of the central Party. Those Christian farmers have been defying the family planning policy for years. Fines and even more extreme measures have been futile; I suspect they are also encouraged by Western charities. I daresay those farmers raise more children than pigs, although the distinction is admittedly fine."

Ju made a face like too-strong tea.

"Beijing would love to get them off their boats and into a community where they can be more closely monitored," Ning continued. "So I decided that more vigilant enforcement of the one-child policy would call attention to the population problem along the river and thus favor my case for a dam."

"You yourself told me the raid last night did not go well. A policeman was injured."

Ning chuckled morbidly. "The police are inept, but no matter. The point is that these efforts will not escape notice in Beijing. In fact, one could argue the injury of a policeman strengthens my case."

Like most Chinese, Ju was not particularly aggrieved by the wounding of a state security officer, but she shuddered at the callousness of her husband's comment. "It won't work," she said. "There are thousands of river people up and down the Li between here and Guilin. They will revolt."

"I considered that as well," said Ning. "Securing the support of Beijing is only the first step. There are tens of thousands of people who rely on the river; if they can be convinced it is in their interest to remove the pig farmers..."

"The virtuous will have neighbors," said Ju.

"Quoting Confucius again?"

"It is written in the Analects. The farmers bother no one."

"Ahh, but their pigs bother my nose! Have you walked along the river lately? Dog shit smells like jasmine compared to swine feces."

"It has always been so. In one end and out the other. No one cares."

"Not now, they don't." Ning raised the teapot toward Ju's cup. "But imagine if there were some sort of accident with the pigs. You know swine ailments are rampant these days."

Ju covered her cup with her hand. "This plan will come to no good, Ning. The river is sacred and must not be defiled."

"Dear wife, I beg of you to go light some incense in the temple and leave these worldly matters to me."

"Even to consider this plan requires atonement," she said. "You must release a captive creature into the wild."

Ning laughed. "Very well. Tomorrow I shall take a goldfish down to the river. Let us hope the cormorants don't catch it!"

Chapter Five

Fang Dazhu poured himself a tumbler of *báijiǔ* as the new station secretary bowed and dropped a bundle of files on his desk. He watched her walk toward the door, taking in the sway of her tiny bottom, then called her back: *"Mei!"*

She turned and bowed again. "Please do not wear denim in this office anymore. Skirts are more appropriate. Or a close-fitting dress."

"Very well, Honorable Fang." Had Dazhu been paying attention he might have caught her sullen pout as she pivoted toward the door, but he was deep in his own head. He crushed the stub of a cigarette under the toe of his black boot and wondered how many days he might wait before he could reasonably fuck her. He wondered if she was married, not that it mattered. All that really mattered was the immense pleasure of the first shot of the day—his favorite time of day, always on an empty stomach so the alcohol would course straight to his brain like an injection. Up went the glass, and down, and then warm bliss. He closed his eyes, smiled and clicked his long polished fingernails on his desk. Dagger-like nails conveyed status for a

Zhuang man because they indicated the owner did not perform manual labor. Even though his father was a rice farmer and his given name was decidedly rural (it literally meant Big Pole), sub-chief Fang kept his claws impeccably manicured. In fact, his once-a-week visit to the manicurist generally ended with at least a hand job and, depending on the day's schedule (his, of course, never the manicurist's), full sex. So many benefits to good grooming—yet beyond his fingernails Dazhu was no paragon of hygiene. He made his wife cut his hair to save money—all the barbers were men so there was no opportunity for sexual favors—and she expressed her contempt for him by deliberately botching the job so he came away looking like an English punk rocker minus the safety-pin earrings. His face was sallow and pock-marked, the skin sagging like tree resin as if the alcohol itself had, over the decades, congealed in lumps under the jagged real estate of his cheekbones.

The piercing whine of a downshifting scooter deflated Dazhu's reverie. He swiveled in his chair and peered out the grimy window behind his desk. The scooter turned into the empty parking space next to his Buick, followed by Yun Jian's Ford, and when the rider removed his helmet, Dazhu smiled. He turned back to his desk, poured another shot, lit a cigarette and pretended to study files until Mei ushered in the cop and his charge.

"Yun Jian, how thoughtful of you to honor me with a *wàiguórén*," said Dazhu, using the Mandarin slang for a foreigner. "I was about to go home. Perhaps he should come with me and enjoy some of my dear wife's chicken feet." Dazhu knew that Westerners abhorred the country's national dish, and he always made a point of offering it to them.

"My apologies, Honorable Fang," said Jian with a stiff, unconvincing bow. "This man was driving a motorcycle without a license. He could have come from anywhere."

"So I see," Dazhu replied, nodding at the window.

"It's a scooter," said T.K. "Not a motorcycle."

"A scooter in name only," said Jian. "I clocked him at one hundred."

T.K. smiled. "Nineteen Sixty-five Lambretta TV-200. Made in Milan for the British racing market. I've seen a lot of Indian copies over here, but that one's original." The sub-chief showed no appreciation. "She'll make a hundred and twenty in a tailwind," T.K. added, as if it were a boat.

Dazhu stared at T.K. and gestured at a straight-backed metal chair in front of his desk. "Please sit down, Honorable..."

"...Dean," said T.K., taking a seat. "T.K. Dean. Is that *báijiǔ*?"

"Indeed it is. Last month's distillation. Would you like some?"

"How kind of you."

"Mei! A glass for Honorable Mr. Dean!"

Mei swayed in with a small round glass. Dazhu's eyes again followed her out. He uncorked the bottle and tipped three fingers into the glass. T.K. smiled and reached for the offering but Dazhu cut him off. "First, I should like to see your passport."

T.K. slumped. "I have it," said Jian, handing it over. T.K. looked around the room. The office smelled like antiseptic floor cleaner but was still dingy. The walls had brown stains the size of small islands, the light switches vignetted in an aura of greasy fingerprints. Metal filing cabinets were dented and rusty. Above him, a lazy horsefly dodged the churning blades of a ceiling fan; spiders lurked in the corners. T.K. kept one eye on the full shot glass and one on the sub-chief, who was pawing through his passport with considerably less care than Jian had shown, hastily turning pages with fingernails that reminded T.K. of chicken feet.

"So you are here on business."

T.K. nodded.

"What is your business?"

"Scooters. I import restored scooters to the States. From China and Vietnam mostly, but also Thailand, India. I'd love to open up Burma..."

"Scooters! Like the one you are riding?" Dazhu nodded again at the window.

"Yes. Actually I was just out for a test ride on that one. Your people here do nice work."

"And Americans want to buy these...scooters?" Dazhu asked with disdain, rising from his desk and walking around to face T.K. In Asia scooters were a way of life, not a lifestyle choice—a step up from a bicycle and a step below a car. "They cannot afford cars in America?"

"They're mostly for fun. Trendy."

"I see," said Dazhu, now leaning on the front of his desk, perched over T.K. but not looking up from the passport pages. He flipped back and forth between several pages, counting to himself.

"You have entered Libya fourteen times."

"Tripoli Airport. I was transiting on Afriqiyah Airways. Which sucks by the way—you know you can't get a drink on those Muslim flights…"

Dazhu thrust his arm forward and slapped T.K. across the face with his own passport. "I know the difference between transiting and entering, these are entry stamps! Do not take me for a fool!" T.K. sat motionless. Jian, who had been watching impassively near the door, arched his eyebrows.

"Oh, but I am a terrible host," continued Dazhu, smiling now. "Your drink." He gestured to the glass while pouring himself another shot. "To scooters!" said Dazhu, raising his glass.

"To scooters!" Their cheap crystal clinked dully. They drained their shots together and knocked the glasses on Dazhu's grimy desk. Dazhu watched the ecstasy flash across T.K.'s face. He knew it so well, knew just the moment to resume the interrogation.

"Do they also restore scooters in Libya?" he asked. But T.K. was silent, sensing any conversation about Libya would invite another slap. "Well, never mind that. May I see your phone?" He did not use the polite interrogatory *ma*.

"You can see it, but you can't use it," said T.K., pulling the phone out of the gun pocket of his bomber jacket. "It stopped working."

"Really!" said Dazhu, taking the phone. "I wonder why?"

"Cheap Taiwanese crap," said T.K.

Dazhu pried off the back and noticed the red indicator dot for moisture. "Ahh, here is the problem. Your phone got wet."

"I sweat a lot."

"Oh no, the phone must have been completely submerged to turn the dot red."

"I might have dropped it in a bucket of beer."

"That could do it. I have often wondered why they don't put these phones on chains, like an old pocket watch." He nodded at T.K.'s wristwatch. "I see you are fond of our dear Chairman." It was one of those kitsch Cultural Revolution watches, where Mao's arm waves and the sweep second is a red star.

T.K. looked at his watch. It was five minutes after six. Mao was smiling, waving his arm. "I collect them," he said. "Got maybe a hundred. They actually have a pretty good quality movement, seventeen jewels. Of course the case is a piece of shit, plated steel, and nothing's polished. The main problem is the oil they used was pre-synthetic, so after fifty years it gums up the spring. A little cleaning, new oil and some adjustments and they'll work to within three minutes a day."

"And these Cultural Revolution watches—they are another import business of yours?"

"I just like to know what time it is."

Dazhu smiled. "Let's talk about ten o'clock last night."

Jian shifted nervously on his feet.

"Are you aware of what happened on the river last night?"

T.K. shrugged: "*Bùrán.* Nope. I was in town."

"Where?"

"Demo Bar on the Gua Hua Lu. You can ask." T.K. felt certain the bartender would assume he had been in the crowded Western-style nightspot, like most nights.

Dazhu stared at T.K. "Mr. Dean, do you have a rash?"

"Huh?"

"Your face, it looks flushed."

"Too much sun."

"I see. Do you know a local man named Chen Yong?"

"Well that's a very common name."

"Allow me to specify. This Chen Yong lives on a riverboat with his wife, Zeng Ming, a lovely bloom I might add"—T.K. stiffened—"and their son Jintao."

"I don't know them."

"Are you sure?"

"Positive."

"Chen Yong is a pig farmer who also repairs scooters for a living. Or did. He was killed by police last night in a raid on his houseboat. Before he was shot he managed to grab another officer's gun"—he paused briefly to glance at Jian, still standing by the door—"and wound a second."

Jian listened without blinking. His throat felt dry, and when he swallowed, his Adam's apple vibrated. Dazhu drummed his nails on the desk, then stretched out the fingers of his left hand to inspect them.

T.K. broke the silence. "Look, there's a scooter repair shop on every corner in this town. I'm telling you I don't know this guy. Didn't. Don't."

"In addition, a man was seen fleeing the riverbank last night on a scooter. He was tall, possibly Western."

"This place is crawling with tourists on scooters. Many of them are tall, especially compared to—" He bit his tongue. T.K. felt relieved the police apparently had no positive I.D. from last night, and his level of concern dipped accordingly. But at the same time a new and unfamiliar concern gripped him. It came from outside his own head, out in the world that he had spent a lifetime chronicling but never really engaging. For the first time in decades he felt concerned about someone else, although the feeling was tenuous, like a toddler just learning how to stretch and walk.

"Another drink, Mr. Dean?"

"You read my mind," he said, snapping out of his reflections long enough to be thankful Fang Dazhu could not actually read his mind. He downed the stinging shot, which kindled his thoughts on the new concern overwhelming him. In his mind he saw Chen Yong bleeding in a pigsty, heard his wife

Ming moaning in the hold of the houseboat and their sleeping boy Jintao, tossing with nightmares, on the tattered floor mat that served as a bed. And this cretinous sub-chief, who leered at his secretary and had probably interrogated Ming, meaning—what? Had she been arrested? Or worse? God only knew what this creep would do to her; then again it might pale compared to what she'd been through already. To actually care about other people was a concept so foreign to T.K. as to represent a concern in itself, if not an actual fear. But as the alcohol settled he shook off this strange musing and realized that the source of his concern was indeed more personal and familiar. He understood that his primal concern was the unbearable but now distinct possibility that he would never see Ming again.

Dazhu poured T.K. another shot, then walked back around his desk. He raised his nose and sniffed the air. "I smell pig shit," he said, taking his seat and swiveling toward the window. "Jian, do you smell pig shit?"

"Possibly, sir."

"No no, it is unmistakable. So vile." T.K. downed his shot as Dazhu swiveled back to address him. "Mr. Dean, is that pig shit on your boots?"

Designs
The Second Part

CHAPTER SIX

It was early fall of the previous year, typhoon season in the south, and the seed pods of the Chinese lantern bushes blazed orange along the dirt roads leading out of town. T.K. thought they looked like tiny paper jack-o-lanterns, and in Guangxi they were the closest botanical equivalent to the fall foliage of his New England youth. Autumn in Vermont had been his favorite time of year. To him fall meant not the end of summer but a new kind of life: The musky smell of composting leaves, the apple trees groaning under endowments of scarlet fruit, and the smoke from woodstoves spiraling above farmhouse chimneys all felt like something was beginning—something vaguely dangerous and more serious than summer. Then came winter, the season of fast sports on snow and ice; what could be more alive than cheating death down a mountain on skis?

His father, tall and tan with eyes like cold black coffee, did not share Teddy's appreciation for autumn's ochre charms. For him the shortening days fell like a weighted curtain. One October afternoon when Teddy was not quite thirteen they were walking through the sugar bush looking for ambrosia beetles on the maple trees, and his father lapsed into melancholy. "We're headed into the tunnel," he muttered solemnly. "Won't be long now."

"What won't be long?" Teddy asked in the unconsciously pedantic way of children.

"Winter," said his father. "And the days."

Teddy wanted to point out the many ways winter could be enjoyed, but he bit his tongue, knowing his father was not bendable on this point. Instead, sensing his father's despair over the quickening twilight and somehow wanting to make it better, he said optimistically, "Every place on earth receives exactly the same hours of night and day. They're just distributed differently. For example, on the equator the sun rises and sets every day at six o'clock. They don't get our long summer days, so it all evens out."

"Did you read that in one of your books?"

"*Popular Astronomy* by Simon Newcomb, first published in 1878. Pre-Einstein but a classic."

"Are you trying to say you're no Einstein?"

"Mrs. Blanchard says I'm too young for the Theory of Relativity. But I know what it is."

"Do you know what an ambrosia beetle is?"

"Yes sir. Dark brown with fuzzy backs and no pincers. They indicate stressed trees."

"Then keep your eyes open for them."

"Yes sir."

His father's melancholy increased as the days grew shorter until by Christmas he had withdrawn completely from his wife and son and even, it seemed, from his own self. His thoughts became ashen and circular as the chimney smoke, rising into nothingness but leaving a black aura like soot around his brain. He would start drinking as soon as it got dark, which was around four o'clock. At first Teddy was hurt and wondered what he had done to cause his father such pain. Then one day Teddy gored his hand with a pair of branch loppers and his father gave him a shot of whiskey in a tumbler he kept in the sugar shack. "You'll need stitches," said his father, wrapping a rag around the wound. "I'll get the truck. Drink this." Teddy took a tentative, choking sip.

And then everything was made clear. The revelation that an amber liquid could make caring superfluous, could create a new form of presence from absence, impressed a curious youth as occult knowledge, or alchemy. It was like a first orgasm and he wanted to cry out, *Why didn't anyone tell me about this before?* And he stopped worrying about his father.

Teddy welcomed the autumn evenings, which gave him more time for stealth reconnaissance missions. He would ride his bicycle into town, past houses and cemeteries with the same family names on every tombstone and mailbox, ditch it on the Common and creep around the village pretending he was an international spy. On moonless nights he practiced jumping over picket fences from a standstill, like a deer, then watching women in colonial kitchens feed logs into glowing cast iron stoves. This undercover excitement culminated in Halloween, his favorite holiday. Every year his mother, who had never held any job other than raising her only child, helped him make elaborate costumes from scratch, always clever takes on whatever adventure books and biographies he was reading. Two years in a row he won Best Costume at his school—once as "MacMummy," wrapped head to toe in Scottish tartan plaid; then as "Muhammed Mobutu Ali," in Everlast boxing shorts and gloves with a leopard-skin cap and ivory scepter. The blackface for that disguise was mildly controversial and the local paper, playing it safe, refused to run his photo, even though Teddy had raised over $200 in Unicef coins while trick-or-treating. That was a state solo record; Teddy always worked alone.

T.K. thought it odd that such distant memories could be summoned merely by the sight of Chinese lantern plants in Guangxi. It was one thing to deliberately conjure a memory—*What was my eighth-grade science teacher's name? Right, Mrs. Blanchard*—but T.K. wasn't *trying* to remember Halloween as he dodged cattle on a scooter along a dusty road in Guangxi. Instead, the random sight of orange seed pods triggered brain synapses that activated acetylcholine neurotransmitters that untangled vast strands of long-ago memories of bicycle rides through leaf piles in rural Vermont. He realized that the greatest accomplishments in Italian motor technology, from Ducati to Piaggio to Lamborghini, were mere teething toys compared to the gearbox of the brain, where billions of molecular moving parts kept up their silent combustion, by day and by dreams, and could even be lubricated with alcohol, itself a miracle of nature—literally the shit of yeast, expelled after eating sugar. God he loved chemistry!

Around one more bend and on the right, behind a battered, steam-shrouded noodle stand, was the Hung Far Lo Moto Shop. T.K.

pulled up to the entrance, parked next to a stunted papaya tree, dismounted and strode in. The showroom was a battered dun color, the cracked terrazzo floor overlaid in cigarette butts. Two rows of mint-condition vintage scooters gleamed incongruously. *"Nǐhǎo!"* said the salesman, a squat middle-aged man in a shabby, pilled golf shirt.

"Nǐhǎo," said T.K.

"You want to buy a scooter?"

"I always want to buy a scooter."

"I have one that is perfect for you," said the salesman, pulling T.K. by the arm to a red-and-white Vespa wrapped in garlands of chrome running trim. "1967, last year for the VBB model. All original. Mint condition. Seven thousand yuan."

T.K. stared at the machine and shook his head. "Two for the price of one?"

"Huh?"

"Or is it three?"

"I don't understand."

"It's a bodge job." He said *bodge job* in English.

"Bodge job?" repeated the salesman haltingly. "What does it mean?"

"A British term of art for shit."

"Shit?"

"*Pìhuà*. Rubbish. Cobbled together from whatever's lying around. How many wrecked bikes did it take to make this Frankenscooter in your back room?"

"Oh no! All original. Not from parts!"

"Yeah, that's what they always say on the 'Bay. May I?" He pulled a small magnet from his pocket and ran it along the leg shields and lower frame. Whenever he let go, the magnet fell to the floor. "No sticky, no steel. *Pìhuà*. In English, a Bondo resto."

"Bondo resto?"

"A Bondo restoration job. Silly Putty."

"Ahh, *Bondo resto!* Very funny!"

"Not when it cracks in half at rush hour on the Hollywood Freeway."

"I show you another, much better, all original," said the salesman, scurrying across the showroom.

"Skip it, I'm here to meet someone. Let me give you a few pointers on how to sell a bodge job. You do nice work, albeit evil work, but Satan's in the details. First: The Piaggio Motor Company of Pontedera, Italy has never made a two-tone Vespa. Ever. Lambretta, yes. Vespa, no. So when you paint a Vespa with these crazy color schemes—the yellow on white, the blue on buff, the red on black, the pink on anything—you're giving away the game right there. I don't care if it's a chick magnet;

it's wrong. Ditto on the two-tone seat; never happens in real life. Here's a big one: You're advertising this as a VBB but it's got a Sprint fender and cowls. The VBB was much rounder; the Sprint had more of a squared-off Seventies look. I get that the average chowderhead won't know the difference, but thousands of hardcore Vespa collectors in Europe and America do. You could argue they should get a life, and you might be right, but instead what they do is flame sellers like you on eBay. If you're gonna chop and swap, stick with one model. Now take a look at your center stand. It's a ten-inch stand on a bike with eight-inch wheels, which is why the front tire is off the ground, ready for blast-off; it's a scooter, not a cruise missile. While we're on the center stand, look at those yellow plastic boots. They only exist in Asia. It's a dead giveaway. You guys need to find a supplier of black rubber stand boots. Now look at all that chrome: You've got chrome crash bars, a chrome fender guard, a chrome grab bar, a chrome stinger on the exhaust. It looks like a Pakistani taxi."

"People like chrome," said the salesman.

"People in Asia like chrome. Also Germans. For everyone else, a little goes a long way. Same goes for that stupid winged Piaggio crest logo tacked on the front. They make those in Nam and it screams bodge. I could go on: the plastic floor mat, the leg shield glove box which VBBs never had, the rubber gasket around the gas cap, the knockoff Veglia speedo with Tron font...but time is money. I'm here to meet one of your mechanics—guy by the name of Chen Yong."

"Chen Yong? Ahh, you need to repair a scooter?"

"Something like that."

"Chen Yong is the best. If we don't have the part he can make it."

"Clutch plates out of coffee cans—I've seen them. Guaranteed to last a hundred miles."

"Pardon?"

"Never mind. Is Yong here?"

"One moment please."

The salesman disappeared through a back door. Minutes later a slim, fine-featured man with a long goatee emerged, wiping his hands on the front of a greasy apron. A gold crucifix dangled from his neck. He was older than T.K. had imagined—fifty if he was a day—and the age creases around his mouth deepened as he smiled. He was tan—too tan for a garage mechanic, thought T.K.—but without the round features common to the Zhuang. When he spoke Mandarin, it was obvious he was Han. "*Nǐhǎo*. I am Chen Yong. How can I help you?"

"Good afternoon, Mr. Chen. I have a Lambretta that's making a funny clicking sound at high speed. Maybe a bad variator roller."

"Is it here?"

"Out front."

"Let's go for a ride."

With Yong on the back, T.K. swung the Lambretta into the road and buzzed through the glazed tile *páifāng* gate that marked the western end of town. The road hugged a tributary of the Li, past tire shops and farm supply outlets, until the looming karst peaks forced a sharp turn before the landscape opened onto paddies. T.K. pulled over at a clearing next to a small pond where a woman stooped in the shallow water under a camellia tree, tending a flock of ducks. He shut off the engine and both men dismounted.

"I heard nothing," said Yong. "No problem with the rollers."

"My scooter's fine, Mr. Chen. I wanted to speak to you where we could not be overheard."

Yong frowned. "Who are you?"

"My name is T.K. Dean. I'm an American journalist. I got your name from the Christian International Aid people in New York."

"They are very good people. What is this about?"

"It's about the family planning law. I'm writing a book."

"About the law?"

T.K. paused. He looked over Yong's shoulder at the woman in the pond, tossing grain to her ducks. "About abortions."

Yong's eyes twitched involuntarily at the word, then he recovered and gazed over the rice paddies. The breeze had stiffened, teasing his long, wispy goatee out like a windsock. "You mean *qiǎngpò duòtāi*—forced abortions."

"*Duì*. That's right. I understand your wife, Zeng Ming, had one."

"My wife's story is hers to tell."

"Can I meet her?"

Yong hesitated, scanning the road, the paddies, and the jagged landscape beyond. "I'm not yet an old man, Mr. Dean, but I am beyond the age of wondering what's beyond the next mountain. It's different for Ming. She is still young. And we have a son. I'm sorry. It's too dangerous. I have already said too much." He pivoted toward the scooter. T.K. took his arm.

"Yong, someday your son will have a wife and they will want children of their own. If the law is to change, the abuse must be exposed. I'm asking you to think of your grandchildren." Yong cast his eyes to the ground. "They tell me you are the best moto man in the south," T.K. said.

"I am very careful in my work," said Yong, lifting his eyes to T.K.'s.

"So am I. My business visa identifies me as a scooter importer. It would be natural to be dealing with you. I'm asking you to trust me."

Yong sighed, shoved his hands deep into his overall pockets and nodded west toward the Li. "We live on the river. Fourth houseboat off the Jimacun Road, beyond the pigsties. Come tonight after dark."

Chapter Seven

T.K. returned to his rented flat in town above the Demo Bar. The apartment was dingy and sparse, but it was owned by the downstairs watering hole, allowing T.K. to settle his drinking and sleeping tabs in one convenient transaction. The space had large windows overlooking busy Gua Hua Street and a rear stairwell that exited to an alley along the concrete banks of the stream that flowed through town. The kitchen windows overlooked the back alley and the stream, so he could, if necessary, surveil arrivals both front and rear. The wall-mounted water heater never ran out, and the bathtub was large. On the other hand, T.K. found the traditional Chinese squat toilet to be a pain in the ass, literally. After all these years in China he never got used to them, could never understand the appeal. Supposedly they are better for you, as in less likely to cause hemorrhoids, but considering that he had had precisely no hemorrhoids in his entire life the precaution seemed unwarranted. He once read that Mao, who in his life never travelled anywhere outside China except Russia, despised Western-style commodes and even had the toilet in his lavish

Moscow guest quarters removed and replaced with a proper hole. Maybe he had hemorrhoids to go along with his cataracts. Mao was also a connoisseur of fart jokes, so go figure.

T.K. pulled a bottle of China Pabst Blue Ribbon out of the fridge and emptied it into a tall glass. It was two o'clock in the afternoon. He wondered for approximately three seconds if it was too early to start drinking, then decided it was fine and poured himself a generous shot of *báijiŭ*. He sat at his small desk, opened his laptop and logged on to Cryptocat. The first email in his cue made no sense:

Oops, scratch that. Forgot my bras need to keep the key for now.

It was from Meg. T.K. folded his brow trying to understand the meaning. Then he scrolled down and realized it was attached and related to an earlier email from her. The reverse chronology of emails, blogs and pretty much everything computer-related irritated him. It was a major reason he hated personal technology. Life was supposed to start at the beginning and proceed to the end, not the other way around. He also vaguely suspected all the gadgets were threatening world order and breeding new humans (or maybe humanoids) who would never understand the thrill of riding a bicycle through leaf piles on an autumn night in New England, or leaning into curves around karst mountains on a vintage moto. The earlier email said:

hi teddy. finally got all my stuff out of the apartment its all yours now. will mail key or leave with dman next time uptown. This email was sent from my iPhone; please excuse any typos.

T.K. wasn't ready to excuse Meg for anything, actually, including typos. And that email should have been first in the cue. It was all backwards. In fact if only he had been able to read that email ten years ago, before the marriage, it would have saved so much trouble for both of them. He wrote back:

How could you forget bras?

In seconds she replied:

hanging to dry in bathroom.

It was two a.m. in New York. *You're awake?*

can't sleep.

What are you wearing?

No reply. T.K. knew he would never see her in a bra again, or even know what bra she was wearing against her soft, not-too-large but perfectly shaped breasts. He switched his keyboard to pinyin and typed:

Dāng nǐ yǒu quēxiàn, bùyào hàipà fàngqì. – Kǒngzǐ

The program automatically rendered the keystrokes into simplified Chinese:

当你有缺陷，不要害怕放弃. –孔子

His wife answered:

quoting confucius again? ru going to tell me what it means or make me use translate?

T.K. wrote back:

"When you have faults, do not fear to abandon them."

No reply. Maybe she fell asleep.

He scrolled through emails from Christian International, confirming the hookup with Chen Yong, then logged out of the secure site. He took a drink and shifted his gaze from the browser window to the apartment window. Down on the Gua Hua Lu, the old woman who ran the tea shop across the street was trying to extract money from a German tourist who had taken her picture. Neither spoke a word of the other's tongue so the conversation proceeded in the universal sign language for cash—the rubbing of thumb against forefinger, the pantomime of counting bills—until the German with the twenty-thousand-dollar Leica got tired of negotiating and finally said *"Ich spreche kein Chinesisch!"* and walked away, the old woman cursing him and flailing her arms.

T.K. opened Google Earth and zoomed into the Li riverbank, scanning for Yong's pig farm and houseboat. But the satellite data for that area was old and low-res, revealing little more than grey smudges along the edge of the wide, black river. He loaded the weather page on his browser and saw a typhoon spiraling like a galaxy over the South China Sea. It was too far away to directly threaten Guangxi, but today's wind had been carried on its back—zephyrs reaching like tendrils all the way to the tea plantations that stepped up the mountainsides far into Yunnan province. The sky had darkened, and drops of rain began pelting his window. T.K. finished his drink and his beer, opened Word and started to write.

Chapter Eight

Zeng Ming crinkled her nose and dumped a bucket of cabbage heels over a bamboo fence into the fetid pigsty. Her seventeen pigs, the smallest of which weighed more than twice Ming, had anticipated the meal, recognizing the bucket, and were already grunting and jostling around the fence when she arrived. Six pregnant sows, each with a dozen massive teats dragging in the slop, maneuvered their swollen flanks to body-slam the others out of the way. In the jungle code of pigs it was survival of the fattest.

Ming stood for a minute watching the pregnant sows rooting their snouts into the scraps, then looked up over the river and the mountains, where dark clouds had blown in on the southerly typhoon's shoulder. It was starting to rain. She trekked back to the riverbank and eyed the two thick jute mooring lines, bow and stern, that tethered her floating home to the land. The houseboat pitched and rolled in the wake stirred up by the wind—the river was wide here at the bend and behaved like a large lake in bad weather—and the ropes hummed and strained along their length between the deck cleats and the granite blocks that anchored them ashore. Across the river, slots between the karst peaks funneled howling furies over the water; a bright red Chinese flag, mounted on a pole at the stern of the houseboat, snapped tautly in the gust. The noise distracted Ming. As the wind shifted, the five stars in the canton seemed to whip around each other like electrons in an atom, forming a yellow blur. She knew she should be proud of her country's flag, but its contradictions only amplified her loss, her longing for truth. The flag, as every Chinese schoolchild knew, was designed by a peasant in a 1949 contest. According to legend, the large star signified the Communist Party, guiding the four smaller stars that represented Mao's Bloc of Four revolutionary classes: peasants, proletarian workers, small business owners and national industrialists. Ming wondered how many Westerners knew that capitalists had their own stars on the Communist Chinese flag; she suspected none of the stars on the American flag represented communism. But of course in 1949, Mao's enemies were not capitalists so much as feudal landlords and foreign imperialists, especially the vile Japanese. His flirtation with the free market was a marriage of convenience; by the 1960s, what remained of China's capitalist class had been "appropriated," but their stars still burned on the flag, the flag that never represented Mao's true goals any more than it represented the reality of China. Ming thought an honest flag for the twenty-first century should have only two stars—one very large one representing the single class of government-sponsored capitalism, and a smaller (very small) star for the factory workers. Maybe that could be the flag for the whole world. At any rate, China had no place for peasants anymore.

"I was never a peasant!" The words floated through the veil of the flag, as if on the wind.

Ming was a little girl, sitting on her grandfather's lap in his Shanghai study, surrounded by his books, brushes and inks.

"Peasants do not study economics at Nanjing University," her grandfather Zeng Liansong said, dipping a calligraphy brush in the inkwell. "Peasants are not managers at the Shanghai Waste Recycling Company." He daubed a black character on rice paper and squinted through thick glasses that magnified his eyes like a cartoon character. "Nor was I an artist."

"But grandfather," said Ming, rubbing his bald head, "you are the most famous artist in all of China."

Liansong laughed. "Which tells you nothing about art, and everything about being famous."

"I don't understand."

Liansong dipped his brush in the ink and drew a new character:

"What is this?" he asked Ming.

"*Zhōng!* Middle." He dipped his brush and added a character:

"Now what does it mean?"

"China!" she said. "Everyone knows that! *Zhōngguó.*"

"The Middle Kingdom," said Liansong. "But notice what makes it a kingdom. The second character represents the king on his throne, inside a box that signifies the borders of his domain." He drew it again as he spoke. "But the important stroke is the little one inside the box"—with a quick, delicate flourish he added the small accent mark at the bottom. "That represents the king's seal; without it, he is a pretender to the throne."

"But China doesn't have a king anymore."

Liansong twirled his brush in a glass of water. "Let me tell you a story about the flag. It began on a very hot night in the summer of 1949."

"Mama!"

Ming blinked. The voice called from inside the houseboat, where Jintao was working on his studies. She shivered and crossed the sagging wooden gangplank, stopping on deck to wrap another turn of mooring line around each of the rusty Bollard cleats. The steel boat was the same grey as the sky, and ringed in a dull necklace of truck tires chained to the gunwales. It was well over a hundred feet long but most of the deck was an open cargo hold; the "house" was really just a flat-roofed crew cabin aft of the hold, roughly twenty by twenty feet, its walls pierced by a few dirty jalousie windows sheathed in iron bars. Outside the cabin, laundry twisted on a line strung between hatch fittings. Plastic window boxes filled with geraniums hung over the stern rail between tire fenders, and smoke rose from a Z-shaped stovepipe through the roof. The houseboat was, in fact, a converted self-propelled coal barge of the type used on rivers and canals throughout China. The boat's powerful machinery—twin diesel engines, capable of moving fifteen hundred tons of coal at upwards of ten knots—had long since been removed; it was nothing but a bodge job.

"Mama!"

Ming quickly pulled the laundry off the line and crossed into the cabin where twelve-year-old Jintao sat at the small kitchen table, algebra workbooks spread out. "Mama, I can't solve this problem." He was small for his age, and he had to sit on an old ring-style life preserver to reach the table. Long locks of hair draped over his dark eyes and seemed, in their limp surrender, to confirm the melancholy that Ming felt sure defined his nature. The cabin lurched as a large wave caught the boat broadside, and Ming suddenly felt sick. She staggered to the squat toilet, which drained directly into the river, and threw up. When Jintao heard his mother retching, he looked up from his homework but did not rise. He could never understand why some people got seasick. The smell of pigs could certainly make you sick, but a boat? He loved living on a boat, mainly because it held the potential, however slight in this case, for a journey, and more than anything else Jintao wanted to go somewhere. It didn't matter where, and it didn't matter that the barge had no visible means of propulsion. At night as he lay on his mat, he would fall asleep to the sway of the wake and imagine the dirty old coal barge was moving downstream, toward the ocean. Often, in his dreams, he would rise in the morning and find the boat far out to sea—no pigs, no claustrophobic karst mountains, just endless blue water in every direction.

Ming returned, wiping her face on a rag. "Show me the problem."

Jintao read from his workbook: "The population of China at the beginning of the Song Dynasty in AD 1000 was 87 million. By 1800 under the Qing Dynasty, the population had grown to 268 million. What was the rate of population growth, and what would the population of China be in 2010 if that rate had continued?"

"So you are calculating exponential growth," said Ming. She drew the equation on his pad:

$$PR = \frac{(Vpresent - Vpast)}{Vpast} x100$$

"Start by subtracting the Song Dynasty population from the Qing Dynasty population." She punched the numbers into his calculator. "That gives you a population increase of 181 million. Okay?"

"Yes."

"Now divide that by the Song population and you get 2.08. Multiplying that number by one hundred equals 208. Divide by the number of years, eight hundred, and you get an increase of 2.6 percent per year. Do you understand so far?"

"Yes."

"Now you need to apply that rate of increase to the period from 1800 to 2010. Here is the formula:

$$P = C(1+r)^t$$

"So 1 plus r is 1.026. Let's put that in the calculator. Go ahead, you do it. Now punch the key and enter the exponent, which is the number of years."

"Number of years?"

"From 1800 to 2010."

"Oh! 210."

"Good! Put it in. Hit the *equal* key. Now multiply that by 268 million, which is the population in 1800. What do you get?"

Jintao stared at his calculator, counting the zeroes. "Almost six billion. That's a lot of people! Is that how many people live in China?"

"No, my son. Only about 1.3 billion."

"Then my math is wrong!"

"Your math is correct. What has changed is the rate of growth. The problem is theoretical."

The gangplank creaked; Yong was home. He lifted his Flying Pigeon bicycle onto the deck, went inside and smiled at Ming and Jintao. Over tea with Ming, he told her about his meeting that morning with T.K. Dean.

"If he is from Christian International, he must be a good man," said Ming.

"Not from there exactly," Yong said. "But they know who he is."

"Maybe he can help us," said Ming.

Jintao put down his pencil and wondered what kind of problems could not be solved by algebra.

Chapter Nine

It took a while for T.K. to find the houseboat in the dark and the driving rain. The riverfront was lined with coal barges converted into homes, all of them facing pigsties oozing their stink into the river as the deluge crested. But finally he found a barge with the surname Chen painted on the cabin:

陈

He turned the Lambretta back out to the main road and parked a dozen yards downriver, on a gravel landing where boatmen launched bamboo rafts for overpriced tourist rides—a highlight of the trip was scudding past the spot on the river with the twenty-yuan-note landscape, the only spot along the bank not given over to pigs. He walked back to the houseboat and crossed the groaning gangplank, making note of its sound. Before he could knock on the cabin door, Yong was there, motioning him in.

"Good evening, Mr. Dean. Welcome."

T.K. smiled and wiped the rain from his face on his sleeve.

"This is my son, Jintao," said Yong. The boy rose and bowed.

"And my wife Zeng Ming."

She stood behind her son in the shadow cast by the table lantern, her hands on Jintao's shoulders, and in that moment T.K. remembered fall nights in a Vermont kitchen, his mother cooking dinner and loading wood in the stove while he did his homework at the kitchen table. Then Ming stepped into the light, and T.K. didn't think about his mother anymore.

She was tall by Chinese standards—taller than her husband, and much younger—with a long, slender face and large eyes almost too wide-set for her brow to accommodate, which gave her a sort of beauty rather more unusual than classical. Her skin was pale, no way Zhuang, and T.K. thought she glowed as if surrounded by an aura, and he just wanted to keep looking at her, more out of admiration than desire. Indeed, for though he never felt he had any special intuition about women, something about her energy made T.K. understand immediately that she was newly pregnant.

"*Nǐhǎo.*" Her voice was deeper and more confident than he expected, almost an operatic alto—unusual, thought T.K., as Chinese women tend to squeak in the presence of strange men. They shook hands, hers small but firm in its grasp. "Please sit down," she said. "Would you like some tea, or at this hour perhaps you enjoy something stronger."

"The stronger the better," said T.K.

Ming smiled, then pulled a crock of cheap *báijiǔ* and a small cup off a shelf. The cabin was one room. In a corner near the door was a small coal stove for both heat and cooking, a blackened steel wok perched on top. Opposite the stove, a sink with a manual plunger tap brought the river into the home; a squat toilet behind a reed screen sent it back. Ming and Yong slept on two cots, Jintao on a reed mat. The only light came from the kerosene lantern on the lacquered table. The walls were bare except for a crucifix and a calendar with a stylized color reproduction of Mao, the same portrait that hangs over Tiananmen Square. Below the image of the Chairman was the epigram from his Little Red Book:

全世界无产者，联合起来！

Which is generally translated into English as the alliterative "Workers of the world, unite!" but which in Marx's original German actually refers to "proletarians" and which in Mao's Mandarin version means literally "landless people."

"Those without land, unite!" said T.K., raising his glass.

Yong smiled and poured himself a shot. "We live on the boats because we need every square meter of land for the pigs. If pigs could swim we would graze them in the river as well."

T.K. laughed. "In English we have a phrase, 'If pigs could fly.' Nobody ever asks if they can swim."

"I would not let even a pig swim in this river anymore," said Ming. "Jintao got a rash the last time he jumped in, and this year there were no lotus plants on the bank. But here we are. They pushed us all the way to the edge of the land, and when they ran out of land they pushed us onto boats."

"I know who you mean by *they*," said T.K. "But whom exactly do you mean by *us*?"

"Those of us who refuse to abide by the one-child law," said Yong. "Most of us are Christian as well—a double scar."

"I understood that the policy has only been enforced in cities, that peasants could have more children."

"We are not peasants," said Yong. "We are from Shanghai. Ming's grandfather was a famous artist—"

—"we are peasants now," said Ming. "We came here because peasants were allowed two children if the first is a girl. Then we had Jintao, so no chance for a second. Jintao looked up from his homework. "But now they are saying even peasants may have only one child, boy or girl. Too many are moving to the cities, they say. If only peasants would stay in their place it would be fine. But people aspire to a better life."

"If you can call it that," said T.K. On one level he understood the motivation, having grown up on a farm before spending most of his adult life in New York and Beijing. But in China the road from rice paddies to urban opportunity generally ended at a dead-end factory job and a filthy shared room in a concrete Stalinist dormitory.

"When the peasants first see Guangzhou from the train station," said Yong, "they look at the tall buildings all flashing neon, and they think they are in some kind of dream."

T.K. nodded. He too loved the animated neon skyscrapers that defined the horizon of modern China—dozens of cities larger than New York that few people in the West had even heard of. It was like every city was a logarithmic multiple of Times Square, and he often wondered why there was so much pushback to lighting displays in the West, where cityscapes outside of "entertainment districts" were comparatively boring.

"Yeah, no neon lights on the factory dormitory blocks," he said.

"They're lucky if they have electricity at all," said Yong, glancing at his kerosene lantern. "Still they come, hoping to make it big. And the fact is, if you have money in the city you can get around the one-child law. They say Zhang Yimou has seven children."

"From four women," said T.K. The well-known film director's priapic personal life was the subject of much resentment and secret admiration in China.

The rain lashed at the windows and found holes in the roof. Ming put a pot under a drip that started over the table. "Ain't that a hole in the boat," said T.K.

Jintao looked up from his studies.

"It's an American expression," T.K. said to him. "When things aren't going well."

The boy smiled.

Yong rose and shoveled a load of coal into the glowing stove. T.K. poured himself and Yong another shot; Ming declined.

"You remind me of my grandfather," she said.

"I'm only thirty-six."

"I mean, he distilled his own alcohol, from sorghum and rice fermentations. When I was a little girl, I used to watch the alcohol dripping from the copper pot in his courtyard. It always seemed like so much work for such a small bottle."

"A little goes a long way. Of course, a lot goes even further."

"When the bottle was full, my grandfather would ask me to fetch it. He always said, 'Be a good girl and bring me the Paramount Leader.' "

T.K. laughed. Deng Xiaoping's given name means *little bottle* in Mandarin. He turned to Jintao. "You like school?"

"Very much," he said, looking up from his notebook.

"So did I. You like to read?"

"Yes, but we have very few books. I have read them all."

"I see. Well there's always the Bible. You have one of those, I assume?"

"Of course."

"When I was a kid and I ran out of books I used to read the Bible, over and over. Old Testament is best. In America you don't even have to pay for it; people giving 'em away on street corners. Now you take your Deuteronomy—for my money more adventure per page than Robert Louis Stevenson. Wars, pillage, stonings, sacrifice, kidnappings, it's all there. Even a plague of hemorrhoids."

Jintao laughed.

"You can't make this stuff up," said T.K. "God has a one-track mind: 'The Lord thy God shall deliver them unto thee, and shall destroy them with a mighty destruction, until they be destroyed.' It does get a little repetitive."

Jintao laughed again. Ming said: " 'The tender and delicate woman shall be forced to eat the child that cometh out from between her

feet.' "

"You read Deuteronomy too?"

"We live it," she said.

"So you will have more children," said T.K.

It was a statement, not a question. Ming looked into T.K.'s eyes and recognized in that instant that he knew she was pregnant. She didn't understand how he knew, nor did she care; whatever force was between them felt as real as the heat from the coal stove on her skin.

"I want to replace the ones they took from me," she said.

"More than one?"

"Twice they took me away." She glanced at her son.

"Jintao," said Yong. "It is time for bed." The boy rose and moved to the sleeping corner of the room.

"Mr. Dean," said Ming.

"Teddy," he said.

"Teddy. Perhaps we can speak again sometime when Jintao is at school."

Yong shook his head no. "It is dangerous to come in the daytime."

CHAPTER TEN

T.K. motored down the Jimacun Road to where the pavement ended and a cemetery had been carved into the foothills of a karst peak. The rain had blown through overnight and this morning the sky was bright, the air fresh. Ming was kneeling at a tomb, praying, in jeans and a white silk Hello Kitty blouse that clung to her breasts in the breeze. Her bicycle was parked behind a bamboo grove. Beside her was the kerosene lantern from the barge. The tombs were built into the side of the mountain; each had a rough stone wall and an arched, weathered wooden door bearing carved inscriptions. On most of the doors, relatives had tacked small red banners and other memorials. Aggressive tendrils of morning glory seemed on the verge of consuming the graves, at least until Tomb Sweeping Day next April. A fog of mosquitos vibrated around T.K.'s head as he joined Ming at the tomb.

"Someone you know?" he asked.

"What else does one do at a cemetery?"

"When I was a kid in New England I used to try to find the oldest grave. The farther back you go, the more children."

"That's so sad. I would like to see England."

"*New* England. In America."

"Oh, you are not British?"

"I only drink like a Brit."

"You remind me—"

"—I know. Of your grandfather. Let's go."

T.K. turned to the road but Ming pulled him toward the tomb and opened the wooden door.

"We're going in there?" said T.K.

"This one is special." She glanced up and down the road. "It's a secret. To the Silver Moon Caves."

"The tourist trap with the Zhang Yimou sound and light show? We'll be seen."

"These caves go for miles," said Ming. "We are not going to that part. This entrance was found by Kuomintang partisans in the 1930s. They hid it behind a false tomb wall. The Red Army never found it. Not even the police know about it. Look at the inscription."

T.K. bent over the door and scanned the vertical characters. "I can't read the name, it's scratched out, but it says *gōng*—a respected older man. Born October 31, 1887 and died April 5, 1975."

"Chiang Kai-shek," said Ming. "Those are his dates. Follow me."

They crossed the portal and entered a dank crevice gored through the limestone. Ming lit the lantern and moved ahead slowly into the labyrinth. She smelled of jasmine—not store-bought perfume but like the actual flower on the vine, blooming along a wild hillside. The humid air of the cave intensified the bouquet, and T.K. was happy to follow her. The rough path sloped downhill, made several turns, then narrowed before it opened into a yawning chamber the size of a squash court. In the center was an underground spring that glowed blue-green from the limestone. T.K. switched on his phone light and aimed it at the ceiling. "Holy shit."

Menacing rows of stalactites dangled like arthritic fingers, dripping slime into the pool. Thousands of slender tomb bats hung from the rock, preening and grooming. Occasionally one would alight and flit erratically before roosting again. The bats, the fluorescent pool, the dripping stalactites all made the chamber seem like a living organism with its own breath and circulation. "You really don't need a sound and light show directed by Zhang Yimou," said T.K.

"You can never have too many colored lights in the land of red lanterns," said Ming.

They sat on a flat rock. T.K. tossed a stone into the pool; the ripples caused the blue light reflected on the walls of the cave to oscillate as if in a dream. "How deep is it?"

"No one has found the bottom," said Ming. T.K. had not shaved that morning, and in the dim light she silently admired his rough, full beard, so unlike Chinese men, and wondered what it would feel like to touch it.

"Do you have children?" she asked.

"No. But I have fond memories of childhood, if that helps."

"You are not married?"

"Yes and no. In the middle of a divorce. It was a marriage of convenience: She had a beautiful smile, and I had a rent-controlled apartment on the Upper West Side. Neither of us really knew what we were doing."

"Americans don't stay married."

"Some do. I suppose my parents would have, but my mother died when I was a boy, and my dad a few years later."

"I'm sorry."

"So tell me about your grandfather," said T.K. "Last night Yong started to say he was an artist."

"His name was Zeng Liansong." Ming stared into the lantern and pictured her grandfather's study.

"Tell me the story of the flag again, Grandfather!"

And so Liansong retold his story. "Well it was long ago, in the summer of 1949," he began. "It was late, and the stink and humidity off the Huangpu was unbearable, so I went up to the roof hoping to sleep better under the heavens. In those days you could still see stars from the Nanjing Road! I was thirty-two years old, which probably seems very old to you, but I still had no idea what I wanted to be when I grew up. I was working secretly for the Communist Party, which in Shanghai was still very much underground. In the north, things were different. The Red Army was driving out the Kuomintang, and the Communists assumed there would soon be a new government. The *People's Daily* posted a notice seeking designs for a national flag; the winner would earn a prize of five hundred yuan and possibly get to meet Chairman Mao. I didn't think much about it, but as I lay on my cot on the roof that night, I noticed how a few stars in the sky were very bright while most others appeared much smaller. Then it hit me: the Communist Party was the *dājiùxīng*, or savior star, of our country. I thought that a large star guiding smaller stars would make a good flag design. So I folded up my cot, went back to my room and took out my brushes. I couldn't sleep anyway! Look, here was my first design."

From his desk drawer he pulled out a tattered page from an old ledger book. On it was painted a design similar to the Chinese flag of today, but with the field of stars in the center.

"Right away I could see this design was boring," said Liansong to his granddaughter. "But I didn't know why. I was an economist, not an artist. Still I thought, 'If that crazy man Soong on the second floor, the one who eats his mahjong tiles when someone robs his *kong*, can make good watercolors, how hard can art be?' So I thought about it a long time, and finally I realized the problem. Putting the stars in the center was the problem. As soon as I moved them to the corner, in the canton, the flag came alive. You see it was just like the king's seal in the character for *kingdom*. The off-center stroke adds energy. That's when I knew that power and beauty are often found in that which exists around the edges. So now you know everything about fame *and* art."

"And did you meet Chairman Mao, grandfather?"

Liansong shrugged. "To my surprise I beat almost three thousand entries, some of them by top Party officials. Mao wanted the flag to be designed by a peasant, so that's what they called me. I took a train to Beijing. I stood with the crowd and the news reporters from around the world at Tiananmen Gate on the first of October, when the Chairman announced the People's Republic and unveiled the flag."

"But did you meet him?"

"Well I prefer to think that he met me."

Ming pulled her grandfather's round tortoise-shell spectacles from his face and tried them on. She had to hold them tightly to keep the heavy saucers of glass from sliding down her nose, and when she looked through them, the familiar world of his study was refracted into a shifting mirage. The paneled walls were now like the sides of an aquarium, and as she moved her head, everything in the room swam. Then she was back in the cave, looking at the rough stone walls shimmering from the light of the glowing tarn.

"Zeng Liansong," said T.K. "I should have known. When did he die?"

"Nineteen ninety-nine. He was eighty-one. I still have his beret. He wore it every day."

"Well if he wore a beret then he must have been a great artist. How long has your family been Christian?"

"Since the nineteenth century, give or take a few Taoists. Yong and I met at the Moore Memorial Church in Shanghai. My grandfather was a Methodist. At first he saw communism as a secular extension of Christian compassion, but over time he grew disillusioned—not just with Mao but even with the market reforms of Deng. He saw early that if the economic changes were controlled by the state, they would mostly benefit a few connected people at the top. He always thought the countries of northern Europe had figured out the best mix of capitalism and socialism. He wanted to go there, but he never got a passport. I think they were afraid he would defect, which would have been embarrassing."

"How old are you, Ming?"

"Thirty-one." She closed her eyes and took several deep breaths, absorbing the cool air of the cave. She wore a red bra, visible under her sheer blouse, and T.K. felt he would be content to simply watch her breasts rise and fall for a long time. "My husband is a good man," said Ming as if in response to T.K.'s thoughts. "But there is only so much he can do."

"Do you want to tell me about the abortions?"

Eyes still closed, Ming nodded. "The first time, I was six months' pregnant. We were living in town. Jintao was two years old. The Family Planning Commission keeps menstrual records of every woman; you must report to the clinic once a month. If you already have a child and you get pregnant, you must pay a fine, or else they come for you." She cleared her throat and swallowed. "It was the middle of the night."

***

"Wake up! Open the door!"

The tiny apartment rattled. Ming sprang upright in bed as Yong ran to the door. "Who is it? What do you want?"

"Family Planning Commission! Let us in or we'll kick the door down, and you will have to pay the landlord for that as well!"

"You can't come in! Go away!"

Boom! Boom! The door swelled against the force of boots. Finally the wood around the hinges splintered; Yong flinched as the door flew open in front of a dozen armed men. Several grabbed Yong and pinned him roughly to the floor as others streamed into the bedroom. The leader waved paperwork in Yong's face. "Your wife is pregnant. You already have a son. You have refused to pay the twenty-thousand yuan fine. Therefore we must abort." Ming screamed from the bedroom.

"I do not have money for the fine!" said Yong.

"That is not my concern," said the leader.

Ming struggled against her captors but there were too many. They dragged her by her arms and legs, still in her nightgown, outside to a waiting van as Yong screamed in protest, still pinned to the floor.

The Family Planning Clinic on Pantao Road was no more nor less than an abortion mill. In a back room, a row of hospital cots with dirty sheets and leather restraints faced a surgical wash station with cold running water and a bar of hand soap next to a rubber glove dispenser. There was a swivel stool. A rolling cart displayed a selection of forceps, hemostats and syringes. Next to each cot was a red plastic pail. Ming had been injected with midazolam in the car, so by the time they dragged her into the clinic she was groggy and compliant. They tossed her on a cot and belted her down. A man took her right forefinger and rolled it in a red inkpad, then pressed her print against an abortion consent form. The faucet across the room dripped dully; Ming thought each drop of water hitting the metal sink sounded like a heartbeat.

Another woman lay on a cot, moaning. A doctor came in and stood over the rolling cart, preparing a syringe. He approached Ming but did not acknowledge her. The needle was so long, she thought. He pulled up her nightgown to expose her belly. Silently, two orderlies appeared on either side of the cot and pinned Ming's shoulders to the thin mattress. The needle bit like a rabid dog, but Ming thought about Yong and little Jintao and refused to cry. The doctor pulled out the needle and tossed it into the red bucket on the floor. Everybody except the moaning woman on the next cot left.

In a few minutes it felt like her insides were on fire, and she urinated all over the tiny bed. She was so thirsty, all she could think about was water. The baby stopped moving. She panted and finally broke down, wailing in anguish, before passing out. She dreamt she was drowning in a lake or ocean—it must have been an ocean because the water was so salty.

She awoke in hard labor. The moaning woman was gone. Ming had no idea how many hours had passed, but daylight filtered through a clerestory window. "Help!" she cried. "Please, help me! I am in labor!" But no one came. After several hours of contractions, the same doctor who injected her came in, with a nurse. This time he scrubbed at the sink and put on gloves, while the nurse fitted gynecological stirrups to the cot and pulled off Ming's soaking wet underwear. She spread Ming's legs and positioned her ankles roughly in the cold metal brackets. The doctor pulled the swivel stool between her legs and sat. He spread some lubricant on his gloved right hand and inserted it all the way into her. Ming gasped.

"Tuī!" he commanded. "Push!"

Ming obeyed.

The doctor turned to the nurse and scowled. "The fetus is breeched," he said. "Get me the forceps."

Just then came a huge contraction and Ming pushed like never before. "Never mind forceps," said the doctor, hand still inside Ming. "I have it." He turned his arm and slid out his hand, clutching the bruised leg of the dead fetus.

"Now push out the rest!" he ordered Ming. One more contraction and the bloody placenta was on the cot. The doctor scooped it all up, fetus and lining, and tossed it into the bucket, on top of the needle from the night before. He peeled off his gloves and threw them in the bucket too. Then he kicked the stool away and left with the nurse. The faucet had stopped dripping and the room was silent.

Ming was still in the stirrups, passed out, when Yong arrived later in the day. His face was bruised and beaten. He fell onto Ming and wept, then removed her feet from the stirrups and covered her with the soiled top sheet. She awoke and squeezed his hands in her own. "What did they do to you?" she asked.

"It's nothing," he said.

"The baby," said Ming. "Is it a girl or a boy?"

Yong looked at the bucket on the floor. He reached in and removed the latex gloves, holding them like a pair of scorpions. "A boy."

The doctor came back in and handed Yong a piece of paper. "The bill for my services," he said. "You must pay within the week or we will contact your employer. Now you both must go. Take her." He turned to leave.

"Doctor," said Yong. The doctor turned back to Yong.

"You forgot something." He tossed the bloody gloves in the doctor's face. "For your next patient."

***

Ming opened her eyes and was surprised to find herself in the arms of Teddy. She withdrew, shivering. "It is so cold in these caves," she said. "We buried the baby in here."

"In this cave?"

"Come." She raised the lantern and led T.K. to other side of the pool. There, in a small grotto that glistened from weeping springs in the wall, were two piles of smooth river rocks topped by wooden crosses. "Brother and sister," said Ming. "We had no land at our apartment. They would have thrown them in the trash."

"What happened the second time?"

"It was three years later. This time they waited until I was nine months' pregnant. Maybe on purpose, I don't know. The injection didn't kill the baby; she was born alive. They tossed her in the pail and let her die." Ming knelt and prayed in silence at the grave, and T.K. knelt beside her.

After a few minutes she rose. "We must go." When they reached the tomb entrance, Ming blew out the lantern and said, "Cover your eyes." She pulled open the door and sunlight exploded. Outside, the wind was still blowing hard, and two red memorial banners, tacked to the front of the door, danced like cardboard Halloween skeletons.

Chapter Eleven

T.K. went back to the barge many nights, always parking his Lambretta down at the raft landing. He brought *báijiǔ* and he drank it with tea and he talked for hours with Yong and Ming and Jintao, like he was a member of the family. He carried books for Jintao, starting with the fourteenth-century classic *Water Margin* by Shi Nai'an. "It's about a bunch of outlaws in the water marsh who save China," he told the boy. "My favorite outlaw is Wu Song. He kills a tiger with his bare hands after drinking eighteen cups of wine." He taught Jintao how to hold his breath for a long time, and they took turns seeing who would breathe first. Yong laughed; Ming worried it was dangerous.

With Yong's introduction T.K. met other houseboat refugees of the one-child law, most of them receiving aid from Christian International. Sometimes they would come over to the Chen barge to play mahjong for cigarettes—not polite American Jewish-lady mahjong but cutthroat Old Hong Kong style, with lots of cursing and violent slapping of the shin-bone tiles on the table. Some of the tiles were so battered that a clever player could remember the dings and dents from the back side, which led to many accusations of cheating followed by counter-arguments that it was all part of the game and you should get over it and maybe try to memorize them yourself instead of whining so much. Above this feral parlay they told their stories until way past midnight. They were the Dickensian dregs at the bottom of the Chinese barrel: men with missing front teeth from the beatings they endured, wearing unmatched sandals crusted in pig manure and pilled polyester shirts with sweat stains; young wives stooped over like grandmothers from the toll of wrenching abortions and miscarriages; and half-naked children with speckled red rashes, many homeschooled because they could not afford public school fees. Land was so scarce that they had to wean piglets in the coal holds of their barges; there were too many pigs in the pens, and the newborns would be trampled. Even so, being landless meant they had nothing of value from which local officials could extract taxes, so they were mostly left alone. But some told of strange disappearances of young women after undergoing forced abortions. The police generally said the women had committed suicide by jumping off the Sea Dragon Bridge into the Yulong River; the stone bridge, built in the Ming dynasty, was a popular place for wedding photos and to kill yourself. But bodies of the women never surfaced, at least not around town. The Yulong flowed into the Li, which eventually fed the Pearl and the South China Sea, but what were the chances a body would float all that way, past Guangzhou and Shenzhen and Macau and Hong Kong, without washing ashore? Some of the neighbors had cheap smartphones and they would go on Sina Weibo and read all sorts of rumors about women being taken as sex slaves for party officials, like something that might happen in North Korea. But you never knew what to believe on the Internet.

T.K. mostly just listened. Listening, he felt, was a lost art in journalism. Maybe it was too many hours of *Sixty Minutes*, or Watergate, or talk radio, but most reporters today were practitioners of the *gotcha* interview—it was about their own cleverness, or the preordained "lede," not the story unfolding right in front of them if they would just slow down. T.K. found if he stopped talking and *listened*, he would enter a sort of attentive trance—a creative zone, maybe even a cone, where the outside world fell away like road signs on a highway and he merged with the world of his subject, to the point where he genuinely pretended to care. Or maybe he really did care? So limited was his personal experience with empathy that he had no clue.

Sometimes he would fall out of the zone and steal a glance at Ming, observing her belly as it swelled more every day, and see that she was looking at him. They had developed a silent language between them that said everything and left everything unsaid. If it was love it was as unrequited as any two points in the universe could be, and both of them were content to leave it that way, as if the thought itself were somehow more real than any physical embrace.

One day, after a few weeks of these night visits, T.K. found himself drawn toward the barge in the morning, toward the light of Ming. He knew it was unsafe to be seen hanging around the river by day, but he also knew that Yong would be at work and he could have her to himself. *Have her* as he understood it simply meant to be in her presence, for like children of divorce who vow to make their own marriage work, he had sworn never to inflict the searing grief of infidelity, the pain he lived with constantly, on another married man and certainly not on one so kind as Yong. Meg's affairs, when he learned of them, had devastated him beyond what he considered all reason, not least because he had never really loved her. His constant travels and lack of concern for Meg's feelings should have prepared him for the inevitable break—her inevitable need for proximity—yet when he discovered her proximate with another man, only to learn there was also another woman, he lost all perspective. He briefly entertained an Arabist fantasy of murdering both lovers in a fit of revenge. Even more briefly, he thought of killing himself. And yet on some level he understood that Meg, like him, was only seeking a life of genuine experience. He had escaped the monotony of monogamy with work and drink; she with athletic sexual adventures. Was either less real than the other?

T.K. would not even admit to himself that he coveted Yong's wife, out of a vague recognition that even an internalized longing might constitute a form of betrayal. Yet he found himself that morning pointing his scooter to the river. When he arrived at the Chen barge, Ming stood in the pigsty holding a long knife. She saw him and waved. He dismounted and hopped the low bamboo fence into the sty.

"In New England we shoot them first, then bleed."

"We have no guns in China," said Ming.

"Guns are dangerous."

"I hate sticking the pigs. So much blood."

He held out his hand for the knife. "Which one?"

"No," she said. "It's my job." She approached a porker of about two hundred pounds from behind. His nose was groveling in the stink and he ignored her. She reached down and pulled up his snout, then jerked the knife smoothly across his throat. The massive beast shrieked and gurgled. Blood spewed like a geyser as Ming jumped back. The pig's eyeballs rolled backwards and he collapsed, hooves twitching patterns in the muck like a child making snow fairies. In seconds he was still; in minutes he was stiff.

T.K. watched Ming's fine, pale arms, like bisque porcelain, swivel deftly as she cut through the hog's rear hoof tendons and threaded an iron grapple bar through the trotters. T.K. thought her strength came not from muscle or bulk, for she was like a reed, but from the very sinews and ligaments between her bones. In that moment she reminded him of great baseball players, maybe Ted Williams, in the days before baseball players lifted weights and looked like football players. She gestured the bloody knife toward the barge.

"Run the line from that winch down here." T.K. scaled the gangplank and unspooled a thick jute rope from a deck winch. Ming grabbed the line and tossed it over a sheeve bolted to the limb of a twisted banyan tree, then tied the bite end to the grappling hook. She gave T.K. a thumbs up and he hauled on the crank until the pig dangled free, dripping the brick-red remains of life from his open throat.

"You can help me shave him," said Ming. "There is another sharp blade in the kitchen."

Over two hours they shaved the hog clean, one on either side. "You never have any help?" said T.K. as they worked.

"Jintao when he's not in school. He hates it. We only kill two every year for our own bacon. The processors take the butcher hogs live."

"On our farm we did four hogs a year," said T.K. "High point of the fall."

Ming frowned.

"I'm joking. I hated it too. Strong drink helped."

"Why do you drink so much?"

T.K. rested his blade and pondered the question. "Because it's there, I guess."

Ming kept moving her blade. "So it's a mountain."

He shrugged and looked up at the karst peaks rising behind Ming. "I guess so."

"Why don't you just go around?"

T.K. laughed. "Why didn't Hillary go around Everest?"

"Because he couldn't get into China then."

"And now you can't get out."

"What makes you think I want to leave?"

"Jintao," said T.K. "Jintao makes me think you want to leave."

"Where would we go?"

"Where everyone goes, I suppose. California."

"But you live in—" She caught herself.

"—New York," he said.

"I only meant—"

"I know," he said. He knew exactly what she was thinking because it was the same thing he was thinking and they both also knew it sounded better to think it than say it.

Her knife went still and her heart pounded. She looked at T.K., admiring his rusty complexion, the way his long hair curled back behind his ears, the tracing of veins in his large hands. She wondered what it would be like to wake up in America. She wondered what it would be like to wake up next to him.

"China is changing," she said. "Things will get better."

"For some," he said. "For some it already has."

"My grandfather never ran away," she said. "My family will not run away."

"And running away from Shanghai to this doesn't count?" He waved his knife around the pigsty, above the squealing drift of swine.

"And you, Teddy? Why do you stay in China?"

If he were a man without filters, with no concerns, he would have said *Because of you.* Instead he said, "Because it's there."

She laughed. They laughed.

Two months passed. T.K. had filled a dozen reporter's notebooks with tiny shorthand, which he would transcribe into his laptop back in his flat, to the din of New Year's fireworks in the street below. One night on the new moon he brought Jintao a translation of an American book. The cover was in English:

Donald Duk

by Frank Chin

Like all Chinese students, Jintao had been studying English and knew the Western alphabet. He read the title slowly, out loud: *"Donald Duk?"*

"It's a play on the English name for *Tánglǎoyā*," said T.K.

"Old Chinese Duck!"

"Yes. Except he's not known as Old Chinese Duck in America."

"But this is a book about him?"

"Not exactly. It's about a Chinese American boy your age whose surname is Duk. His immigrant parents named him Donald, thinking it was a good American name, not realizing what they'd done. I thought you might like it. Can you read traditional characters?"

"Pretty well."

"Good, because it's a Taiwanese edition."

As Jintao leafed through the pages, T.K. heard the gangplank creak. He looked at Yong. "Are you expecting visitors?"

"Just you."

Ming looked up at the ceiling. "*Someone is on the roof!* Teddy, the coal hold! Get in!" She silently pulled the mattress across the floor; beneath it was a trap door. "Down there. Quick!"

T.K. pulled on the ring and lifted the steel hatch. A ladder tailed down ten feet to the bottom of the barge and a few grey piles of coal that Ming used for cooking. In a corner was a pile of straw where piglets would soon be weaned.

"Ming, you must go down as well," said Yong. "I'll deal with them."

"What about Jintao?" said Ming.

"He will be safe, they want you. Go! Now!"

T.K. hugged Jintao, still reading the book, his Chinese residency card as a place mark. "We will read together again. I promise." The boy smiled.

Ming and T.K. climbed down the ladder and Yong closed the hatch over them, sliding the mattress in place just as the banging started on the cabin door.

"Police! Let us in!"

Yong opened the door and two cops fell in, wielding truncheons. "How many people here?" said the first.

"Just myself and my son," said Yong.

"Where is your wife? She has not menstruated in over three months."

"She went to see her family in Shanghai for New Year. She has not returned yet."

"Don't lie to us! China Railway has no record."

"She didn't take the train. Local bus to Guilin and got a ride on a lotus wood truck. We have no money for the train."

"You must come with me. Your son can stay here." The officer turned to his colleague and said, "Search the barge."

In the hold below, Ming and T.K., crouching and blackened with coal soot, listened as Yong and the officer crossed over the gangplank and the other cop moved through the cabin, overturning the meager furnishings. "He will find the trap," whispered Ming.

"Shh," said T.K.

Then Ming felt a stabbing pain in her gut and doubled over, wincing. T.K. caught her before she hit the floor. "What is it?"

"I think I'm in labor."

"Already?"

"Oh God! Help!"

T.K. tried to cover her mouth but it was too late. She wailed. Jintao burst out: "Mama!"

The cop yelled "Hey!"

Above Ming and T.K., the mattress was moving across the floor.

Ming gasped in pain and fright. "You must leave," she said, pointing toward the bow and the black reaches of the hold. "Up there is a ladder to the deck. Jump in the river. Hurry!"

"What about the baby?"

"Life is not meant for this baby."

He forced himself to let go of her and made his way through the anthracite fog to the bow, stubbing his toe on a clinker. He was up the ladder and into the river as the rear hatch opened and the cop climbed down.

Ming had crawled behind a coal pile onto the straw for the pigs, but it didn't take long for the policeman to find her, curled up next to a lifeless purple fetus.

"Shit!" the cop said, looking on the bloody scene with disgust. "Who else is down here?"

Ming said nothing.

"Tell me!" He kicked her in the breast and aimed a flashlight forward, revealing the bow ladder and a ghostly palimpsest of footsteps through the coal dust. He scrambled back up the ladder. Jintao was crying on his mat. "Mama! Papa!" The cop ignored him and bounded across the gangplank where Yong was being held by the officer Yun Jian, whose ears were still ringing from the New Year's fireworks.

"The woman is below, with a dead baby!" said the cop from the boat. "Someone else escaped. Search the river!"

"Ming!" shouted Yong.

"I see him!" said another cop standing by the shore who pointed his revolver in the water and released four rounds. The muzzle popped and flashed in the dark night and Officer Yun Jian flinched as his mind rewound to the boy with the firecrackers in his hand, the smoke and the pain, the black stains on his fingers and the large, coarse hands of his father slamming into his face. In that pause, Chen Yong reached around and grabbed Jian's gun from his holster. He pulled the trigger in the direction of Jian, but like most Chinese citizens he had never fired a gun, and the weight of the weapon surprised him—it wasn't like a gun in a movie—and the bullet hit another officer in the left arm, shattering his ulna. Yong himself did not scream. Three bullets from three guns hit him squarely in the head, which atomized into a mist of blood and brain that sprayed across Officer Yun Jian, who grabbed his gun from the dead man's hand and bent over to retch in the crimson earth.

In the same moment that Officer Yun Jian was reliving his explosive childhood, Theodore Kincaid Dean was rewinding his mind back to a boy named Teddy who could hold his breath for more than seven minutes—people were counting—in a cold Vermont granite quarry. Now T.K. dove deep, down to the poisonous slime at the bottom of the Li, deeper than he hoped bullets could go when slowed by water, and kicked with the current downstream until his lungs flatlined. Nobody was counting but he felt certain he had beaten his own personal best. When he came up, sucking for life, there was no one around and he was very close to his scooter. And in between the breathless Vermont boy in the river and the terrified Chinese boy puking beside the ruined corpse of Chen Yong was another boy clutching a book called *Donald Duk* and crying on a reed mat in a deathly quiet houseboat.

"Papa! Where are you? Mama?"

Doubts
The Third Part

Chapter Twelve

The Shenzhen passport control agent had to fish around in his drawer to find the stamp, which was rarely used. But there it finally was, and with a maestro's drop of the hand, a resounding clunk, T.K.'s Chinese visa, with its detailed engraving of the Great Wall, now bore the large scarlet letters *PNG*.

The sour-faced agent robotically fed the passport back through the window slot to T.K., who ran his hand over the fresh ink as if in disbelief, causing the *P* to smudge slightly. "*Persona Non Grata.* That's a first."

"I would call it the last," said Fang Dazhu, who stood behind T.K. with an immigration security agent. "As in, this is the last time you will ever set foot in Mainland China. I am so glad I was given the opportunity to escort you to the border myself." In mock graciousness he extended a hand toward the barrier that separated Hong Kong from Shenzhen. "Now if you would be so kind as to step through the gate."

T.K. slid past Dazhu, taking in the cop's fermented breath and the bloom of ripe blackheads on his sallow cheeks. As he passed he raised his nose with a sniff and said, in Zhuang: "Is that pig shit I smell?"

"You are very lucky, Mr. Dean," said Dazhu. "It could have been much worse for you. They do not toast with *báijiǔ* in the labor camps."

He would miss *báijiǔ*. In the end leaving China felt, he was quite sure, like death. Just one step across a technical white line, modernity's mediocre version of the Great Wall, and half a lifetime in China lay a romantic ruin at his feet—a Piranesi etching of school in Beijing, trains in Tibet, the river journeys and hutongs and temples and scooters and lamb testicles bubbling in hotpots and cricket fights in Shanghai and a whole fucking language and dialects—all of it gone as surely as a wasted life. What was left? Renting Chinese movies on Netflix? Yong was dead. Ming and Jintao? As good as.

T.K. waited until he was on the other side, then turned to face Dazhu. "If you touch her I'll kill you."

Dazhu doubled over in laughter. "You Americans are so dramatic! Everything like a Hollywood movie. How do you say it? *Bang bang shoot shoot?* Ha ha!" T.K. slung his pack over his shoulder and pivoted toward Hong Kong immigration. "Oh Mr. Dean!" Dazhu called out. "One more thing."

T.K. eased back toward the border warily, keeping his feet firmly planted in the New Territories.

"You may be interested to know of a rather strange development," said Dazhu. "When we found Zeng Ming with her dead fetus, she claimed it was from one of their pigs."

"I didn't know she was pregnant."

"Well naturally we assumed she was lying, as are you," Dazhu continued, "although the fetus was too small and damaged to tell for sure; all those abortions make it so difficult to conceive properly."

T.K. dropped his bag.

"So we took it in for DNA tests," said Dazhu. "And the really crazy thing is, it actually was a pig fetus."

Chapter Thirteen

"*Dédé! Plus de l'eau!*" Mensah Bocoum squatted on a log and waited for his wife to refill the dented aluminum pot of water next to his sharpening stone. They spoke French to each other, not that either spoke it well, but she was Ewe and he was Kabye and they could not *hear* each other's native tongue, as Africans liked to say. Although one of the smallest countries in Africa, Togo still had some forty distinct languages, not including sub-dialects or French. No wonder nothing ever gets done in this country, thought Mensah.

And yet what was there to talk about? Dédé knew how to cook and find snails, and she had given him many children. He knew how to farm and hunt for bush meat. What more was there to say?

Dédé, pretty and slim but stooped from a life of hauling water on her head, dipped a long-handled ladle deep into a fifty-five-gallon plastic drum under a bamboo drain pipe running off the metal roof of their round mud hut. Somewhere down there in the bottom was still some rain water. On her back, tied with a large African-print shawl made in China, was her latest baby, a boy hopefully named Stephen, not *Étienne*, in the hope that someday he would learn to speak English. She carried the ladle to Mensah and transferred the water into the pot at his feet. Mensah dipped his hand into the water, splashed some on the smooth rock and ran the blade of his machete back and forth across the wet surface. The daily morning ritual: sweet tea, porridge and twenty minutes honing his machete, then off to farm. A razor-sharp machete was essential for cutting maize stalks and clearing brush around his cocoa tree seedlings. Usually when someone in the village cut off a hand or a leg while farming, it was from using a dull machete, which is harder to control. Mensah's stone, smooth as glass from years of service, had belonged to his great-grandfather, who had worn a German uniform in World War One when Togoland, as it was then called, was a colony of the Kaiser. After the war the Brits and the French divided Togoland down its mountainous spine into two narrow slivers, the way Mensah's father taught him to split a bamboo stalk with a machete. The western sliver became part of the British colony of Gold Coast, ultimately Ghana, where English was taught; the eastern part became a French colony until independence in 1960. Nobody asked the Ewe or the Kabye or any of the other Togolese ethnic groups which country they wanted to join, or if they wanted to join anything larger than their village at all.

Mensah flipped his machete over, splashed more water on the stone and began working the blade in a circular motion. The larger circle of his domain, not including his eleven acres of maize and cocoa, consisted of his round mud hut, Dédé's cook fire, three molded plastic chairs and a small patch of oil palms, coated in the same fine red dust that covered the village huts and stained your handkerchief every time you blew your nose. It hadn't rained in weeks even though this was the rainy season, and the dust was everywhere, turning the landscape into a dull frieze of unfired clay. The dust and the near-empty rain barrel were nagging reminders that the Sahara was moving south, and the savannah was drying up. Maize yields were way down, and the ears were small even with fertilizer.

In a clearing across the narrow dirt road, Mensah's twelve-year-old son Emmanuel was kicking around a half-inflated soccer ball. It was the only ball in the village, and the nearest hand pump was nine miles into the market town of Asuso, where there was also electricity to charge mobile phones. Once a week, Emmanuel walked into town to sell snails his mother had gathered under banana leaves at night, and to buy matches, sugar and packets of laundry soap. If there was enough money left over after that, he could get the football pumped up for five francs. He and his friends kept the football pitch cleared with machetes. Between matches against neighboring villages, Emmanuel practiced his moves. He was the best goalie in the district, which everyone including Emmanuel attributed to his shirt—a filthy pinstriped charity castoff with a number 2 and the word JETER on the back. It wasn't a football team that anyone in Agbandé recognized—definitely not a West African team or even a UK Premier League club. But someone in the village who could read French said JETER meant "throw," so everyone figured it was the jersey of a goalie. That's how Emmanuel became the goalie; it must have been divined. This was his only shirt as he did not go to school and thus had no uniform, and it was a fate he took seriously, this shirt that commanded him to throw. Someday he hoped to guard the goal for Étoile Filante du Togo—the Meteors—his favorite professional club in Lomé.

Lots of villagers had left Agbandé and moved to Lomé, the crowded and suffocatingly humid capital city on the coast, looking for work. Some had made it into Ghana, which had free elections and a much better economy. Mensah heard Togolese men who spoke English could work as chefs in the big hotels of Accra, since Ghanaians only knew how to make disgusting British food whereas the Togolese had learned from the French how to reduce sauces and bake long bread loaves. Not that Mensah could work as a chef; Agbandé had no power or running water, and Mensah himself had never eaten anything that was not prepared by his wife or his mother over an open fire. Besides, he spoke even less English than French and could read not a word of either, or add and subtract figures.

Still he was a good provider for his wife and six living children. He had once been named Farmer of the Year in his district; the yellowing certificate was the only decoration on the wall of his hut (one advantage of a round hut is there is only one wall). He helped the local agricultural agent keep track of rainfall patterns. He also had a .22-caliber rifle and a thin groveling dog, which meant he could track and kill bush meat, at least when he could afford to buy bullets; yesterday his dog cornered a ferret in the maize field, and with one shot Mensah had put serious protein on the table. This morning he had eaten the ferret heart for extra strength with his porridge, as he was unlikely to get any lunch today.

A battered Toyota Hilux, dust-red as the road, listed into the clearing, diesel knocking. The door opened and from behind the wheel stepped a trim tall man in a camouflage uniform and smart cap with black boots. Kodjo Ayassor was a guard at the Kéran National Park down the road. His job was to protect Togo's dwindling herd of some two hundred elephants from ivory poachers, but it was a poorly paid job that came with an old but powerful Remington .350 Magnum carbine, so what in other *milieux* might politely be described as a "revolving door" existed between poachers and guards at Kéran National Park. What Togo lacked in sheer elephant numbers it made up for in its Lomé container port, which was busy, poorly monitored and highly corruptible. Traders would often pack ivory in a container under a load of iroko wood, bound for Myanmar or Vietnam where the ivory would make its way into China and the lumber ended up being re-exported from Asia as expensive "Burmese teak"—sort of a double reverse smuggle.

While patrolling the park at twilight the day before, Kodjo had discovered a slaughtered bull elephant next to a watering hole. The bull had been shot between the eyes and lay in the mud with stinking gore dangling from his face where poachers had hastily hacked out the tusks. Kodjo knew other elephants would return soon to mourn the dead patriarch; he would need to work quickly before the international wildlife monitors showed up. That's where Mensah came in.

"Are you ready?" said Kodjo in Kabye.

Mensah drew his thumb across the blade of his machete, mentally registered approval of his workmanship, and picked up his rifle. He slipped his plastic sandals off his calloused feet. Dédé handed him his rubber farm boots, which had holes in the heels. Baby Stephen was asleep on her back. Mensah kissed the boy's head and squeezed into his boots. "Let's go."

The road through the park was rutted and overgrown, but with no rain there was little danger of getting stuck; Kodjo didn't even need to use four-wheel-drive. In half an hour they arrived at the small spring where elephants gathered to drink. Overnight, hyenas had already reduced the massive bull corpse to a pile of bones that a flock of pied crows were picking over, veiled in a swarm of tsetse flies. The two men descended from the Hilux with their guns. Mensah swatted and cursed at a stray fly. Better access to cheap drugs had sharply reduced human deaths from fly-borne sleeping sickness, but drugs weren't always available, and villagers still feared the early signs of the fatal disease—fever and itching, followed by massive swollen lymph glands on the neck.

Kodjo led the way down a path to a sandstone ledge that overlooked the watering hole. "We shall wait here." They sat on a large rock and said nothing. A crocodile quietly surfaced in the pool. After about an hour, a rustling in the bamboo on the other side of the water drew their gaze. A cow and her calf soon emerged and lumbered over to the defiled remains of the bull. The cow must have been at least fifteen years old judging from the length of her tusks; they were brown, probably soft, and not as valuable as bull ivory. But the calf, who was maybe three, had a brilliant set of new ivory. Baby tusks, called "blood ivory," were prized for the purity of their tone, which could seem to glow in the right light.

Ignoring the swarm of tsetses, the animals hovered over the corpse and keened. Mensah thought their rumbling sounded like sobbing, and it made him sad. He knew that when he died, his own family would fall over his body, like he cried over the coffin of his second-born son, who died last year. He felt bad for the baby elephant; it deserved better. Everyone deserved better.

The first muzzle blast came from the big Remington carbine, sending the crows and even the flies into panicked flight. The .350 slug hit the mother squarely between the eyes. Before the big creature's knees even collapsed into the ground, Mensah let loose with his .22 into the head of the baby, which wailed like a muted trumpet, stunned. The tiny bullet had pierced the hide, kicking up a puff of dust, embedding in its skull but stopping just short of the brain. Kodjo drew back the bolt on his carbine and fired a merciful .350 fusillade into the calf. It was like a firing squad. As the baby elephant crumpled to the dirt, the crocodile slid below the water.

"Hurry!" said Kodjo. They shouldered their guns and jogged to the killing scene. Mensah withdrew his machete.

"The cow first," said Kodjo. Mensah understood: Ivory begins to dry out as soon as it's removed from the jaw; better to save the prized baby ivory for last.

He bent over the dead cow and pulled open her jaw, trying not to look into her frozen eyes. It had to be done right—no violent slashing and chopping like the reckless maniacs, probably Toareg Muslims, who dismembered the bull yesterday. The right way was to insert the tip of the machete into the base of the tusk, where it entered the gum, and stay close to the bone without damaging the ivory. As the blood spilled and Mensah worked, Kodjo moved to the truck, slipped on a pair of latex gloves he kept in the console, then reached into the bed and hefted out a sack of Furadan with a large poison skull emblem on the side. The powerful granular pesticide in the endocrine disruptor family was banned in North America and Europe but widely available across West Africa. Half a teaspoon could kill a human; a single grain was enough to drop a large bird—and birds easily mistook the grains for seeds, which was the whole point as far as Kodjo was concerned. Vultures can locate an elephant carcass within half an hour of its death, and game wardens counted on flocks of the birds to help track poachers. Already the obnoxious scavengers were circling over Kodjo's elephants and diving down boldly for a closer look. He opened the bag and spread the poison grains across the hides and on the ground, then turned his gaze to the bush, scanning for land-based intruders: Humans would be drawn to the gunfire, lions to the blood.

When the cutting around the first tusk was complete, Mensah said "Twist it." Kodjo grabbed hold of the massive curved prong and pulled in a circular motion, like stirring a giant pot over a fire, while Mensah kept the blade firmly against the gum. In seconds the tusk popped out, perfectly intact. The other one was trickier as it lay on the bottom—the cow had landed on her side—and dead elephants cannot just be flipped over by two men. One option was to hack off the head, but that was messy and time consuming, and Mensah was skilled enough with the blade to remove a tusk from the wrong side. In ten minutes he had it free. Vultures were now dropping down to the kill for a taste. But after one grain of Furadan they would stagger in confusion, then collapse dead. Soon the elephant pyre was draped in a convulsing black aviary of dying vultures, as if the elephants themselves had been tarred and feathered.

"Now that one," said Kodjo, pointing to the calf while shouldering the cow tusks over to the truck. The baby tusks came out quickly—the gums on a three-year-old elephant are soft—and by the time Kodjo had the mother's ivory loaded, Mensah had finished with the calf. Kodjo dunked a length of muslin in the watering hole, watching carefully for crocodiles, then wrapped the wet cloth around the blood ivory, adding them to the stash in the truck. They threw a tarp over the contraband, then arranged a few sacks of cocoa nuts over the tarp.

They climbed into the truck. Mensah looked back at the scene. If not for the pesticide he would have brought home some elephant meat for his family; what a waste. Even the vultures could not be eaten once they had consumed the grains.

Kodjo avoided the park's main gate and left on a back road that led through the small village of Womoso, a cocoa depot. In front of a small storefront with a hand painted sign of hair clippers indicating a beauty parlor, a woman was braiding long extensions into another woman's hair. On the door of the health clinic was another hand-painted sign, depicting a man presenting a beaded necklace to a woman who shoos him away. *"Si votre cadeau est pour le sexe, vous pouver le garder,"* she was saying. And below: *"Vous ne méritez pas le SIDA."*

No, no one deserved AIDS, thought Mensah. Everyone deserved better.

"Kodjo," said Mensah as they jostled along, "do you ever think about the elephants?"

Kodjo looked at Mensah like he was the full moon but said nothing, then turned his eyes back to the road. His mouth tasted like red dust.

"I mean, what happens when they are all gone?" Mensah continued. "Then what will we do?"

Kodjo kept his eyes on the road. "Pangolin."

"Pangolin?" Mensah's dog sometimes cornered one of the strange armored anteaters, which were delicious in stew but hard to clean because of their sharp keratin scales.

"The Chinese love the meat," said Kodjo. "And the scales are valuable too. Chinese women take them in a powder, to promote the monthly blood."

"Why would you need to promote the blood?" asked Mensah. "When it comes, it comes, and then you know she is not with child and must try again."

"I do not know," said Kodjo. "Maybe it is different in China."

"Pangolin!" said Mensah. "To me it is only bush meat."

"Also crocodiles," said Kodjo. "Very valuable."

"I don't mind killing crocodiles," said Mensah.

"I hate crocodiles," said Kodjo.

When the truck turned in to Agbandé, Kodjo handed Mensah a hundred thousand francs—more than he made in a year of farming. The money would let him buy a mechanical press to extract valuable clear oil from the inner seeds of his palm nuts. And the money from selling palm oil would pay for Stephen's school uniforms and supplies, so he could learn to read and write French and English. Because he deserved better.

Chapter Fourteen

"*Gwailo!*"

The hack outside the Hong Kong-Shenzhen border crossing had the window of his Toyota rolled down and was addressing T.K. with the Cantonese word for "foreign devil."

"*Gwailo! Nei huei bei bein dowah?*"

God how T.K. hated Cantonese. All those tones and vowels, so unnecessary, so impure. In truth except for the Mid-levels bar scene he despised Hong Kong, which he felt was China for beginners. It was too easy, and now its vaporous dim sum stands and screeching vertical trolleys and bloody night markets and spitting, coughing, snot-voiding impatient masses would torment him with memories of the real China he would never see again. He hopped in the cab, ignoring the driver's attempt to ask him where he was going in Cantonese, and said in English: "Nathan Road, Kowloon."

"Ah, Nathan Road!" said the driver finally in English. Like Montrealers, Hong Kongers all speak English when the promise of commerce is aimed like a weapon directly at their Babel-ing heads. "You do shopping?"

"Something like that."

"Very good deals there. Pussy, computer, genuine copy watch, everything nice price. No smoking please." He tapped a No Smoking sign that took up most of the glass divider behind his seat, with type large enough to read from Macau.

"I don't smoke."

"Okay, just checking. People come through Immigration, wait long time, need cigarette."

"Actually I got through pretty fast. Private escort."

"Oh, you must be VIP!"

"Something like that. Can I pay in RMB? No Hong Kong dollars."

"Okay, but surcharge. Should have changed at border." The Cantonese have a way of scolding strangers that is almost Aryan, thought T.K. "Also you need dollars for pussy on Nathan Road."

Night fell like leaded crystal on the neon ride down to Kowloon. At the corner of Carnarvon and Kimberley, T.K. told the driver: "Pull over by the dumpling stand, I'll walk from here." He climbed out and followed the crowd a block over to Nathan Road, swimming with the current again, into the VAT-free zipper-sign slipstream of laptop emporiums, overpriced seafood restaurants, watch vendors and wide-eyed tourists from the Real World Where Cars Drive on the Right (*Look Left!*)—all of it, from the Rolexes to the gawkers and at this point even himself, surrounded by quote marks of questionable provenance.

He crossed into a nondescript mobile phone shop, unbranded, where a young woman behind a glass counter was working a Sudoku puzzle and wearing an epidermal China Mobile mini-dress whose frayed hems dated it to a long-ago Canton Trade Fair. The phones were undoubtedly fake or grey-market, the SIM cards pirating minutes through Bulgarian piggyback accounts. Perfect. "Good evening," he said.

The girl looked up, ready to frown as usual at the sight of a customer, but this one was handsome enough to warrant a smile, plus he wasn't fat and wearing a tracksuit.

"I need your cheapest smartphone and a prepaid SIM with data minutes."

She closed her Sudoku book in annoyance, reached under the counter and plopped a white plastic "iCallU" Android phone on the counter. "Same company makes Galaxy," she said mechanically, which was true in the sense that the same company also made Etch-a-Sketch toys at a factory in Shenzhen. "Two thousand with minutes."

"How much in RMB?"

"Same."

"Wow. Last time I checked, the exchange was about sixty percent." The girl shrugged. Since the handover, China deliberately pegged the Hong Kong dollar and the Macanese pataca lower than the yuan, which made it convenient for wealthy mainland officials looking to gamble in Macao or park their millions in Hong Kong real estate; apparently this phone store never got the memo. He could change money down the street at the real rate but then they'd scan his passport, and who knew where that information went? Hong Kong Schmong Kong—he was still technically in China and he didn't much feel like sharing. He fished twenty crumpled hundred-yuan notes, the wrinkles aging Chairman Mao by some twenty years, out of his jacket. The girl unwrapped the phone and a fresh SIM card. "You want me activate?"

"Please."

"I need see passport."

"Define *see*."

"Oh, just need verify you have one. Only scan Chinese passports. You not Chinese, right?"

The question stung him momentarily. No, he would never be even an honorary Chinese again. "American."

"Oh, you fooled me—no tracksuit."

"I'm not very athletic."

"Americans wear gym clothes but don't look like they go to gym. I learn that word—*couch potato!*"

"That's two words."

"Okay, American couch potato. For you, only lookie-look passport." She'd clearly been down Lookie Lu with other well-traveled skeptics; nobody bought an "iCallU" phone to impress friends, and two thousand yuan was a lot of money for an Etch-a-Sketch knockoff. T.K. opened his passport to the photo page and held it up. She reached for it but he pulled back.

"You said *look*," he reminded, wagging a finger. Not that it would probably matter but he really didn't want her to see the PNG stamp on his China visa.

"Okay okay fine." She fiddled with the phone and handed it over. "Your number here," she said, pointing to the SIM card packaging. "You can buy top-ups now if you like."

"Thanks." He opened the browser and made sure the data plan had kicked in. Google Maps: check. WhatsApp: good. He punched in a Hong Kong number from memory and tapped out a message:

Hey TK here.

Moments later a text came back:

Where ru?

Kowloon.

Meet me FCC 1900.

CHAPTER FIFTEEN

By seven o'clock that evening the Main Bar of the Hong Kong Foreign Correspondents' Club was packed as usual, with the usual crowd: jowly Brit press hounds old enough to have worked in radio when radio mattered; Aussie photographers hunchbacked from decades of slinging Nikon necklaces; and fecal-breathed French columnists who'd been slurping at this trough since Dien Bien Phu—all of them hitting on women in "the financial press" young enough to be their granddaughters. God, journalists were a lecherous lot, thought T.K. Something about the mandate to be *objective* had somewhere along the line translated to *objectify,* nowhere more so than here, where on any given night the bar poured enough gin and tonic to cure malaria. What the hell, T.K. told himself. As good a place as any to get drunk.

"Zuolin!" T.K. summoned the white-jacketed Manchurian bartender, who was older even than the palsied war correspondents he served—so old that his wife had bound feet, which he still believed to be the height of eroticism. "Another gin Rickey please."

Zuolin bowed. The drink arrived at the same time as a tap on T.K.'s shoulder.

"T.K!"

He turned and smiled. "George!" T.K. stood and looked into the eyes of the man who was his best friend, although that wasn't saying much as he counted only two friends in the world. George was as tall as T.K. and equal to him in every other definition of stature that mattered: intellect, wit, humor, a skeptical regard for the spiritual world and a firm believer in the world of spirits. George Chambers, felt T.K., was a man perfectly suited to his name: He had the omniscient bearing of a judge, an ability to quickly synthesize information to form an opinion and render it with finality. And yet beneath the smirking confidence burned the embers of a restless child who seemed never quite sure of himself after all. His eyes rattled around like marbles in a skeeball game, permanently distracted, unable or unwilling to filter. To George, rooms full of people were like a shopping spree at Barney's New York; where to begin? In a lesser intellect this orbital disposition would characterize a crushing bore, but in George Chambers it came off as endearingly virtuosic. They embraced, T.K. noting the working cuff buttons on George's bespoke nailhead suit.

"I can't believe they let you in here," said George, running his eyes down from T.K.'s battered bomber jacket to his wrinkled khakis and spattered boots.

"I had to promise I'd spend a lot at the bar."

"We must all make sacrifices. I take it you arrived early?"

"Minutes ago. Only on my third Rickey."

George was still staring at T.K.'s footwear. "Is that some kind of shit on your boots?"

"Pig. I scraped most of it off on the doormat."

"Good lord. I hope you've been immunized."

"They call this the distressed look," said T.K. "All the rage now."

"Glad to see fashion catching up with you," said George. "You were never one to shirk the shitholes. As I recall you were the poor bastard assigned to excavate the cistern at Psalmodi."

Psalmodi was the archeological dig in southern France where they had met one college summer—two would-be journalists off on a European lark. The site was a Gothic Benedictine monastery on top of a Romanesque church on top of a Carolingian church on top of an ancient Roman villa. A bodge job of incongruous layers, but mostly in ruins except for one side of the twelfth-century Gothic nave which was being used as the outside wall of a barn on a sunflower farm in the marshy Camargue, near the walled city of Aigues-Mortes. The monks had abandoned the place in the seventeenth century when rising swampland bred too many mosquitoes and caused malaria outbreaks. That summer George discovered a Romanesque stone lintel carved with the scene of Christ entering Jerusalem. Not to be outdone, T.K. unearthed a Huguenot mass grave from the seventeenth century—the skulls had been bashed in, poor Protestant bastards—and a stash of unexploded World War II ordnance that required a call to the Gendarmerie

National. They slept in tents and had no hot water, just a hose shower behind the stables. Everybody got ringworm. Everybody fucked everybody else, including the professors. Everybody got blind drunk every night, emptying wine casks in the barn. Then they had to work the next day in the broiling hot sun, hung over. The only toilet was in a tomato greenhouse—*dig rats* weren't allowed to go into the farmer's house unless they had to use his manual typewriter, which had a weird French keyboard with accent keys—and if you had to take a shit in the daytime it was well over 120 degrees in the hothouse. To cool off on breaks they would take turns napping in a marble Roman sarcophagus under an olive tree; the stone was nice and cool, much better than the tents in the hot sun. Everyone except T.K. and George slept backwards in the stone coffin—feet on the head side—because it was considered too creepy to lay in a coffin the "correct" way; you might never wake up. T.K. and George scoffed at the superstition and napped like corpses, properly arranged.

At the end of the dig they went to Nice and took their first hot shower in months, watching what they thought were suntans go down the drain of the pension house. That's when George learned that no amount of soap gets you clean without hot water. Later when they both got jobs at the *Detroit News* and co-reported metro stories exposing corruption in the police department, they wanted to byline themselves "The Dig Rats," but the city editor refused. "I'm happy to call you the Dimmer

Twins," said the editor, "but only in the newsroom. You know, like Mick and Keith, only dimmer." The name stuck.

"The cistern," said T.K, frowning. "That was the worst job I never got paid for."

"Why do I think your current look of distress is more than just a fashion statement?" George asked.

"What are you drinking?"

"Beer."

"Beer doesn't count."

George smiled. "To think I've been waiting four years to hear you say that. I'm saving myself for dinner. Kathleen is joining us. Can't wait for you to meet her. Now out with it; what's going on? I haven't seen you in ages and you show up on the island caked in shit with a brand new Hong Kong SIM."

"You go first. Tell me how much you miss journalism."

"I'm afraid that would be a short conversation, my friend. My God how that world has changed."

T.K. glanced around the bar. "Look at these cadavers. Could they still be gainfully employed?"

"If you count blogging. Actually most are spies I suspect," said George. "The U.S. Consulate is right across the street."

"Spying—now that's a growth industry," said T.K.

George, who had been following T.K.'s gaze around the room, snapped out of some reverie. "You remember when we worked at the *News* they were still correcting page proofs with a red pencil?"

"They still do in the book business."

"Your witness, counsel."

"Remember that copy chief who kept a collection of rubber stamps on his desk?" said T.K, picking up on George's nostalgia riff. "He had all his possible comments made into stamps, and to save time he would stamp his notes on stories. My favorite stamp said, HED TOO STRONG."

"He should have planted that right here," said George, poking two fingers on T.K.'s forehead. "Really neither one of us was cut out for being stamped by editors, and I'm afraid I never had the discipline to write books."

T.K. signaled Zuolin for another round, amused by the implication that he was himself remotely disciplined. Of his many attributes, he thought, self-discipline was conspicuously lacking. Then again, it was true that he applied discipline to his work, both in his careful attention to detail and his single-minded ability to focus on the empty page. Why is it always both ways, he wondered. Why don't the inherent good qualities simply overpower the bad? It was easy to understand how there could be truly fucked-up humans like Hitler or, more prosaically, Republican Congressmen, but why do so many basically decent people trail this waterlogged raft of shit behind them? People were not bottles of eighty-two Pétrus; they didn't improve with age, and the lush overtones of slothfulness and greed were not high notes in the human condition. He wondered if they had any old Pétrus in the cellar of the club. Yiqian, the wizened sommelier who spoke French better than Zhou Enlai, would have bought it himself in France years ago, not recently at some overpriced Tokyo auction, and it could be on the list at a reasonable markup for members. He hoped George was picking up the dinner tab.

"You know Nietzsche had it wrong," said T.K. "Dionysus, not Apollo, was the god of creativity."

"I'll drink to that," said George.

T.K. clinked his glass against George's beer bottle and said, "So what's new in the world of venture capital?"

"On this side of the world? More like *adventure* capital," said George. "Every other twenty-year-old over there"—he jerked his head in the direction of Mainland China, vaguely across Victoria Harbor—"is an engineer, and I'm counting the women too; they can gin up a circuit for a hand sample of anything you want in about an hour, but ask them for their own ideas and they turn to stone. *Buy cheap, sell dear, move it fast.* That's what passes for entrepreneurship over there. I keep looking, and I'm not alone. There's billions in VC cash sitting on the sidelines here. But enough about my business. How goes the maple syrup empire?"

T.K. winced. "Did you know that when sap comes out of the maple tree it's like water?"

"I did not know that."

"And do you know how many gallons of sap it takes to make a gallon of maple syrup?"

"Again I confess ignorance."

"Forty."

"That's a lot of sap. Good thing trees are big."

"So how do you think you get all that water out of the sap?" prompted T.K.

"Beat it with a stick?"

"You boil it. For hours. It's a process of reduction. Like writing. You write a four-thousand-word story and the editor reduces it to a thousand."

"Well in my case they usually just cut from the bottom. But I get it, you're saying the energy costs kill you."

"Energy, people—same difference in Vermont. The heat comes from wood. Somebody has to cut it, split it, stack it, then keep it burning. When my dad went to Vietnam there were dozens of kids around town, too young to fight, who kept the sugar house running. Now they're gone. Me too."

"The last time I checked, Americans were looking for jobs."

"Yeah, folding sweaters at the Gap Outlet. Nobody wants to stoke sugar shacks in February."

"Jesus. I'm so glad I'm not you."

"I'm not me either. I sold the whole operation to Pepsi last year."

"Pepsi?"

"Pepsico, the multi-national corporation, not to be confused with Mexico, which is a subsidiary of the United States. Pepsico owns Quaker Oats, which owns the Aunt Jemima syrup brand."

"Please don't tell me she isn't real."

The soft long vowels from behind them were Australian. George and T.K. pivoted on their stools and faced a tall, slim blonde in a short black skirt suit. "Darling!" said George, standing to peck his girlfriend. "This is my old friend T.K. Meet Kathleen."

"A pleasure," said T.K., rising and turning to shake hands.

"Oh my God, separated at birth!" Kathleen said, her eyes bouncing between T.K. and George.

"Please darling, we don't look *that* alike," said George, "although I'd wager these Chinese think we're twins."

"A pleasure to meet the other Dimmer Twin," she said to T.K. "Unless you're planning to disabuse me on the existence of Aunt Jemima."

"I'm afraid I have to ruin our relationship straight off. But if it makes you feel any better, there was once an Aunt Jemima, although she was actually a white man."

"Relationship saved! *Zuolin, a mojito please.* A man?"

"She was a popular sketch character in minstrel shows after the Civil War—the whole slappin' mammy bit. Generally speaking all minstrel performers were men."

"Like the Old Globe," she said. George sat back, amused at the repartée between his old friend and his new girlfriend.

"By most accounts the first Jemima was a German immigrant in blackface named Pete Baker."

"Jesus," she said. "Next you'll tell me Santa Claus was a bearded white man."

"So was God, before he was pronounced dead. They're everywhere, those old white men."

"Just look around this bar!" said George.

"Why do you know so much about Aunt Jemima?" said Kathleen.

"I am a font of useless information."

"I positively *live* for useless information."

"Oh shit, don't tell me you're another journo."

"Financial press," she said.

"Naturally. Isn't everyone these days?" He caught her frown and said, "I mean—isn't everyone who's ambitious and talented?"

"She's a Murdoch man," said George. "I mean woman. Sorry dear. Former Hanoi bureau chief of the *Australian,* now posted here."

"Great," said T.K. "Have you hacked my phone yet?"

"Not to worry old boy, your number's too new," said George.

"I'm famished," said Kathleen. "What time is our table?"

George flipped over his wrist and studied his Rolex, which was not from Nathan Road. "Now."

Drinks in hand, sloshing only a bit behind them, the trio ascended the wide circular stairs to the main dining room and secured a quiet table under a round shuttered window, beneath the burnished teak trestles of the old ice house ceiling.

"Can you believe they used to store ice in this place?" said Kathleen.

"Adds new meaning to the word *coolie,*" said George.

"Oh George!" said Kathleen. "I can always count on you to say something politically incorrect."

"Well darling you can be damn sure the Brits didn't haul that ice. I'll wager they consumed plenty of it though, right T.K?"

"I'm not a betting man but I'd call that a safe wager. Cheers!" They clinked glasses as the waiter arrived.

"Good evening," said T.K. "Another Rickey, please. And send over Yiqian with the wine list, or a bottle of Eighty-two Pétrus, whichever is faster."

"Just bring around a good Côte-Rôtie and a Meursault," said George to the waiter. "2000 on both if you have it."

The waiter bowed. T.K. was at this point absorbed in his place setting, studying it like an ancient rune on starched white linen.

"Something the matter?" asked Kathleen.

"Oh nothing," he said. "Just that I haven't used a fork in so long, or held a glass with a stem."

"Don't worry, it's like riding a bicycle," she said. "It all comes back."

"But if you're concerned," added George, "we can arrange for a bib and high chair."

"I'd feed you myself but I'm afraid I've no experience as a mother," said Kathleen.

"And I was a terrible son," said T.K. "Perfect!"

"I'm sure your parents loved you all the same," said Kathleen.

"In their own way," he said.

***

His father had been drinking that day, in his own way, meaning starting after breakfast. T.K. remembered the pancakes and maple syrup—the last meal his mother would ever make, on the day that divided then from now. It was early March: The sap was running high and the sugar shack was in full boil. T.K. was helping his father stoke the stove; his mother had come out with bacon sandwiches for lunch. Teddy was bent over the woodpile, heaving four-foot logs across the floor to his father, who was pushing them into the flame. The furnace was loud, and Teddy didn't hear his mother walk in, and he tossed a log that scuttled under her feet and knocked her over onto the concrete slab. She didn't appear to be seriously hurt but she must have twisted an ankle because she couldn't get up. Teddy and his father dropped their work and rushed over to help her. But in his haste, his father forgot to shut down the dampers on the stove, and the sap was nearly done boiling. When sap boils too long it boils over—like water but much faster, and much hotter, like grease, and it's thick and sticky and stays where it lays. If it lays on your skin it can burn a hole down to the bone, like acid. *Hot maple syrup is an accident waiting to happen,* his father used to say, almost as if, in his melancholy, he was literally waiting for it to happen. The evaporation pan on the stove held four hundred gallons of sap, which boiled down to ten gallons of scalding syrup—ten gallons that erupted like lava over the edge of the pan and onto the floor and his mother's prone body.

Her pain was brief, according to the doctor. "It was over so fast," he said. Teddy was sixteen, old enough to suspect that it would never be over, especially for his father, but not old enough to see any path through the sugar bush of his own grief and guilt.

***

The waiter arrived with the wine and slid out the corks. T.K.'s eyes followed the pour like a tennis ball as George looked on.

"Sorry mate, no rice wine tonight," said George. "Rumor has it this stuff is made from genuine grapes."

"Only one way to be sure," said T.K., raising his glass. "To China!"

"*À la Chine!*"

They toasted China, and Hong Kong, and Australia, and Detroit and Psalmodi and Aunt Jemima, and in minutes the white was drained.

"Waiter!" said George, fingering his phone, distracted. He gestured at the Côte-Rôtie. "Another bottle, please. And no more for you T.K. unless you spill the beans on what the hell you've been up to."

They drank more bottles and ate racks of lamb and T.K. told them about Ming and Yong and their son Jintao and the two abortions.

Kathleen had stopped eating. "Oh that poor woman," she said. "And beyond the sheer beastliness of the doctor, how creepy that the government actually keeps track of a woman's menstrual periods. It's like something out of Orwell."

"But not all that different from the West," said George.

"Meaning what?" she said.

"Meaning in most of the so-called free world, women are allowed to have an abortion up to a certain gestational period."

"And?"

"And how do you think they determine that period? Ask the fetus?"

She frowned. "I assume a doctor can tell."

"No doubt with ultrasound a good estimate can be made, but the fact is, in most countries there is a legal definition that's based on the woman's last menstruation. So if you're allowing the state to regulate abortions based on a woman's menstrual cycle, by definition you're allowing the state to monitor a woman's menstruation—at least any woman seeking an abortion. Otherwise the law is technically unenforceable."

He carved away a lamb rib. "Put another way, if a woman seeking an abortion says her fetus is X weeks old and a doctor rules it $X+1$ weeks old, what would be her legal recourse? Only the record of her last menstruation."

"So what's your point?" said T.K., refilling his glass.

"My point is that even free societies, by virtue of laws which are enforced by evidentiary proceedings, must necessarily invade privacy, often in ways we rarely think about. It's simply the price we pay for a uniform civil code. Indeed one could argue *must* invade privacy to apply justice fairly and equally; the alternative is arbitrary justice, which is totalitarianism."

"So let me get this straight," said T.K. "You're saying that free countries compromise privacy to protect freedom."

"Yes."

"And totalitarian countries like China also, by definition, compromise privacy to protect the interests of the powerful."

"In both cases one could argue the ends justify the means, no?"

"So basically you can be free, or not free, but either way you can't expect privacy unless you're a Taoist monk living on a mountaintop."

"Well there are degrees, but yes."

"Now *that's* Orwellian," said Kathleen with a shudder.

"And I haven't even finished my story," said T.K. Then he told them about the miscarriage in the coal bin of the barge, and the savage death of innocent Yong in the pigsty under a new moon.

"They just blew the back of his head off?" said Kathleen. George was typing on his phone, distracted, but half listening and shaking his head in a gesture of empathy.

"Like the fucking Zapruder film," said T.K. "They took me to see his body in the morgue. Wanted to see if I recognized him. I said 'How am I supposed to know?'"

"The Chinese police get rather persnickety when when a citizen points a gun," said George, looking up from his phone. "And can you blame them?"

"Well here's the grand finale," said T.K. Then he repeated the last words of the sub-chief Fang Dazhu at the border crossing that morning: *"And the really crazy thing is, it actually was a pig fetus."*

"Wow," said Kathleen. "Do you think he was lying?"

George looked up from his phone. "Those Mainland cops are all professional liars, you know."

"No," said T.K. "I don't think he was lying. Something in his eyes—I think he was as surprised as me, and maybe was hoping my reaction could explain it for him. I don't know."

"Well if *he* wasn't lying then *she* was," said George, logically. "The whole pregnancy story."

"No," said T.K. "She was pregnant. Don't ask me how, but I know she was. She was. I need to find her and Jintao."

"You love her, don't you?" said Kathleen, her turquoise eyes large in the candlelight.

"I don't know. Maybe you could reduce it to that."

"Reduce it?" said George. "My friend, it's not maple syrup. Nothing's more complicated than love."

"Or as irreducible," said Kathleen, feeling proudly philosophical.

"What I mean is, what I feel for her seems far larger than love, if that's possible. I can't put my finger on it. It's like trying to describe China in a sentence. Frankly I've never felt this way about a person before."

"Did you—you know?" said George, fluttering his eyebrows like Groucho Marx.

"No," said T.K. "It was strictly platonic. Maybe even Socratic."

"Well that settles it," said Kathleen. "Any man who feels that way without sex is definitely in love."

"Are you sure you're not gay?" said George.

"I guarantee you he's not," said Kathleen.

"Because it's okay—we're a tolerant bunch," said George.

"Look, thank you for your concern, but I've got some important drinking to do tonight, and you all must have work in the morning."

"*Work,*" said Kathleen like a spit take, draining her glass. "I hate it when that happens."

Chapter Sixteen

In his sleep that night, T.K. dreamed he was in the cave with Ming. Her lantern had run out of oil and the damp underground air washed over his eyes like calligraphy until all was black. Volts of neurons arced across his retinas, which glowed red. It was like staring into a fire, and after a while he noticed stars burning on the image within his head. The stars of the Chinese flag.

Then a low, tugging vibration through his legs jerked him awake, and he opened his eyes and realized he wasn't in bed after all but was in fact riding the outdoor escalator up to Mid-levels and the Soho bar scene. He was drunk—that much was certain, but then wasn't that the plan? As long as things were going according to plan, he thought, there was no need for concern. *"Courage!"* he said to himself, pronouncing it in his mind the French way, and he gripped the handrail tightly as the conveyer doggedly pulled him up, above the red Toyota taxis blaring Canto-Pop along Queen's Road and the blinking video parlors on Stanley Street and the ziggurats of worker-bee studio apartments with their Murphy beds never made and kitchenettes never used.

At the Wellington Street entrance, a strange little man got on the moving stairs just in front of T.K. He was *curious* in every sense of the word, the sort of person whose appearance and attire seemed carefully designed to draw attention. He was Chinese, middle-aged, and he wore a beige slubbed silk suit, a black silk Mandarin-collar shirt with knitted frog buttons, a wide-brimmed Montecristi straw fedora, and sharply pointed brown loafers of the type known in England as *winkle-pickers*. He had a long silver Fu-Manchu moustache—a real one grown only from the upper lip and braided, not the "horseshoe" version favored by American bikers that grows down the sides—and he wore round tortoise-shell Pu Yi glasses. He was, deliberately it seemed, the embodiment of the venerable "Chinaman" stereotype. It was as if instead of jumping on the escalator at Wellington Street he had leaped directly from the pages of a Sax Rohmer novel. As the stairs droned up toward Soho, he turned to face T.K., smiled wanly, and addressed him formally in Mandarin:

"Dean *xiānshēng?*"

"Who wants to know?" said T.K., glad to be speaking Mandarin again.

"Permit me to introduce myself, Mr. Dean. I am Wang Weicheng from Christian International Aid in Shanghai. I may be able to help your friend."

T.K. belched, with remembrances of roast lamb and Rhône appellation. "I don't have any friends."

"You have a friend on the mainland, no? With a child? They could be in grave danger."

"Do you know where she is?" said T.K., suddenly feeling sober in a relative sense.

"Not yet," said Weicheng. "We knew her husband Yong of course. A pity about him. But you see, we don't know his wife's name, and can't find her since the barge incident. With your help, we can be sure she and the boy are safe. You can't go back to China. I can."

"I only deal with Christian International in New York," said T.K. "I don't know you from Fu-Manchu." He said it before he could stop himself; it just seemed appropriate.

The man smiled at the joke, not offended by the reference. "If I may be so forward, please check your phone. He should be sending you a text right now that will verify my identity, with a photo."

T.K. checked his Mao watch. Midnight.

"It's noon in New York," added Mr. Wang. "He will be having lunch at Nom Wah tea parlor, as usual."

T.K. pulled out his phone. The escalator hummed. A minute later came the confirmation. He looked at Mr. Wang and the picture on his phone. "Her name is Zeng. Zeng Ming."

"And the boy? Does he use his father's surname?"

The boy. At his mention some stray neuron, undimmed by the cloak of Syrah and gin Rickeys, fired a glimmer of concern across T.K.'s brain, like the glow of approaching headlights over a hill.

"Duk. His name is Donald Duk."

"I will be in touch with the New York contact," said Mr. Wang. And at the Hollywood Road footbridge he disembarked and vanished around the grey hulk of Victoria Prison.

T.K. continued up to Mid-levels and got off at Staunton Street. Standing at the roadway, just off the conveyer, was Kathleen.

"You again!" said T.K. "Why do I get the sense everyone is following me?"

"George went back to his office and I was hoping you'd buy me a drink. Kind of figured you'd wind up here." They walked west toward Aberdeen, dodging throngs of expat bankers, still in their sack suits with neckties askew, spilling out of pubs and bistros and barking lame jokes.

"Who was that man on the escalator?" said Kathleen. "Okay, I followed you."

"Name of Wang. Definitely not Cantonese; native Mandarin speaker. From Christian International. Says he can help me find Ming and Jintao."

"Funny, he wasn't wearing a cross," she said. "Don't those Christian types always wear big crosses?"

"Maybe it's tattooed on his ass, I don't know."

"Listen, you need to leave Hong Kong."

They stopped at the corner of Peel Street.

"Don't tell me I'm PNG here as well," said T.K.

"Seriously. It's not safe here."

"Not safe? I spent half my life in Mainland China, dodging security police. This place is like a fucking frat house! I mean look at these people. Bunch of Limey stockbrokers in half-canvased suits. These poofs wouldn't know how to pull back their foreskins without calling a lawyer."

"Maybe you've been on the Mainland too long. I don't think you get it. Hong Kong today is like the worst of both worlds. It's a free-for-all, that's for sure, but it's not as free as it looks. The Mainlanders are moving in. Look at those luxury condos up on the peak; why do you think they're all dark?"

He glanced up the mountain looming behind them. "Maybe they're not drunks like us and they go to bed at a decent hour."

"Maybe nobody lives in them," she said. "Maybe they're banks."

"Banks?"

"Investments. A place for Mainland billionaires to park their fortunes outside of China, just in case."

"Just in case of what?"

"The real revolution."

"And your point is?"

"My point is they're taking over, and they're doing it with money, not torture confessions and forced abortions. They own everything but they don't live anywhere. They live on the Internet."

"What's that got to do with me?"

"I don't know exactly, but Hong Kong today is not what it seems. All this posturing and fulminating over free speech and property and human rights—it's a smokescreen, to keep people loyal to the brands."

"The *brands?* It's not fucking maple syrup here. These are real people, not Aunt Jemima.'" T.K. was growing weary of the exchange. He wanted a drink, but as he stepped away Kathleen pulled him back.

"Listen to me! East and West, it's like Coke and Pepsi—all the same sugar water." Sensing his doubt, she strained for more analogies. "Arsenal and United, the Yankees and the Red Sox—it's all bullshit. Fake rivalries to whip up the crowd and make more money."

"Hold on. The Yankees are genuinely evil, with the possible exception of Derek Jeter. You wouldn't know that, you're Australian."

"Whatever! The truth is, there's no East or West in Hong Kong anymore. On the level where things really count—"

"—as in counting money?"

"They're in the sack together. Look at the newspapers. By law the journalists here are free to criticize Mainland policies, but the advertisers are all trying to do business on the Mainland; that's where the money is. And they can't risk pissing off the Mainland powers by advertising in *Ming Pao* or the other independent Cantonese papers. So they run ads in *Ta Kung Pao* or *Wen Hui Po*, party organs that nobody in Hong Kong reads, just to curry favor on the Mainland. The free papers are down to skeleton staffs; they exist just to create the illusion of press freedom. You can't trust anyone, I don't care what their passport says."

"Even George?"

"For fuck's sake, he thinks of you like a brother." She paused. "But the fact is, I don't know what he really does either. For what it's worth he's got a Consulate security pass in his wallet."

"You know, for such agreeable people you Aussies are a sneaky bunch."

"What can I say, I work for Rupert Murdoch. Can I help it if he falls asleep before me and leaves his wallet out?"

"You sleep with Rupert Murdoch? That dirty old bastard!"

"George!"

"Oh, your boyfriend. My Dimmer Twin. I think you've been reading too many spy novels."

"Look, I get it," she said. "There's no Dr. No. It's not some evil plot. No one's in charge. These business deals are so convoluted, deliberately."

"A bodge job."

"It's a bodge alright. Honestly I don't know what holds it all together."

"Ming and Jintao and a billion other Chinese," said T.K. "Until the wheels fall off."

"What did you tell that man on the escalator?"

"Ming's name."

"I think that was a mistake."

"I got a text from my source in New York."

"Who's that?"

"Mr. Howe. *H-o-w-e*, not *H-a-o*, but I assume he's Asian. Never actually met him or even talked to him. We communicate by text. But he's never done me wrong."

"How did he get your new Hong Kong mobile?"

T.K. dropped his head. "Fuck."

"I was also wondering how George knew your number was new. Did you tell him?"

"No, but it's an 852 country code; my China phone went for a swim that night on the barge. Bought a new SIM today on Nathan Road."

"But you could have had a Hong Kong SIM before; lots of people keep both. He knew it was new. Did the store scan your passport?"

"Nope."

"The clerk could have written down your number."

"She saw my passport for like three seconds. Never touched it. She'd need a photographic memory."

"The average Chinese knows like ten thousand characters. How hard could it be to remember a passport number?"

"For fuck's sake Kathleen, it's nine digits."

"That's what I mean. Everybody knows everything, except us. We don't know how George knew about your SIM, we don't know who the man on the escalator is, we don't know why Ming gave the police a pig fetus. But I'm telling you, it's dangerous here. There is no one who can help you."

Across the street, a Chinese man in a kitchen uniform was arguing with a fishmonger over the accuracy of the merchant's bamboo scale. Next door, a karaoke bar was blasting Faye Wong's haunting Chinese cover of the Cranberries' "Dreams." A hit song by an Irish alt-rock band sung in Cantonese by a Mandarin native who starred in a Hong Kong film called *Chungking Express*. Welcome to Central. Kathleen was right: You could have a passport from Pluto and it wouldn't turn heads in this fucking burg.

T.K. checked his watch. Chairman Mao was smiling, waving. "Look," he said, "my room's in Kowloon and there's still time to catch the last ferry. I should go." He squeezed her hands. "Thank you." She smiled. He kissed her on the lips, quickly, which to his surprise gave him a brief erection, and he slanted down the steep incline of Peel Street toward Queen's Road.

From Man Hing Alley, a long-haired Cantonese man in a Trotsky t-shirt staggered out of Bar 71, the watering hole favored by local activists and assorted left-wing journos. T.K. briefly considered stepping in for more fortification but he kept moving: Need to make that last ferry, he thought. If he tarried he'd have to take a red taxi through the Cross Harbour Tunnel, and then he couldn't do what he needed to do on the boat, which was, among other things, take a roaring piss every five minutes. Getting old sucked.

Down to the harbor, T.K. tried to square his fuckup with Mr. Wang. Booze? Never stopped him from slaying tigers before. Was it age? Age and booze—maybe the combination. Maybe he couldn't drink so much anymore. That would definitely suck. God, would he have to smoke dope instead? How boring! He had only recently started to consider the hazards of age; maybe contemplating age was itself a hazard of age. Behind it all lurked the nagging suspicion that his growing concern for Ming had somehow contributed to his mistakes, as if empathy had compromised his defenses. Just thinking about it all felt like driving into a tunnel; he shuddered and made for the ferry terminal.

At the dock T.K. bought an upper-deck ticket and merged into the crowded waiting room. As he unshouldered his backpack he noticed, behind him, the long-haired man in the Trotsky t-shirt. The guy had been looking at him too, but as soon as T.K. caught his eye, Trotsky averted his gaze. At first T.K. wondered if he knew the fellow—he had, after all, frequented Bar 71 himself over many years—but he definitely couldn't place him. While it could not be said that he never forgot a face, Theodore Kincaid Dean rarely forgot a bar patron. No, he had never raised a glass with this guy, that much was sure.

Soon a ferry horn pierced the low din of the waiting room, and the growl of massive propellers twisting in reverse signaled the berthing of the last Star Ferry. The gates opened and the crowd pressed forward over the gangway. Attendants in blue sailor suits and white gloves asserted their ostensible authority by puffing into shrill whistles. T.K. found a seat on a wooden bench upstairs, along the starboard rail, removing his laptop from the backpack. As he sat down he noticed Trotsky had taken a place directly behind him.

The horn blew again and the ship lurched away from the dock, spewing foam against the bulwarks of Admiralty. Minutes later the great blinking hive of Hong Kong Island loomed and then receded as the boat bore on toward the mirror image of humanity on Kowloon. A young Chinese couple, clearly in love and just as clearly blotto, staggered up to the rail in front of T.K. and held hands over the life rings. T.K. slowly pulled a thumb drive from his jacket pocket, hoping to conceal it from Trotsky, but the old bench seats had open backs and he was sure his tail could see everything. With as much sleight of hand as he could muster, he drew the thumb drive in front of him and slowly inserted it into his laptop, taking care not to suggest by body language what he was doing. Then he began quickly dragging files onto the drive: his book, his notes, his photos, his emails, his browser history (would historians of the future research browser "histories?"), his contacts, his hex-code mobile backups—his life. When he was done, he removed the drive and clutched it tightly in his right hand.

Now what? He felt Trotsky's eyes on him, but turning around was out of the question.

Then good fortune arrived as the young woman at the rail leaned over and barked a fountain of rickshaw noodles (with fish balls) into Victoria Harbour. In apparent solidarity her gassed lover rolled his eyes, groaned and emptied his own noodle burden (he had ordered with pig skin) overboard.

Unfortunately for Trotsky, just as the boyfriend was heaving hog noodles forth, the boat heaved in the opposite direction, and the partially digested mass of stir-fried pig bits, Blue Girl beer, gastric acids and assorted bile made an apparent U-turn in midair, as if captured in a video and run in reverse, back over the gunwales into the boat. But the boat was making twelve knots, so the noxious supernova of vomit did not return into the face of the young man who launched it but went cartwheeling past T.K. and directly onto the coordinates of Trotsky.

"Diu!"

The general-purpose Cantonese vulgarism for *fuck* confirmed for T.K. that his Bolshevik friend was not Mandarin and was most definitely distracted by the bits of emesis now hanging like stalactites from his eyebrows and moustache, and from the eyebrows and moustache of the silk-screened Trotsky on his t-shirt. Just as stunned were the upper-deck passengers, who reacted, first to Trotsky's profanity and then to his unlucky condition, with gasping disbelief. Everyone except the young drunken couple, who were still drooling over the rail, now dry heaving arm in arm.

Trotsky nearly vomited himself as he contemplated the impasto of alien stomach goo clinging to his face. In his hygienic panic he forgot about T.K., who in that moment stuffed the thumb drive into the coin pocket of his khakis and slipped his laptop, still open, over the rail into the dark waters of Victoria Harbor, followed by his new ICallU phone.

Chinese-made electronic appliances sink at the rate of about one foot per second in sea water. As such T.K.'s laptop and phone impacted the muddy bottom of Victoria Harbor in less than one minute, unlike the young couple's barf which washed up along the Avenue of Stars in Tsim Tsa Tsui the next day. Trotsky was still in the men's room under a faucet when the boat docked in Kowloon; T.K. hustled up Nathan Road to his hotel, thanking God that some people could not hold their liquor.

Detours

The Fourth Part

Chapter Seventeen

George threw open the blackout curtains on the unpromising dawn of Guangzhou. Seventeen floors below his hotel room the Pearl River oozed toward Hong Kong and Macau. The water was chartreuse and seemed to glow slightly, like one of those artist's representations of the surface of Venus in a science museum. Giant hairy brown blobs resembling pipe tobacco floated lazily downstream; a motorized sampan navigated deftly through the morass, piloted by a man in a sedge hat with a long net who scooped up passing aggregations of who-knows-what.

"Jesus," George said aloud to himself. *"Everybody out of the pool."*

Half an hour later he was loading a plate full of bacon at the breakfast buffet downstairs before joining Hu Tianhua at a small table. The Chinese businessman had circulated past the congee buffet and returned with a bowl of the white gruel, topped by mud carp paste, pig's liver and an ash-blackened century duck egg. The two men eyed each other's breakfast warily.

"It's good you Chinese are so fond of the hog's liver, Harry," said George. "Leaves more bacon for me."

"That's perfect," said Tianhua. "I love deals where everybody wins."

"I used to think the Brits had the best bacon until I came to China," said George.

"And to think we were eating tree bark fifty years ago." Tianhua gazed around the room, filled with Western businessmen attending the massive Canton Trade Fair. Everyone on a first-name basis, so unlike China, so essentially wrong, but as the tired and profoundly dishonest American aphorism goes, the customer is always right. Hence his adopted Western name, Harry—no Harold or Harrison or Hartwell, just Harry, Harry Hu—which he had carried since his USC undergrad days, although his frat brothers called him Knock-Knock as in:

"Knock knock."

"Who's there?"

"Harry. Harry Hu."

Tianhua liked this George Chambers, who reminded him of his frat brothers, although he didn't trust him, but that was fine. Confucius said "To trust is good; not to trust is better." Or was it some Italian? Either way. The truth was he didn't really need George's venture capital to launch new businesses in Guangxi; he had his own sources of finance. But he hoped a partnership with the American would give him better access to Western trade secrets that would make him more competitive.

How quaint that Americans called that "stealing," he thought. In China, imitation was the sincerest flattery. It's why officials in Beijing could never understand Hollywood's obsession with "intellectual piracy." The best Chinese movies blatantly stole whole scenes from other movies, as an *homage* to the earlier director. It was an honor to have your work copied. He would like to so honor his American competitors.

George understood Harry as a businessman of flexible and refreshingly guilt-free ethics, which bode well for the sort of win-win deal both had in mind. Beyond that he was not very impressed with Harry's business proposals—coat hangers were not exactly a growth industry—but he wasn't looking for an equity play. He wanted Harry to use his local mainland connections to push through a hydro power plant on the Li River. If Harry thought the investment was for a new hydro-powered coat hanger factory, fine. Because there *would* be a coat hanger factory.

He inhaled the last strip of bacon and stirred his coffee. "Tree bark. Sadly it's become the cliché food of starving people the world over, hasn't it? Whenever there's a famine, we always picture people eating tree bark."

"I guess we invented that," said Tianhua, "along with gunpowder and the compass."

"You know the West had very little idea what was going on in China those years," said George. "Oh, Kennedy was getting reports of scattered food shortages and poor harvests, but even he didn't know the extent of it, and of course Mao refused help."

"He would have lost face," said Tianhua. "That's the worst thing you can do in China. Better to let thirty or forty million peasants starve to death than lose face."

"Speaking of peasants, what's going on with your friend in Guangxi?"

"You mean Mr. Nong, that corpulent party leader agitating for a dam?"

"Yes."

"He's a fool."

"But a clever one, I gather. Hydro power up there would open up a huge cheap labor pool without moving more of those yokels to the coast. Nong would profit handsomely from the land rights. So would anyone who might get in first with a factory."

"Agreed. Still it remains to be seen if he can pull it off."

Tianhua wondered why George really cared about hydro power on the Li. Surely not for a coat hanger factory. Chambers was a high-tech venture capitalist; coat hangers were hardly part of his portfolio. Well, no matter, he thought. So what if neither knew what the other was really up to? This deal was win-win.

Chapter Eighteen

Six fat rats, looped on the fermented remains of a Korean grocery, staggered like Sunday-morning drunks down a storm drain on Fifty-seventh Street. A sanitation worker had interrupted their bender by hoisting the grocery's trash bags into the hold of a garbage truck. The pungent bags popped and snarled as the hydraulic compactor smothered them into an evil paté. Who was the genius who forgot to put alleys in New York, wondered T.K. The truck lurched forward past him, and as the worker moved down to the next *Rattenkeller*, T.K. tossed his burner phone into the stinking rear end.

Two doors down was the T-Mobile shop. "What's your cheapest pre-paid phone?" he asked the clerk.

"That would be the Alcatel. Nineteen dollars after rebate. It's not a smartphone."

"I don't need a smartphone, just texting."

"The Alcatel would be perfect then. Unlimited calls and texts. Then burn, baby, burn."

T.K. resented the shopkeeper's implication that he was a drug dealer who cycled through mobile phone numbers daily to avoid tracing, but the truth is, he was cycling through mobile phone numbers daily to avoid tracing, so he stifled himself.

"I'll take it."

"Will you be porting a number?"

"No, I need a new number." Duh.

Another day, another phone. At the corner of Seventh Avenue he hopped onto the R downtown.

The cut-glass saloon doors creaked open, brass hinges grouching under decades of urban grime. Meg Dean walked into Fanelli's, trailed by the bleat of a taxi horn and the mumble of tires on the cobblestones of Mercer Street.

"Hello Meg." T.K. shifted in his barstool and stood.

"Hi Teddy." They embraced tentatively. She kneaded the shoulders of his bomber jacket and took in his jade eyes, sensing trouble. T.K. was always on alert—she thought of him as a deer with one eye on the tree line—but now he seemed even more on edge than usual, as if caught in the headlights. Still, years of Teddy maintenance had taught her not to go there.

"You always did look good in battered horsehide," she said, unhitching her shoulder bag and slumping into a stool. "Anyway, how are you? You look tired." She on the other hand looked ravishing—auburn hair bobbed smartly with insouciant locks tracing the dangle of her long jaw.

He shrugged. On the wall behind them, framed portraits of long-ago Italian-American boxing champions—or were they Italian?—their accomplishments now obscured by time and a patina of cigarette tar, begged for attention. "I'm a man without a country, but other than that I feel fine. I think. It's good to be back, sort of. When did New York become a giant fucking shopping mall?"

"Around the same time China became a giant fucking factory. Sad, isn't it?"

"I never buy anything. I feel so out of place."

Fanelli's was one of the last holdouts of the old days in Soho. It looked the same as always, but the customers were no longer Abstract Expressionists with turpentine-scented hair and cadmium-daubed khakis. Now the drinkers wore selvedge Japanese denim, and the tables and barstools were ringed in small fortresses of boutique shopping bags. The watering hole of wits and wiseguys had become a rest stop for marathon shoppers.

"All the writers are in Queens now," said Meg. "They got pushed out of Brooklyn by the bankers from Manhattan. South of Harlem, nobody lives in Manhattan except Eurotrash and people who think *Vanity Fair* is hip. I mean, we got used to Greek diners getting elbowed out by Starbucks. Now even the high-end restaurants—those places the *Times* jacks off on that serve forty-dollar octopus galette with coffee dust—are closing to make way for new Microsoft stores."

"Microsoft stores?"

"You've been gone. Microsoft is still playing catch-up with Apple. Now they've got to have their own slick stores in every trendy neighborhood. Naturally landlords are tripling the rent; goodbye octopus galette. Pretty soon there won't be any food left in Manhattan, just five-dollar coffees and personal devices. The lofts down here are all owned by Asian billionaires, but they're never around, thank God."

T.K. smirked. "Déjà vu all over again."

"Huh?"

"Nothing. Speaking of apartments, did you ever get my key back to the doorman?"

"Shit. No. I have it," she said, unzipping her bag.

"Hold on to it for now."

She stopped rummaging and looked up.

"Just keep it for now," he said. "It may come in handy, and I may not be in town for long."

"Whatever you want," she said, pulling a thick Fedex envelope out of her bag. "Here's the paperwork. All the places you need to initial and sign are marked, then just stick it all in Fedex."

"And then it's official?"

"As soon as the court clerk enters it. Not sure how long."

"Thanks for taking care of all this, Meg. It's hard to stay on top of an American divorce from China."

"My pleasure—I mean, you know. It's fine."

"Yeah, I know," he said, wondering who if anyone was fucking her these days, and whether he or she was decent or an asshole. "Can I buy you a drink?"

At Broadway and Tenth Street a Bichon Frisé emptied its bladder onto the crocuses in front of Grace Church. The little white dog, brown eye smegma encrusted on its cheeks, was walking an older woman with hair extensions and so much cosmetic surgery that her nose looked chiseled away like the Sphinx of Cheops. T.K. hurried past. It was a typical blustery day of spring, that brief and uncertain season when the weather and everything else in New York seems never quite groomed, as if the whole city forgot to look in the mirror and rinse out the eye goo that morning. In Union Square the organic farmers were trying in vain to convince New Yorkers they liked rhubarb, it being too early even for peas or lettuce.

He entered the dingy lobby of his agent's building and stepped into the tiny elevator, not much larger than an old phone booth. The car had a scissor gate that you had to haul shut and latch, and dull black Bakelite pushbuttons for each floor that stayed depressed until some physical mechanism in the shaft forced them back out as the elevator reached the requested floor. The same mechanism tripped a bell that announced each level. The stubborn persistence of this analog relic amused T.K. and somehow felt perfect in a business where editors still corrected manuscripts on paper with red pencil. He pushed eleven and waited as the car groaned slowly upward: *ding...ding...ding...*

It shuddered to a stop and the door opened directly into a cluttered business suite; a pert young assistant in yoga pants peeked out from behind a tower of bound galleys on her desk and ushered T.K around an obstacle course of book piles into a small office with a clear view of the Empire State Building. His agent, the venerable Trixie Gatebush, was facing the window, her massive girth invisible in a high-backed Embody chair except for two stiletto heals bouncing under the desk. She swiveled and smiled. "Teddy!"

"Trix! Don't get up, I'll worship you from afar."

"Nonsense!" She rose and air-kissed him. "Welcome home. Now sit down and tell me everything." She was wearing a black minidress, black stockings and black patent leather high-heeled riding boots—her signature look for more than forty years through countless fluctuations in body weight. Her heart-shaped face, framed in frosted curls, still looked fresh yet not implausibly young—whoever did her surgeries was the best—but the arthritic hands gave it away. Her English accent—South London, cloaked in Cheltenham posh—flaked like shingles in the wind.

"You know this place is a fire hazard," said T.K.

Trixie lit a cigarette and waved her arm dismissively. "The fucking publishers don't want the books anymore after six months. What am I going to do, shred them? This is my life! I might as well jump out the fucking window."

"Then who would torment all those editors?"

She pursed her lips and spit smoke. "What's left of them. Honey, we're all in the same sinking boat." Obligatory end-of-book-publishing-as-we-know-it point made, she moved on. "So why no calls, darling? Where's my book? You know Harper's got a first-look and they're practically strip-searching me for clues, but they can't commit without at least an outline. I keep telling them 'He's in China, he's working on it.' "

"Sorry, I ran into some trouble over there." Cleary brought him a can of beer.

"Darling you always run into trouble. That's why people buy your books."

"I wasn't aware people still buy books."

"Something has to go on the nightstand besides the remote."

"So we're in the home furnishing business now?"

"As Amazon would have it. Actually independent bookstores are buying lots these days. Of course most of them get returned."

"And they end up here."

"It's a bit of a Potemkin village, granted. But we keep the lights on. What sort of trouble?"

"I got thrown out of China."

"Literally?"

"I can't go back."

"Ever?"

"Barring regime change."

"What happened? Are you okay?"

"It's a long story. I'm okay. It's a bit of a cluster."

"Do you think you have enough material to finish the book?" She had carefully buried the last question beneath ostensibly more important concerns about his well-being, but they both knew she was finally getting to the point.

"Yes. No. I mean, I don't know. Basically I've written the abortion book. I'm just not sure that's the book anymore. I feel like it's so much more than that."

"Meaning?"

"Meaning I don't know what it all means. I guess that's the point. China's population has flattened, even dropped; in that sense it's unclear why the one-child law is still being enforced. But it is—selectively. Especially if you're landless and Christian. It's about something else at this point. The people on those houseboats aren't just defying the party line on childbirths; they're rejecting everything. It's like coming out against the Second Law of Thermodynamics; you just don't do that. They're up against forces that are inevitable, and no one's in charge."

"So there's no God. What else is new? If you want to write a book about atheism you better have a good angle. It's been done to death, for Christ's sake."

"No I don't mean atheism. In a way I mean the opposite. Sometimes I think there really is a God but he's not wise and just, or vindictive. He's more of an algorithm."

"Like the way Amazon picks books for its home page?"

"Well I guess that's part of it, yes. But it's everywhere, and completely out of our hands, even though we made it. The funny thing is, the creationists have it exactly backwards: It's we who created God."

"You mean like *Open the pod bay doors, Hal.*"

"No, I don't mean like sci-fi. It's not that computers are taking over. There's no consciousness to it, even cyber-consciousness. It's like this closed feedback loop sucking everything down to a point of infinite consumerism. The governments, the merchants, the media, they're all squeezing into the same blind cave. I don't know what's in the cave; everything and nothing."

"Listen honey, let me tell you what *nothing* means in the book business: *Nothing* is what Amazon tells publishers about the customers who buy their books at fifty percent off list. *Nothing*. Not even e-mails. Everything else is *something*, which is what I typically tell writers their books need to be about. We're down to five legacy publishers; even the biggest is a flyspeck division of a multi-national media conglomerate. They're currently not buying books about nothing. And they're definitely not buying books about how their parent companies are dropping turds all over the world."

He reached into his pocket and pulled out a thumbdrive. "I need you to do me a favor. Hold onto this for me. It's a copy of everything on my laptop, which is now at the bottom of Victoria Harbor. There are two of these; I've got the other one."

"Fine," she said, tossing the drive into her purse. She stubbed out her cigarette in a Harvard Club ashtray. "What are you going to do, Teddy? I mean, it's your life, I just get fifteen percent of it."

"Maybe I should blog."

Trixie swooned. "Oh God, where are my heart pills? Speak not that word in my presence! Darling, our books might be furniture but they're not blogs or tweets."

"What about self publishing?"

"Blasphemer!" She tried to light another cigarette but tossed it aside in a coughing fit. "My pills, *my pills,*" sweeping papers across her desk. "Cleary, where's my fucking nitro!"

T.K. jumped out of his chair. "Trix, what the fuck?"

She was gulping air, but she hadn't finished her tirade. "We don't publish books *on demand in Seattle*—what a horrifying place that is. Have you been? Like Maine with traffic." She tilted back in her Embody chair and began to pound her heaving chest. "The city that invented the ten-dollar book and the five-dollar cup of coffee. What sense does that make?"

"Trixie!"

Her face went blue and cold as an Alpine trout, and she pitched forward onto the floor, spittle pooling onto the kilim. Cleary stood in the door and screamed, dropping the bottle of nitro pills. T.K. leaped on top of Trixie, rolled her onto her back and ripped open her blouse and bra. "Call 911!" he said, forcing some pills down her throat. "And get that fucking elevator up here!"

He stacked his palms over her sternum and pumped thirty times, then blew twice into her mouth. Her chest filled with air, then settled. Nothing. He pumped again thirty times, blew again. Nothing. Again, and finally a short breath.

Cleary reappeared in the door. "Ambulance and elevator on the way."

"Help me move her; we need to get her downstairs fast. You take her feet."

T.K. wrapped his arms around his agent's cold chest and lifted her torso off the kilim, but her lower half was too much for Cleary; the assistant whose résumé claimed she did "all the heavy lifting" for super-agent Trixie Gatebush could not, in the end, lift her boss, but only drag her ass indelicately along the floor. The kilim came along for the ride, pinned under Trixie's butt and sliding across the floor until it snagged on a pile of remaindered books by Jimmy Carter (*Always a Reckoning and Other Poems*), one of Trixie's most prestigious authors.

"The books!" said T.K. "The rug's caught on those fucking books!"

Cleary kicked the Carter books aside. The pair flopped Trixie down at the elevator door, where T.K. saw that her feeble breathing had stopped again. As a siren wailed down on Union Square West and the elevator cable hummed, T.K. again pumped her chest and blew into her mouth. *Ding...ding...ding...*

Finally the door clattered open. Cleary unlatched the gate and they dragged Trixie's sagging frame into the car. T.K. had to hold her upright so they could all fit; the agent's head flopped forward against T.K.'s arms, which he kept pumping desperately against her chest.

"I think you're actually doing the Heimlich now," said Cleary.

"Better than nothing."
Ding...ding...ding...

By the time the door opened on the ground floor, the paramedics were there, but Trixie Gatebush was not.

Chapter Nineteen

"You from New York?"

"New England."

The bald Chinese barber was tightening the noose of crepe paper around T.K.'s neck. "Not get lot American here," he said. "Most Chinese. Why I ask. No hard complaint—you straight hair, I cut okay. Brack man no way—I send Fourteen Street. How you want cut?"

T.K. tried to imagine the improbable string of events that would lead a black man into a Chinatown barbershop. Or for that matter the equally strange events that found himself there. Because the honest truth was he didn't want his hair cut at all, much less by a bald Chinese barber. What he really wanted was a perfect view into the Nom Wah tea parlor directly across the narrow jog of Doyers Street. It was lunchtime; somebody in there, probably ordering dim sum alone, was his Christian International contact. The sad-faced Asian guy at a booth, gnawing on chicken feet? The professorial dude in a too-big hound's-tooth jacket at the counter, checking off his dim sum ticket like he was grading a paper? He assumed his contact was

Chinese, but maybe not: All sorts of New Yorkers and even tourists ate here every day; it was the best dim sum in town. Westerners in particular appreciated the décor because it had none. Unlike virtually every other Chinatown restaurant, Nom Wah had never been "refurbished" in red flock wallpaper and chintzy oriental chandeliers with moving waterfall paintings. The owners didn't even bother to play insipid Canto-Pop music, or any music at all. The place still had the original tin ceiling and no air conditioning, just a grime-encrusted industrial fan in a metal cage over the door transom. Behind the counter, a massive copper-trimmed range hood framed tall urns of hot water for tea, which was scooped out of battered tins.

"Just clean it up a little on the sides," T.K. told the barber.

The scissors flew. T.K. took out his new phone and sent a text to the contact: "Hey I'm in NY. Can we meet?" Then he watched the window.

The barber swung the chair around. "Trim eyebrow?"

Fuck. Now he couldn't see the restaurant.

"No, thanks. Can you shave the neck?"

"No complaint." He swung the chair back so T.K. again faced the street, but the barber pushed his head down to lather up his neck—forcing T.K. to bend his eyes up to the level of the window. Across the street, the grey-haired Asian guy in the booth dropped a chicken foot, took his mobile out of his shirt pocket and studied it.

Bingo.

He started tapping. A message came back to T.K: "Too dangerous."

T.K. sent back: "Where ru?"

"Queens. Can't talk." He put his cell down on the table and went back to work on his chicken feet.

The barber finished. T.K. paid quickly and ducked across the street to Nom Wah. He slid into the old man's booth behind the plate of freshly gnawed chicken feet. "Mr. Howe I presume?"

"Huh?" said the contact, startled at the guest.

"Seven train must be running on greased rails today," said T.K.

"What?"

"You said you were in Queens four minutes ago." T.K. grabbed the cell off the table, swiped it open and held up the text. The contact slumped.

"How did you find me?"

"I just looked up and there you were."

The waiter flopped down an order of turnip cakes with wild mushrooms, then hovered. "Brooklyn Lager, please," said T.K. "And some beef balls in broth."

"Look, I'm sorry," said the contact. He had long grey hairs growing out of his ears and a wooden crucifix around his neck. Next to his phone on the table was a dish of chili oil and a pocket Bible. "I can't talk to you anymore. Things have changed."

"No shit," said T.K. "Chen Yong lost his head, and his wife and kid are missing in action. Plus she appears to have miscarried a pig fetus, which I don't think is even mentioned as a curse in Leviticus." He pointed at the Bible. "Then you hook me up with Fu-Manchu on the escalators in Hong Kong, and then I get tailed by some creep on the Star Ferry. I'm buying a new cell phone every day and I'm seriously considering a rectal thumb drive. Meanwhile I'm trying to glean the Christian spirit in all this, but I'm having trouble."

"You like wild mushrooms?" the contact said, offering his dish.

"No thanks." The contact tore into the slimy mass of fungi. The waiter brought T.K.'s beer.

"Look, I'm sorry," said Mr. Howe between bites. "I don't know anything about what happened to Zeng Ming, don't know where she is. But I can tell you the organization is...different now. Used to be the refugees would come to New York; I had a good contact at the consulate, and we got them asylum and into homes and jobs in Queens. Now I report to a new top man in Amsterdam, and most of the refugees go straight to Europe. I never see them. They tell me don't talk to you anymore."

"Amsterdam?" The beef balls came. "Why Amsterdam?"

"I guess because lots of flights from Beijing. Direct, no transit."

"But they don't stay in Amsterdam. The refugees. There's only so many Chinese restaurants in Holland."

"I don't know."

"Who's your boss over there?"

Mr. Howe frowned. "I have already said too much."

"How did you get my Hong Kong number?"

"Please, you must leave me alone." He shoved his bill over to T.K.'s side of the booth. "Thank you for lunch."

T.K. grabbed the check and Mr. Howe's arm. "Look, you could be in danger, but I can't help if you don't tell me what you know."

Mr. Howe didn't hear him. His eyes had turned glassy and the skin on his cheeks tightened and broke out in welts. He doubled over and clutched his gut, then let out a massive fart that smelled worse than a fart.

"I've soiled myself," he said. And then he rolled onto the floor into a fetal position, twitching and foaming at the mouth, oozing spittle over his crucifix.

Customers recoiled. The waiter, working behind the counter, turned and dropped a tea tin. T.K. jumped out of the booth. "Call 911!" Mr. Howe was breathing but losing consciousness.

"Jesus," said the professor in the too-big jacket. "Maybe it was the mushrooms."

"Too soon," said T.K. "Usually takes twenty-four hours for bad mushrooms to hit like that."

"He order same dish every day," chimed in the waiter.

"Fuck," said T.K. "Where do you get these mushrooms?"

The waiter twitched. "You think mushroom guy tell us that? Big secret. Korean guy upstate somewhere. But never problem. Boss has insurance for poisoning anyway."

The ambulance came fast. T.K. grabbed Mr. Howe's Bible off the table and climbed in beside his comatose contact—no one else in the restaurant had volunteered—and they roared off to Lower Manhattan Hospital. "You a relative?" asked the EMT, a young Hispanic woman with long dark hair tied back, as they zipped downtown.

"Business associate. I don't even know where he lives, maybe Queens. We were having lunch and he went green, then shit his pants. Apparently he eats there every day. Wild mushrooms from some forager upstate, according to the waiter."

"It's always the Asians," she said. "They go for those straw mushrooms, but unfortunately North America has a lookalike called *amanita phalloides*."

"Death cap." T.K. knew them from the sugar bush in Vermont.

"You got it. Native of Europe. Killed several popes and Roman emperors."

"And they don't grow in Asia."

"Nope. Looks just like a straw mushroom to them, and I'm told they taste good too. An unfortunate cultural disconnect."

She pushed the button on her lapel mike: "EMT four-nine to LM ER, we're three minutes away with a probable mycetism. Prepare gastric lavage and high-dose penicillin and silibinin, over. What's his name?"

T.K. was lost in his head.

The radio buzzed: *"Roger, EMT four-nine. LM ER ready and waiting on mycetic patient."*

First Trixie, now Mr. Howe—people around him seemed to be keeling over a lot lately, and he wasn't even counting poor Yong on the houseboat. Was it paranoid to see a connection? Trixie! *Fuck!* He had left the thumb drive in her purse.

"Sir?"

"Oh, sorry. Howe."

"Bad mushrooms are how. What's his name, so I can tell ER."

"That's his name. Howe. *H-o-w-e*, maybe *H-a-o*, I don't know."

"First name?"

"Mister."

She glared, which on her looked kind of sexy.

"I don't know his first name."

"You're having lunch with the guy and you don't know his first name?"

"Asians are more formal that way."

"What's your name?"

"Dean."

"That's your first name?"

"Teddy. Teddy Dean."

"Thanks Teddy. I'm Placenta. Hope I'm not being too informal."

"Placenta." He said it flat, not like a question, testing it out.

"I know. It was the first word my mom heard the nurse say after I was born; her English wasn't so good, and she thought it sounded like a nice name. Ordained by God, you know? So I guess I was born to the trade."

She checked on Mr. Howe's vital signs and frowned. "Weird. His pulse is racing but he's out like a hibernating bear."

"What's that mean?"

"I don't know but he's not presenting like a mushroom case. Usually their heartbeat drops off the map."

The ambulance swung into the ER bay. "You can wait in triage but since you're not immediate family they probably won't tell you much," said Placenta. "HIPAA compliance rules."

"The guy just blew a septic tank out his ass in a crowded restaurant and you're worried about his medical privacy?"

"Not my call. Take it up with your congressman."

"Thanks."

Orderlies swarmed the victim and wheeled him away. T.K. sat down in the waiting room between a sad-looking old black man in a blue parking garage uniform and a pink-skinned Wall Street trader in a blue banking uniform. Both had pinstripes. The TV in the corner was playing a soap opera; T.K. didn't know they still made soap operas. After about an hour, a preppy-looking doctor with a rep tie under his white coat came out and addressed him.

"You the guy who brought in the mushroom eater?" He had a flat, nasal Midwestern accent.

"That's me."

"I'm Dr. Bradley. Your friend is in very serious condition. He went into cardiac arrest twice and we brought him back. If it's mushrooms they must have been some strange fruit. Maybe psychedelics, I don't know; we're waiting on the lab. Definitely weird to see that high pulse rate, almost like a meth overdose. But the cramps, the diarrhea, the nervous-system shutdown, all classic alpha-Amanatin."

"Alpha-what?"

"The toxin in death cap mushrooms. It's actually a peptic acid, but not your average bear. One of the most poisonous substances known to man. It basically unravels the helix of your DNA, causing permanent liver and kidney failure. Unfortunately the symptoms don't generally present for a day or so, and by then it's often too late. Like I said, we're waiting on the lab. And we've got Department of Health all over the restaurant; hopefully we'll be able to prevent any more cases."

"That place is packed every day," said T.K. "The turnip cakes with wild mushrooms are a house specialty. How is it he's the only victim?"

"Well so far anyway. But I don't know. Good question. Possibly only a handful of death caps got mixed in with a healthy box of mushrooms."

"And he was the lucky raffle winner."

"You could say."

"Will he live?"

"Maybe. But if he needs a new liver they don't grow on trees."

The automatic doors to the ambulance bay slid open and Placenta hurried in. "I think I know what it is," she said to T.K. and the doctor. "Liquid nicotine."

Dr. Bradley raised an eyebrow. "Liquid nicotine?"

"E-cigarettes, vaping, you know? The latest thing. I saw a picture in *Other Half* of Leo DiCaprio smoking one while riding a Citibike in Tribeca. I mean, that proves it."

"That proves our patient was poisoned by liquid nicotine?" The doctor seemed annoyed. T.K. hoped he hadn't noticed Placenta's nametag, which was unlikely to raise her credibility in his eyes. For now she was just a lowly EMT of minority extraction who probably went to one of those for-profit "colleges" with ads plastered on every subway car. An EMT of minority extraction named Placenta was possibly a bridge too far for Dr. Bradley.

"No, it proves vaping is the next big thing. Safer than real cigarettes, no tar, which is where the cancer comes from, right? Once Leo and the supermodels start doing it, the suburbs are hooked—and fashion trends last a long time out there. Remember punk rock and pink hair? That was like fifteen minutes in Manhattan, but in Jersey it's been going strong for decades now. Take the inbound PATH train on a Friday night if you don't believe me."

The doctor listened like a cow, taking it all in while refusing to make any expression that might acknowledge this woman's ludicrous rant.

"But it's one thing to vaporize nicotine in an e-cigarette," she went on. "You're getting like trace amounts. It's quite another to ingest the *actual liquid* from the vials. A teaspoon of that shit can kill a child; a tablespoon can seriously fuck up a healthy adult, maybe even kill them, and it's completely unregulated. This shit makes poison mushrooms look like Hostess Twinkies, except it's not just a few Chinese immigrants. Millions of teenagers, half of them with ADHD and poor hand-eye coordination, are mixing up these potions every day. You can buy the shit online in fifty-five-gallon drums from China. It's a hazmat spill waiting to happen, and Barbie dolls have more warning labels than this shit."

Dr. Bradley was still wincing at the f-bomb she dropped in the middle of the ER triage room. "As a clinician and having no personal experience with cigarettes of any kind," he said with an attenuated sneer, "I'm afraid I'm not up on either the cultural or pathological trends related to that foul habit."

Placenta rolled her eyes. *What a douche.* Clearly this guy never left the library in all four years of med school. "Let me spell it out for you, doc. It's like the difference between one martini and drinking a whole bottle of vodka." She was pretty sure he had personal experience with the "pathology" of Grey Goose.

"Why would someone drink the liquid?" asked the doctor, starting to catch on.

"Why do dogs lick antifreeze?" said Placenta. "Some of these e-flavors taste like candy or bubble gum. Also, it can be absorbed through the skin. Happened to my cousin Jose, that's how I know so much. He was filling his vape canister on the bed—dumb idea, I know, but he's not exactly the brightest bulb in the chandelier—because the thing is, he loves to smoke in bed, and when e-cigarettes came out he thought 'Great! Now I won't burn my house down smoking in bed.' Which is true.

Unfortunately he spilled some of the nicotine on the sheets and it soaked into his skin. Woke up in the middle of the night with vomiting and diarrhea accompanied by the heartbeat of a racehorse in the final turn at Aqueduct."

"Just like Mr. Howe," said T.K.

"Bingo."

The doctor looked at T.K. "Did this man smoke these...e-cigarettes?"

"No idea."

Bradley turned back to Placenta. "Thank you, Miss..." he gazed over his glasses at her nametag but he couldn't bring himself to say it. "We'll check for nicotine presence in the blood. Nurse! Get Poison Control on the phone, *stat!*"

***

T.K. leaned into a bitter spring wind as he headed up Beekman Street to City Hall Park. He shivered and dug his hands into his jacket pockets. There in the left pocket was Howe's Bible, a Chinese translation. It was the size of a Little Red Book, the cover made of the same cheap shiny vinyl, only black and with a picture of Jesus instead of Chairman Mao. He flipped it open to the frontispiece and read the hand-lettered Chinese inscription:

Hao Wei

112-26 38th Avenue

Flushing, Queens 11368

He bolted for the Brooklyn Bridge station and hopped on an uptown express just before the doors closed.

The shabby duplex was just off Main Street in Flushing and only a few blocks from the last stop on the Seven train. T.K. climbed the front stoop and banged on the aluminum storm door. A short Chinese woman with a chopstick in her hair bun and a pincushion Velcroed to her wrist answered.

"Hao tài tai?" asked T.K.

"I am Mrs. Hao," she said in Mandarin.

"May I come in? I know your husband. I'm afraid I have bad news."

Her eyes narrowed. "Come in."

The living room had been converted into a sewing shop. Fabric and dresses hung on mannequins and portable wardrobes. In the center was a sewing machine on a long workbench. Mrs. Hao cleared a pile of prom dress patterns off a chair. "Please, sit." T.K. bowed and sat; she took her stool behind the sewing machine.

"Mrs. Hao, your husband is very sick. He's in Lower Manhattan Hospital."

She cupped a hand over her mouth but stayed calm, almost placid. "Is he in pain?"

"I don't think so, not right now. He is not conscious and is being kept alive by doctors."

"What happened?"

"I'm not sure. It's possible he may have been poisoned somehow. Did he smoke e-cigarettes?"

"E-cigarettes?"

"A new form of tobacco with no smoke."

"No."

"Any type of tobacco at all?"

"Never."

"Do you speak English?"

"No. I know the alphabet in lower case and the numbers, for sewing."

"Do you have any children?"

"A son. On Long Island. He is studying economics at Hofstra."

"You need to call your son and go to the hospital with him right away."

"Of course," she said, reaching for the phone.

"Mrs. Hao, I don't want to alarm you, but can you think of anyone who might have wanted to hurt your husband?" *Wasn't that what detectives always say on TV?* he thought.

"Hurt him? Why?"

"Well I don't know exactly. But before he got sick, he told me things have been difficult on his job lately."

"Very difficult," she said, frowning with renewed worry. "The new people, they have changed everything. There is nothing for him to do. My husband said he doesn't know why they still pay him. But why would they hurt him?"

"I don't know," he said. "Maybe he knew something important and secret. Or maybe it was just an accident."

"He did not say anything like that to me."

"He mentioned a new boss in Amsterdam. Did he ever tell you his name?"

"Yes, Blokov." She wrote it down in lower-case Western letters, in case her pronunciation was wrong. "Russian I think. That's all I know."

"Thank you. Can you put your phone number there too? And your son's number?"

Chapter Twenty

Ning considered any day without humidity to be a good day, and by those standards the morning, with air as thin as a zither note, already rated a gold star. But further events, starting with a knock on his door, were about to push the afternoon well into platinum territory.

"Ning!" It was his wife Ju, scurrying in from the front entrance. "There is a truck in the courtyard. A man has a delivery for you."

"Who is it?"

"I don't know."

"What does he have?"

She glared at him.

"Okay, I will go see."

Ning pushed away his teapot impatiently and levitated his immense frame, panting at the effort. The floor groaned under the load shift as if disturbed by an earthquake. Out in the courtyard was a military-style troop transport truck with a canvas awning. Standing next to it was a driver Ning recognized from the lotus wood mill.

"Good day, sir!" said the driver, bowing stiffly.

"Good day. What is it?"

"I have a delivery for you, sir."

"I did not order anything."

"It is a gift."

"Show me the bill of lading."

The man laughed. "No lading for this gift." He gestured around to the back of the truck. Ning stepped over and watched as the man heaved open a long wooden crate and pulled aside a layer of straw. Inside, wrapped in bloody canvas, was a fresh baby elephant tusk.

Ning gasped. "Where did this come from?"

"Vietnam," said the man.

"Of course it did, you idiot. I mean who sent it to me?"

The man withdrew a small card from his shirt pocket and read aloud: "For Honorable Nong Ning, County Committee Secretary, GAD. Please enjoy this small token of my appreciation and gratitude for your hospitality. I trust your carvers will know what to make of it. Looking forward to working with you in the future."

It was signed: *Hu Tianhua of Guangzhou.*

Ning smiled and took the card. The man said, "It's a fine piece. The best I have seen."

"Take it to the ivory workshop," said Ning. "I will come by later." And inasmuch as a man of Ning's girth could do so, he fairly skipped inside to tell his wife.

She frowned, which he expected. Not that Ju held any particular concern for baby elephants—to her their troubles were as abstract and impersonal as the wounding of a policeman or the expulsion of an American who drank too much *báijiŭ*—nor was she morally opposed to corruption in business or government, not that there was really any difference. No, her dismay, as Ning easily predicted, was founded on a vaguely Confucian suspicion of extravagant gestures.

"This is not a gift," she said. "This is a bribe. You will have to pay somehow."

Ning nodded. "As will Mr. Hu. We shall both pay, and we shall both reap. Dear wife, the point of this gift is not to secure a particular favor but rather to demonstrate that Mr. Hu is a man who can get things done."

"Nevertheless, I fear the doing shall fall heaviest on your shoulders."

"Then I shall make it my endeavor to prove you wrong," said Ning. "Now, help me choose a classical theme for the new ivory carving. I'm thinking of a scene from *Water Margin*."

Ju pondered the idea. "Perhaps the outlaw Yang Zhi."

"Of course! His epic battle with Lin Chong in the Liangshan Marsh would make a splendid relief."

"I was thinking of a later episode in the book," said Ju. "The part after he loses the cargo of gemstones mined by the peasants and must sell his precious saber to make amends."

Chapter Twenty-One

Leaf buds were swelling on the elm trees along Fifth Avenue, and around their massive trunks purple crocuses mocked the cold. T.K. wondered how Central Park's trees managed to survive Dutch elm disease, which had arrived in a shipment of logs from Holland in 1928. For that matter why did Amsterdam's seventy-five thousand elm trees thrive despite the fungus, which is spread by a bark beetle similar to the ones his father taught him to find in the sugar bush.

At Grand Army Plaza he headed west past the horse carriages along Fifty-ninth Street. When he was a boy his father still used draft horses to pull the sap wagon through the bush—two gentle chestnut Haflingers with long blond manes. That was before plastic tubing and vacuum pumps took the place of sap buckets and the hauling of hundreds of gallons through the woods every day. In the twenty-first century there were more horses in midtown Manhattan than in a Vermont sugar bush.

The sap would be running now. Maybe he could head up for a few days—take the train to Bellows Falls, then call a neighbor for a pickup at the station. He would call Larry, his high-school buddy who held the stopwatch when he beat the underwater record at the old granite quarry. He would call Larry and say, "Hey Larry, I'm in Fellow's Balls," which is what they called it, and Larry would say, "Well I hope he jerks off soon and lets you out!" Humor forged in the caldron of grade school comes with a lifetime warranty.

Yes, he could go on up to Vermont, where no one from New York or Hong Kong would know how to find him, and just see how the old sugar bush was doing. Or maybe not. He heard Pepsi had installed a state-of-the-art reverse osmosis filtration system that removed most of the water from the sap, leaving only a quick evaporative finish in the boiling tanks. No more hours of cooking over cords of firewood. Now the brief boil was done over gas jets. Now it was all about filtration, not reduction, and he wasn't sure how he would feel about that. Because when you reduce something, anything, it's all still there, just concentrated. With filtration, something gets left behind.

His dad knew his trees alright, and loved to talk about them, and to them. But about the boil he never had much to say—a process of linguistic reduction that reflected the task at hand. In the sugar shack he donned a sticky, grey sap-encrusted "novelty" apron that said HOW CAN YOU HELP? GET OUT OF MY KITCHEN!! but which had become so soot-covered as to be illegible, and in fact indistinguishable from his long grey sticky beard. Before that he had an apron that said FREE KNOCKWURST HERE with an arrow pointing down, but local parents complained after a busload of third-graders came on a field trip and left with slightly more knowledge of the wider world than they had anticipated. It made the local paper. Dad didn't care. Enveloped in steam and impervious to distraction, he bent over his gurgling tanks like a scientist in a Victorian novel—tapping temperature gauges, dipping Brix pipes and condemning logs to the hell of the firebox below. The logs were maple too, from trees that died or limbs that had crashed in winter storms. "If they can't make sugar they can still make fire," he'd say after a bad storm. The dead ones, no matter how large, were called sticks. In the sugar shack when he called out for Teddy to haul in more logs he'd yell *"Sticks!"* and when the boiling tanks needed a top-up he'd yell *"Sap!"* Shifting his attention from the furnace to the tanks and back, he'd repeat his mantra all day long, the cycle of sugaring life: "Sticks and sap...sticks and sap...dead or alive...dead or alive."

T.K. hooked left on Sixth Avenue, pausing briefly to admire the equestrian statue of José Martí at the park entrance. Now there was a man who could read, write and fight! Journalist, statesman, intellectual, horseman, poet, soldier—an advocate for Cuban independence who lived what he preached and died fighting the Spanish at age forty-two, decades before Castro was born. T.K. wondered if he drank. He definitely smoked cigars, which reminded him he needed to check in on Mr. Howe, who was still in stable but critical condition a week after the tea parlor incident. The lab tests had come back positive for nicotine overdose, but how, and why? He'd hit a tunnel with no light at the end, like these endless dull grey days in New York. What would José do?

At Fifty-fourth Street he pushed through the revolving door of the Keyhole Media Building. The air whooshed and sucked him into the marble lobby. It was the end of the day, and workers ricocheted across the cool expanse like freed electrons. Expensive heels clicked on the terrazzo floor, which had been designed by some Italian artist who once re-created the gold Byzantine mosaics from the dome of St. Mark's in a round swimming pool for Brad Pitt and Angelina Jolie.

"T.K. Dean for Richard Cerf of *Other Half*," he told the guard, a snowy-haired black man, behind the desk. "I'll wait down here." The guard grunted and picked up the phone. T.K. slid away from the desk and hovered in a corner. There were no chairs, the better to discourage lingerers. The magazine empire built on voyeurism was distinctly averse to self attention.

Soon the elevators disgorged a fresh cohort of fact checkers and editorial assistants, most of them young women in short skirts and pumps, and one tall, stoop-shouldered man of considerably more advanced age. He had a pencil moustache somewhat permanently distorted into a tilde, following the rake of his careless smile. He wore an impeccably tailored blue chalk-stripe suit whose low gorge, wide lapels and linebacker shoulders marked it as dating from the Reagan presidency. His liberal use of hair wax dated from even earlier stylistic times, but somehow it all worked perfectly on Richard Cerf, a man of honed confidence in himself and, by extension, the absolute certainty that everyone else was equally clear-headed and sane. He had the graceful ability to make people feel at ease even as most people were quite certain that he was distinctly more at ease. The only child of second-generation Okies, he grew up in a southern California trailer park, won a scholarship to USC, edited the daily paper there, married his high-school sweetheart (also an only child from the same trailer park), never had children, and spent the vast majority of his life in this building and a few midtown restaurants and wine bars. "This is my family," he would often say in his corner office, stretching his arms to indicate the whole of *Other Half* magazine and its hundred and thirty staffers. He was older than T.K. by fifteen years. Yet along with George Chambers, he was his best friend.

"Richard!" said T.K.

"Cheers Teddy." They embraced, filed through the revolving door and headed west on Fifty-first Street.

"So how's the magazine business, my friend?"

The editor shrugged. "Not bad considering no one reads anymore. We solved that problem by eliminating words. Mostly we write captions. It seems to be working. Of course it's never good enough for corporate. We had revenue of six hundred million dollars last year—just one magazine, six and change, and margins up the ass—and they came to me last week and said I need to cut a hundred newspaper subscriptions. Too much duplication, they said. How many people need to get the *Times* in one building?"

"Six hundred mil in revs and they're worried about a few newspapers?"

Richard's moustache twisted into a vein of sarcasm. "Fifty thousand here, fifty thousand there, next thing you know the CFO gets a bonus. The priorities are truly astounding. I may have to lay off twenty-three staffers next week so those fuckers on the forty-ninth floor can pay for their vacation homes in Gstaad."

"Well somebody has to ski in Switzerland," said T.K. They crossed Broadway and kept on toward Eighth Avenue.

"Indeed," said Richard. "But this is my family we're talking about. I keep begging Wolfson to fire me instead; it would be a mercy killing, and would save roughly the same as two dozen of these youngsters. But she's a coward, and she needs me to do the layoffs. I'll be the last one out the door."

"You make it sound so appealing. A real job and all."

"Sorry, enough about me. What's going on with your book? Why aren't you in China?"

"One of my sources over there lost his head. Probably my fault. Another source is in a coma in Lower Manhattan Hospital, possibly attempted murder, possibly my fault."

"Jesus. I always thought of you as being so careful."

"Yeah me too. Maybe I'm getting old. Oh, and my agent died. In my arms, a week ago."

"Are you serious? Must have been amazing sex."

"Actually I was giving her the Heimlich Maneuver."

"She was choking on food during sex?"

"No, she had a heart attack."

"The Heimlich Maneuver is for food, not heart attacks."

"I know. There was no room. It was a small elevator. But at least it wasn't my fault this time. Unfortunately I left my book in her purse."

"The whole book?"

"With my notes and contacts. On a thumb drive."

"You don't have another copy?"

"I do. But the point is, I don't know where that thumb drive is now."

"Let's hope you don't have to go rifling through her purse. Never know what you'll find in those things." He shuddered. "Too bad for her, huh? Why couldn't it have been Wolfson?"

T.K. nodded. "Life is so unfair."

They reached Tout Va Bien, the usual place, and descended the steps to the cellar entrance. *"Bonjour messieurs!"* said Mariel, the middle-aged French hostess, in recognition. *"Ça va?"*

The restaurant was actually owned by an Italian, which explained the red-and-green flags and the *Forza Azzurri* soccer banners, but all the employees were Algerian *pieds-noirs*, as in all French restaurants in New York.

"Plus ça change," said T.K., verifying the same autographed black-and-white glossies that covered the walls picturing local newscasters from the 1980s, their big hair gelled and frozen in time.

"The food is still mostly edible, and still cheap," said Richard. They took a small table along the wall and ordered two nondescript bottles of Saint-Émilion.

"Comme d'habitude!" said Mariel.

"Do you have sweetbreads tonight?" asked T.K.

"Bien-sûr!"

He sighed and smiled at Richard. "Now I feel like I'm home."

"I'll drink to that!" said his friend. "Now tell me more about China."

T.K. related the whole story, and in shockingly little time both bottles of wine were drained. So engrossed was Richard in the tale that it wasn't until the third bottle, between platters of cracking cold oysters and searingly hot escargots, that Richard could ask T.K. about his marriage.

"I signed my divorce papers the day Trixie died," he said.

"I'm so sorry," said Richard.

"Not me, really. It wasn't meant to happen."

"This woman in China. The pregnant one. Was she meant to happen?"

"I don't know," said T.K. "We never talked about it. Didn't need to. Richard, you have Meg's phone number, don't you?"

He pulled out his phone and scrolled. "This one?"

"That's it," said T.K. "Hold onto it."

"Are you kidding? Now that you're divorced I plan on calling her next weekend."

Richard glanced around the restaurant. Tables on either side were still empty but he leaned in and lowered his voice. "If you need companionship, I can arrange something."

"Why do I not doubt that?" said T.K.

"I only mean…You've been gone a long time."

"This may come as a surprise to you but the 1.3 billion residents of China have sex too. Thanks Richard, but I'm good."

"There is one special friend, she'd be perfect for you."

"A professional?"

"Very much so. Expensive, and worth it."

"I see."

The door banged opened and a loud party of seven squeezed into the foyer. Mariel and a busboy pushed together a few tables next to T.K. and Richard, and the group sat down—three women in chairs facing the wall, and four men along the booth.

"Guppy?" said Richard, staring at the man at the far end.

"Richard Cerf! How the hell are you?"

"Never better. It's been years! T.K., say hello to Garamond Rockwell of *Crown* magazine. We worked together at the *Sun* ages ago."

"A pleasure," said T.K. He knew all about "Guppy" Rockwell, the columnist, former *Times* Rome bureau chief, public intellectual and author of bestselling memoirs, novels, plays and children's books. Every month at *Crown* he churned out some revelatory but inevitably counter-intuitive discursion on a self-referential field of study like how language and food evolve together ("It's been said we are what we eat, but in fact we tend to eat what we say") that would instantly become a cultural *meme*. He was short and frumpily dressed in a wrinkled oxford shirt and frayed khakis; unkempt locks of dark hair curled over his ears. The general impression was of someone too engrossed in important thought to care about personal hygiene. Nevertheless, and presenting further evidence that life was unfair, women fairly crawled over him. He was once married to Dr. Jessica Stone, who had her own TV show and was once named the World's Most Beautiful Gastroenterologist by *Other Half* magazine. She left Rockwell after a scandal involving the nanny.

"Everyone, meet my old friend Richard Cerf," said Rockwell, "who I believe is still executive editor of *Other Half* magazine, right?"

"Still and forever," said Richard.

"And your friend? Also a lifer?"

"I'm out on bad behavior," said T.K. "Actually I worked at the magazine for a nanosecond years ago—long enough to discover that Richard and I shared a love of *vin ordinaire* and even more ordinary French restaurants. In fact we have spent the last fifteen years researching the definitive guidebook to bad French restaurants, which we will never actually write. And what brings you to this half-star establishment?"

"A small celebration," said Rockwell. "We just had a run-through of my new Broadway musical—I'm writing the book of course, not the music..."

"He's fucking brilliant!" interrupted a slightly drunk redhead opposite T.K.

"...and this is my creative team," he went on, pretending not very well to ignore the compliment. Rockwell introduced the composer, a grizzled old plunker of long-past theatrical note named Sy who was reduced to scoring Smurfs movies, and the assorted other hacks behind this latest addition to the canon of Garamond Rockwell. "It's a culture-clash story," continued Rockwell although neither man had asked, "about an orthodox Jew from Brooklyn who moves to Pennsylvania Dutch country and finds he has more in common with them than funny hats."

"It's called *Hayseed Hasid!*" said the redhead, who had been introduced as the costumer. "Fucking brilliant!"

"It's meant as an ironic take on America's cornball impulse," explained Rockwell.

"Brilliant!" said the costumer again.

Rockwell turned to the bar and spoke loudly in bad Italian to the owner, who was watching the AC Milan game. Minutes later three bottles of Barolo, not *ordinaire*, materialized. The wine went around, and soon what had been two separate parties melded into one big table, at the head of which sat Garamond Rockwell, a man whom T.K. understood viscerally to be a colossal ass.

"What did you say your job is at *Other Half*?" Rockwell asked T.K.

"I didn't, but I was a senior editor. Many years ago."

"So you two are like the last of the Friday Night Guys!" Rockwell exclaimed.

"The what?" asked Richard.

"The Friday Night Guys! I just made that up, but you know what I mean: The old-school midtown magazine editors who used to go out on Friday night and get sloshed on their expense account."

"I remember expense accounts," said Richard wistfully. "Now we share hotel rooms. Last time I bunked up with an ad rep who wore a hairnet to bed."

"The Friday Night Guys!" said the redhead. "That's fucking brilliant, Guppy! You should write about them!" Then turning to Richard she said, wide-eyed: "So you're the top dog at *Other Half*?"

"I'm the second dog," said Richard. "Susan Wolfson would be the top dog."

"And what a dog she is!" interjected Rockwell to much tableside mirth.

"What's the second dog at *Other Half* do?" asked the redhead.

Richard sighed. "I'm dad."

"Dad?"

He nodded. "Whenever anyone has a problem, they come to me: 'Dad, Willie Nelson won't let us shoot him on the bus unless he's smoking a joint, what do we do?' 'Dad, the President won't do the Oval Office interview if we publish another picture of his kids, what do we do?' 'Dad, Julia Roberts wants a hundred-thousand-dollar donation to her charity for exclusive pictures of her hand-inseminating a show horse with a turkey baster, what do we do?' I could go on. I'm dad to a hundred and thirty editorial staffers; half of them went to Bryn Mawr, the other half to Barnard. They owe more in combined student loans than the gross national product of Costa Rica. You could argue that's a terrible waste, but at least they actually *make* something, unlike most people in New York, because every week that magazine comes out—four million hard copies—and lands in store racks and dentists' offices all across America. The pass-along is something like eleven, which means every week some forty-four million people set down their chicken nuggets and run their greasy fingers through those soul-deadening pages. And I'm the dad of it all! It's a pathetic excuse for a family—a magazine—but there you have it."

Everyone picked up their menus and feigned deep study. "I recommend the sweetbreads," said T.K. cheerily. "Best thing not on the menu, and they don't always have them."

"What, I'm afraid to ask, are sweetbreads?" asked the redhead.

"Well that depends," said T.K. "It's become a general-purpose euphemism for several different glandular lobes of both cows and sheep. But here it refers specifically to the thymus of a calf. Breaded and sautéed with capers and lemon. Very delicate taste—perhaps too delicate with that thick Barolo your friend ordered. I recommend an estate Beaujolais."

She shivered. "That sounds positively revolting. Could anything be worse?"

"Than an estate Beaujolais? Perhaps a simple Villages."

"Than those...sweetmeats or whatever you call them." She made a sour face.

"Suit yourself," said T.K., by now pretty drunk, "but you don't know what you're missing."

"Don't listen to him," said Richard. "He's a connoisseur of disgusting food. I recommend the venison steak with green peppercorn sauce. Comes with lots of fries. In fact we could share." The redhead felt the line delivered hard against her heart but kept her gaze on the menu. *He's coming on to me,* she thought. *He's old enough to be my dad.* Richard smiled. She thought his moustache was dashing. That was the word she used in her mind: *dashing.*

And yet there was still Garamond Rockwell, the original object of her affection, who was gulping Barolo and had launched into a monologue about his next book, a novel. His words ran together like a paragraph from *Moby-Dick:*

"It's about a guy maybe British maybe American I'm not sure yet who is a total introvert completely unable to relate to other people he's emotionally broken from events in his past he's not a sociopath he has empathy for other people indeed maybe more than for himself but he's completely in his own head. So he moves to Rome and has an epiphany at the Basilica of St. Paul standing over the crypt of St. Paul who was beheaded by the Romans and suddenly he sort of loses his own head and becomes the world's biggest extrovert and loves everybody and can't stop talking to them."

"That's *brilliant!*" said the redhead, this time mechanically. Now she was looking at Richard.

Garamond paused briefly to allow the rote brilliance to settle in, then continued: "Hippocrates was the first to claim we are all born with one of four humors, as he called them—melancholic, choleric, sanguine or phlegmatic..."

T.K. blew his nose loudly into a handkerchief.

"...and our emotional reactions to everything in the world are largely tempered by that humor—hence the word *temperament*. In other words, we are what we are, and any changes to our personality exist only along the scale of that basic temperament. When you get right down to it, modern psychology hasn't given us much beyond that. But I'm interested in exploring what happens if it simply isn't true. What happens if you really can completely change your personality?"

"That's what wine is for," said Richard, lifting his glass.

"Here here!" said the others, and a toast was made, to the annoyance of Rockwell who sensed he was not being taken seriously, perhaps even by the redheaded costumer whom he assumed would be removing most of her own costume in his bedroom later that evening but not too much later as he was not a young man anymore.

"Okay I'll drink to that," he said, "but of course I don't mean externally driven personality cues. What if you could just...endeavor to change yourself? And what would happen?"

"What's his name?" asked the old composer. "The character who is you."

Rockwell flinched defensively. "It isn't really me. More of a palimpsest. Paul."

"Of course, Paul—like the saint," the composer said. "What's the title?"

"*Saint Paul Without the Walls*."

"*Saint Paul Without the Walls*." The redhead repeated it, her brow furrowed in thought.

"It's the church," said T.K., leaning in to the conversation. "The name of the church in Rome. *San Paolo Fuori le Mura*. An interesting declination of normal Italian gender rules because the word for *wall* is masculine—*muro*—but the word for city walls, as opposed to a wall in your house, is feminine, *mura*, which is technically singular but treated as a plural and preceded by the plural feminine article *le*. Hence *le mura*. It's weird, but that's Italian."

"Oh, now I get it!" she said. "*St. Paul Without the Walls!* Like the walls in his head!"

"*Brava*, my dear," said Rockwell. "*Più vino!*"

The redhead turned to T.K. "So you speak Italian too?"

"Too? Does somebody else speak Italian at this table? Oh, you mean Rockwell. I think he only speaks wine list. I can get by on the boot. It helps I had Latin in high school. Everyone should study Latin."

"Guppy, didn't you go to some Latin high school?" said one of the women.

"Boston Latin," he said, swelling. "It's not really a *Latin* school per se, but it is the oldest public school in the United States. Benjamin Franklin was its most famous dropout. Also Louis Farrakhan."

"To dropouts!" said T.K., raising his glass.

"To everything Latin!" said Richard, winking at the redhead. Rockwell joined the toast, seething that the monologue on his novel had been derailed and vaguely blaming T.K.

The food arrived. The old composer had ordered the sweetbreads. "You only live once," he said, unrolling his napkin.

"We're splitting the venison," said Richard to the waiter, wagging his finger between himself and the redhead. "Can we get another plate?" The redhead felt strongly that venison was all she would be sharing with Richard that evening, although she was happy to flirt. The real question in her mind was whether she would go home with Guppy or this fellow T.K., about whom she knew almost nothing but very much wanted to know more. Like his name.

"So what does T.K. stand for?"

"To come!" said Rockwell from across the table, dissecting a frog leg. "It's an old journalism trope; when a reporter doesn't have some fact he writes *TK* in his copy, turns it in and heads out to the bar. Why it's spelled with a *K* I haven't a clue. Maybe I should do a column on that. Did you know there is no *K* in the Italian alphabet?"

"I always made a point of filling in all my *TK*s before I went to the bar," said T.K. "Personal pride I guess, with my name and all. It's Theodore Kincaid. Teddy if you like. Teddy Junior in fact."

"Did you say you were a junior editor?" asked Rockwell.

"I'm Diane," said the redhead to T.K., ignoring Rockwell.

"Diane!" said T.K. "Do you know I've never met a Diane in my life?"

"I don't believe you."

"Seriously!"

"I bet you say that to all the Dianes."

"Well I might if I'd ever met any. This calls for a bottle of Beaujolais."

"Waiter!" said Rockwell. "A coarse Beaujolais for the junior editor!"

"Say, I've got a column idea for you, Guppy," said T.K. "A thought experiment, if you will."

"I'm all ears," he said.

"Let's say you go to a doctor. He says 'I'm sorry to tell you this Mr. Rockwell, but you've got cancer of the cock.' "

Forks dropped. "Cancer of the *cock!*" blurted Rockwell with exaggerated mirth as his dining partners chortled conspiratorially. "Must be exceedingly rare!"

"I bloody well hope so!" said the composer. "Although I gather in your case Guppy the diagnosis would require microscopic biopsy!"

More explosive hilarity. T.K. ignored their braying and continued: "Doctor says 'You've only got minutes to live unless we amputate. There's not even time for anesthesia'—he's holding a meat cleaver. You say, 'Can I get a second opinion?' He says, 'Well we can bring in my associate for a quick look.' He calls in the other doctor—and it's your *ex-wife* Dr. Jessica Stone—she who caught you boning the nanny tied to the crib and wearing a latex hood.' "

Before T.K. could finish saying "So what do you do?" Rockwell was over the table, Barolos and Beaujolais cascading over the tablecloth, frog legs and sweetbreads mid-air, chairs overturned and diners scattering as the two men throttled each other and rolled across the floor. Rockwell was no match in arm strength for his younger opponent and he knew it, so he was trying to gain advantage by poking an eye out.

And he would have, had not Diane cried, *"It's Sy! He's choking on food! He can't breathe!"*

The fighters peeled apart and scrambled off the floor. The old music man was down to his last song—still in his seat, clutching his throat and turning a deep shade of purple. His eyes bugged out in terror. T.K. swept the table aside, lifted Sy, spun him around and went into a full Heimlich. After three jerks, Sy fired off a sweetbread projectile that ricocheted off the ceiling and landed in the front pocket of Garamond Rockwell's shirt. Dinner was over.

Chapter Twenty-Two

"That went well," said T.K.

He and Richard were walking east on Forty-ninth Street. It had started to rain lightly. The thick steel plates over the open crypts of New York's endless street work glistened, and thin films of motor oil formed rainbow patterns under rushing car headlights.

"Now that was the proper application of the Heimlich Maneuver," said Richard. "You saved that guy's life, what's left of it. Could have been his last meal."

"I guess that was our last meal at Tout Va Bien. I'm sorry."

"No need to apologize. We were never going to finish that guidebook anyway. Anyway it was the best fun I've had with my pants on in ages. Besides, he attacked you. And no one died."

"Because generally someone does die when I'm around," said T.K.

They turned down Seventh Avenue and walked a block in silence, dodging umbrellas. Finally Richard said, "Did you know I never saw a cloud in my entire childhood?"

"Huh?"

"Growing up in LA there were never any clouds. I mean those big puffy clouds like the kind that march up and down the Hudson out my office window. Even when it rained it was just...grey, like the smog. When I came East and saw clouds, I was amazed at how beautiful they were. And I've loved them ever since. Even the dark ones. I guess for most people clouds are sort of a downer, but they've always put me in the best mood. When the sky is bright and sunny I'm bored to tears. Strange, isn't it?"

"You never told me this before."

"To be honest I'd rather talk about women. Why don't I put you in touch with that special friend I mentioned? Do you a world of good. You seem awfully distracted by all this. You need to live in the moment. You're too anxious."

"Anxious people tend to survive."

"She's Chinese actually."

T.K. stopped walking. "Your whore? You mean Chinese Chinese?"

"Chinese Chinese. Her name is Lao. From somewhere in the middle of China where they found those stone soldiers."

"Xian."

"That's it."

"The terracotta army. Thousands of life-size soldiers from the First Empire. They were meant to protect the emperor's tomb. Found by a farmer digging a well in the Seventies."

"That's the place. She talks about it. Had a rough time apparently—one of those grim abortions you've been writing about, now I think about it. I never pressed her for the details."

T.K. turned his gaze down Seventh Avenue to the kinetic sales pitch of Times Square. A giant naked Lady Gaga lay prone across a billboard, her breasts crawling with Lilliputian men who formed a chain-link bra. "What's her number?"

"I'll text you."

"No texts. Just tell me. I'll remember."

"Okay," Richard said, pulling out his phone. "It's a UK mobile, so country code forty-four." He read it off and they parted; as Richard stepped off the curb he turned to T.K. and said, "To the last of the Friday Night Guys!"

"Hey, that terracotta army?" said T.K. "The emperor wanted it secret, so he killed all the artists when they finished. Hundreds of carvers worked their whole lives on the army. Then they were just massacred. Buried alive."

"Life is so unfair," said Richard.

T.K. kept walking south, reciting the phone number in his mind, memorizing it, finally pushing into the mindless surge of hucksters and blinking tourists drawn, like water downhill, to the fetid crevice of Theatre Row.

As he crossed Forty-sixth Street an urge overcame him to turn around quickly. If asked he would not have been able to articulate why, beyond a vague comprehension, recognizable to those who live on the edge of constant concern, that he was at that moment being followed. But in recognition of his own neurotic tendencies, he didn't really expect to see anyone following him. Still he had to look.

And there, not ten paces behind him, was Trotsky.

Or not. That is, not wearing the Trotsky t-shirt he sported in Hong Kong (last seen not-so-sportingly brocaded in vomit on the Star Ferry), but the same guy—the long hair, the faraway gaze and pasty Cantonese complexion, the apparent duty to tail Theodore Kincaid Dean around the world.

"*Motherfucker!*" T.K. sprang after Trotsky, who dropped a tattered New York *Post* and bolted up Broadway. Had T.K. consumed one less bottle of wine that evening he might have caught his man, but as it was he misjudged a traffic light and ended up on the wrong side of a red double-decker tour bus that was lumbering across Broadway. By the time he got around the bus, Trotsky had disappeared into the swell of crowds now pouring out of theaters. *How do all these fucking musicals end at the exact same time?* wondered T.K. with annoyance. He spun around three times, trying to spot Trotsky, and realized he had bigger problems. A few hundred pounds bigger.

Across Broadway, three large Western men in baggy suits were angling through the crowd, eyes on T.K. He thought of finding a cop—there were always dozens in Times Square, mostly to keep the street performers from hassling the tourists too much—but what would he tell them? *Help! I'm being pursued by large unknown men for reasons I don't completely understand but having something to do with abortions in China!* He couldn't picture it. He made for the subway entrance but as he approached the top tread the trio of thugs started down the stairs across the street. The Times Square IRT station was a vast maze, and T.K. thought he could probably lose them down there—he guessed they weren't New Yorkers, they had that bushy-browed, scowling eastern European look that he could spot a continent away—but then he saw the bikeshare stand, two bright blue Citi Bikes left. He swiped a credit card in the kiosk and got an unlock code as two of the men ran toward him. (The third had gone into the subway station.) He sprinted to the nearest bike, several yards from the kiosk, punched in the code and yanked it off the rack. *Fuck!* Flat tire. In New York, if something seems too easy it's usually because you're the millionth person to realize that something is in fact very hard. The men were threading through traffic on Seventh Avenue. T.K. ran back to the kiosk and swiped his card again—but he hadn't put the busted bike back in the rack, so the machine thought he already had a bike checked out and wouldn't give him another code. Fuck *fuck!* He circled back, racked the stupid bike with the flat tire, waited for it to click into place, and ran back to the kiosk for a fresh code. The remaining bike was at the far end of the long stand. The men had crossed the avenue as T.K. got to the bike, praying for tires full of nitrogen. Yes, thank you Jesus! He entered the code. *Red light.* Again. *Red light.* "Fucking Citibank, you bastards!" He tried a third time. *Green light.* He tore the bike from the stand, leaped on—the saddle was adjusted for a short person so he felt like a circus clown—and bounced over the curb into Seventh Avenue just as the first guy was at his side. The man cursed in a language T.K. didn't know, then yelled *"Taxi!"*

"Good luck with that, asshole!" yelled T.K. as he pedaled away, thanking his own luck that his assailants were trying to hail a taxi in Times Square in the rain when the shows were letting out. Still, he knew they'd find one sooner or later, or just drag an old lady out of one. He figured he'd be safe on the cross streets, which were backed up river to river. No way they could catch him in that traffic. At Sixth Avenue he hit the red light and squeezed between two panel trucks, hopping off to adjust his saddle. When the light changed he was off, zigzagging across and down Manhattan in high gear all the way. When forced to take the avenues he went against traffic, pedaling south down the northbound arteries, in case his friends had managed to get a cab.

"Hey asshole, wrong way!" said a suit crossing Madison at Thirty-second.

"Sorry, in a hurry," said T.K. sideways, swerving around the pedestrian.

"Who isn't?" the guy yelled back. "Fucking bikeshare assholes! Fucking Citibank!"

A city without alleys leaves few choices for the pursued cyclist. But T.K. knew all the plazas, vest pocket parks and pedestrian walkways, most of them concessions from developers in return for the "right" to build even higher and more oppressive office and apartment towers than the notoriously squishy Manhattan zoning laws theoretically allowed. Most of these "privately-owned public spaces" boasted vaguely aristocratic names—Connaught Park, Brevard Place, Sterling Plaza, Dumont Plaza, Highpoint Plaza—despite their ostensibly democratic intentions. In truth they were design afterthoughts that looked good on the site plan but in real life were about as amenable as the Khumbu Icefall. Within a year of construction, most of these sunless urban fissures devolved into concrete wastelands with shriveled landscaping, overflowing trash bins and the nose-curling stench of sidewalk-cured urine with no place to drain. But they were everywhere, and if you knew the city you could ride north to south and west to east from Bel Canto Plaza to Alliance Capital Park through Verizon Special Permit Plaza to Dag Hammarskjold Park to Murray Hill Mews to Madison Green to the Saatchi & Saatchi Arcade to Salomon Smith Barney Plaza to Zuccotti Park (birthplace of Occupy Wall Street) and the J.P. Morgan Covered Pedestrian Space almost without encountering traffic.

The incorporation of America was working out pretty well for him right now, thought T.K. as he wheeled around a vest-pocket homeless encampment in the redundantly named Parc East Park. Oh yes, he was living in the moment! Here in the moment was a little boy, clear-headed before the branch-lopper accident and his first Eden-banishing taste of whiskey, riding a Schwinn at night across a Vermont village common. Trash bins now apple trees, dense with autumn fruit! Windblown grocery bags and takeout wrappers, now falling maple leaves! The sharp odor of piss now a musk of compost and chimney smoke! A New England boy now an international spy being pursued by nefarious foreign agents! Yes, that was the boy's reality, the moment in the twelve-year-old mind.

It was raining harder. T.K. pedaled on downtown, shedding layers of concern with every block forward and no sign of his followers. But at Houston Street he spotted them in a cab. They saw him and wheeled a U-turn through the First Avenue intersection. He tore the wrong way down Orchard Street toward Delancey, knowing they would chase him along Allen. The Williamsburg Bridge with its dedicated bike lane, high above the roadway and the train tracks, loomed through the fog. Perfect! Of course the big men weren't far behind; their taxi pulled onto Delancey just as T.K. swerved into the bike lane entrance.

T.K. bore down on the pedals as he scaled the bridge. High above the East River the rain beat down harder. At the top of the span he hurled his cell phone over the side and watched it disappear into the black vapor shrouding the water below. Then came the screech of an approaching train. He looked over the other side and caught a streak of light on the Manhattan-bound rails, which ran down the middle of the bridge between the roadways and below the bike path; a J train was lumbering up the span.

The barricade was only four feet feet high and the Citi Bike just flimsy enough that T.K. was able to swing it over his head and send it cartwheeling onto the train tracks. The conductor, a solid union man named Jesus Algorado who'd been working the BMT line since 1987, had seen a lot of strange things on the tracks but never a bicycle. He slammed on the brakes. By the time the train stopped a few yards short of the mangled Citi Bike, T.K. had scaled the barricade and eased down the other side. A short hop and he was on the train roof; minutes later he was between cars. He slid open the door and took a seat next to a nurse, who was arguing with her husband in her cell phone. It would take time for the transit police to get that fucking Citi Bike off the tracks. They were going be there a while.

Essences
The Fifth Part

Chapter Twenty-Three

Kong Lao pulled a pack of American Spirits out of her purse. "Cigarette?"

"I don't smoke," said T.K. They were in her walkup studio apartment in Murray Hill. It was technically more of a home office since most of her clients came here, paying her eight hundred dollars for an hour of anything-goes sex. The smell of curry wafted up from the restaurant downstairs.

Lao shrugged and lit a cigarette for herself, then wrapped her arms around his neck, blowing smoke in his face. "I bet I can get you to share a cigarette with me, yes?"

"I don't gamble."

"No smoke, no gamble. What do you do?"

"I listen."

Lao turned around. "Then why don't you listen to the zipper on my dress."

"Keep your clothes on. Show me your passport."

"What?"

"Don't worry, I'm not INS. Please, just show me your passport."

She grabbed her bag and got up to open the door. "Go."

"Wait a minute. Here." T.K. pulled ten Franklins from his wallet and tossed them on the coffee table. "Seriously. When was the last time you made a thousand bucks with your clothes on? C'mon."

She hesitated, then said: "I'll show you mine if you show me yours."

T.K. rolled his eyes. "Okay. Here." He held out his passport.

She fumbled through her purse and extended her claret-hued Chinese passport. They traded in one swipe.

"Wow!" she said, paging through his visas. "Libya, huh? Are you like a terrorist?"

"I was transit—never mind."

"Hey, PNG in China! You must be really bad!"

"The worst." He flipped through hers. "You haven't left the U.S. in over a year; you got a green card?"

"No shit! You think I learned English so I could go back to Xian? I'm hoping to get citizenship. I've been studying. 'Four score and seven years ago...' "

"Show me the green card."

She huffed and handed it over.

"E-Thirty-one," he said. "That's for skilled workers."

"You didn't seem too interested in my skills a minute ago. You heard of *Fifty Shades of Grey*? I know more than seventy. Some in color."

"Any relatives in China?"

"No one I care about, or cares about me."

"How did you get here? Who paid?"

"I was a Red Star Scholar. Columbia."

"And I'm Charlie Chan. Tell me the truth. Look, I'm trying to help someone." They traded back passports.

"Everybody needs help," she said.

"A friend, Chinese. She disappeared from Guangxi."

"Guangxi? Oh, not good," she said.

"Why?"

"Well...I don't know. I mean, I can't be sure, but I know CIA is involved there too."

"Spies?"

"Spies I don't know about. Christian International Aid."

"Christian...? CIA? No way! Too obvious. Spies aren't that stupid." He mentally flogged himself for not picking up on the initials earlier.

"You think? If they're so smart then how come 9/11?"

"Fuck."

"Yeah, *fuck*—a good word for it. They are not what they seem to be, those Christians. After my abortion they paid for me to get out of Xian—got me a passport and a plane ticket to Amsterdam."

"Amsterdam?"

"You heard me. That place is damned alright."

"If you don't have any kids, why did they give you an abortion?"

"I didn't say it was a forced abortion."

Suddenly serious, she toggled to Mandarin. "They had a guy meet me off the KLM at Schiphol. He had a sign with my name on it, and a cross. I thought maybe I would have to become a nun. If only. Next thing I know I'm in a brothel—on my knees alright, but not exactly praying. It was owned by Russians. Gross hairy-chested guys. Nothing personal if you've got a hairy chest, but those guys also have hairy backs." She made a face like sucking on a lime. "Good thing most of the customers were Brits, over on the Eurostar for the weekend. That's how I learned English. The dirty words first: *tit, cunt, pussy, ass, cock, cum, suck, fuck.* I know them all in French too: *chatte, cul, baise, nichon…*"

"I get it."

"I could work at the UN."

"You're saying the Christian group sold you into sex slavery?"

"Slavery's a big word. In today's economy you need skills. I figured out I could make extra money on the side if I let them stick it in my ass, which was against the house rules. And believe me, all those Brits want to stick it in my ass. It's all they think about while that train's going through the Chunnel. You know what it comes from? They're all gay. Anyway, that's how I bought my way out of there. First I went to London—closer to my customer base. Then I started a business selling my panties online. I only had to wear them for maybe two hours, so I could make a week of inventory in one day."

"A regular F.W. Woolworth."

"Wool? You like wool panties? Maybe you are Mormon. Some of my best customers are Mormon."

"Save it for the civics test. Here's a free study tip: You need to name two American Indian tribes."

"Apache and Geronimo?"

"Google it." He made for the door.

"Hey, where are you going?"

"Amsterdam. I hear the elms are beautiful this time of year."

"You need some panties?"

Chapter Twenty-Four

The location of the ivory shop directly across the street from the police station was a matter of convenience, for it meant that Nong Ning could collect his monthly bribe from Chou Yishan, the owner and master carver, and then proceed with only a few steps to meet with his factotum, the police sub-chief Fang Dazhu. Ning hated walking almost as much as rice planting, especially on hot days, and this one was proving brutal.

The workshop was a long, narrow space with high clerestory windows, much like a small factory floor, which in a sense it was. From his workbench at one end, Yishan oversaw half a dozen work stations where apprentices in white smocks, dust masks and jeweler's headband magnifiers labored over small carvings. Canto-Pop music bleated from a transistor radio, occasionally overpowered by bursts from several air compressors. A Westerner entering the space might experience a vague sense of anxiety—not so much from the sight of elephant tusks stacked everywhere but rather from the high whine of tiny pneumatic drills wielded by the artists—drills in fact exactly like those used by dentists on human ivory. On the far wall hung a banner in bright red characters:

不要紧，你如何慢慢走，只要你不停止！

It was a quote from Confucius: "It does not matter how slowly you go so long as you do not stop!"

Ning greeted Yishan, a wizened old man with a thin beard like pig's whiskers, and confirmed delivery of the baby elephant tusk. "As for the narrative program, I should like to document some scenes from *The Carnal Prayer Mat*," he told the artist. "Starting with the scene where the magician puts a dog's kidney inside Weiyangsheng's penis to give it size and endurance. Then of course we will show him having sex with several women, alone and together."

"A fine choice!" said Yishan obsequiously. His skill as a master carver was exceeded only by his capacity to patronize influential clients. Both talents had taken years to hone. "And his wife Yuxiang? Shall we depict her?" Yishan knew all the great classical themes, especially the erotic ones; he had carved them countless times, although he assured clients that each version was the first—a brilliant new programmatic theme that only a genius, meaning that particular client, would have considered, as opposed to what it really was: another fuck fest. The customer is always trite, right? What a waste of good ivory.

"Yes, but not her suicide. Show her earlier, practicing her...special skill."

"Ah, you mean her dexterity with a calligraphy brush held in her vagina!"

"Precisely."

"A fine idea, Honorable Nong!" Yishan wondered what principle of Newtonian physics made it possible for a man of Mr. Nong's girth to stoop over the toilet without toppling over. Maybe the tonnage acted like a sea anchor, holding him steady in the current, so to speak. Or maybe he had a Western toilet in his home, so he could sit. "We shall situate her in the brothel where she learned the trick. As an artist I have long felt affinity with her character but have never been so honored as to carve her."

"Tell me Yishan. In your career, have you ever met a woman of such notable...artistic bent?"

Yishan twisted his wiry beard in thought. "There were stories about another student in art school," he said. "She was rumored to be of the sapphic persuasion. Only stories, I suppose. But on your recommendation I shall stay vigilant!"

They laughed, which drew the gaze of a young apprentice—a teenage boy whose dark skin was barely visible beneath a veil of ivory dust. He had long bangs that obscured eyes focused on something far beyond the ivory shirt buttons lined up on his workbench, beyond the walls of the studio and in fact beyond China itself. He was thinking about algebra and San Francisco.

"Who is that small boy?" Ning asked Yishan.

"His father was the man killed by police. Now he has no money for school books. A good worker, with an artistic mind. That is to say, he is often too much inside his head."

"In that case it is probably best he avoid school books!" The men laughed again as Ning took his leave and crossed the street to the police station. The asphalt parking lot radiated curtains of heat, which curled like gravity around the black hole of Fang Dazhu's Buick. Ning entered the station, smiled at Mei (who bowed slightly) and let himself into Dazhu's office. The sub-chief was pouring a tumbler of *báijiǔ*.

"Honorable Party Secretary!" said the officer. "You are just in time for the first drink at the end of a long day."

Ning checked his watch. "It is still morning," he said.

Fang glanced at the wall clock. "So it is! You know we start work so very early around here."

"I am certain your days are long and your nights undoubtedly...longer," said Ning, taking a seat in the only chair without armrests, which Dazhu kept in the office specifically to accommodate his immense honorable guest. The chair was sturdy, in fact specially reinforced for Ning, but not so comfortable as to encourage loitering. "Nevertheless I am hot and would like a glass of water."

"Mei!" shouted Dazhu. "Water for the party leader!"

Ning wondered how long a drunken police sub-chief who raped his subordinates could keep his post. Times were changing, officials less likely to tolerate indiscretions, especially in big cities. But out here in rural Guangxi? Hard to say. And he was Zhuang, not like normal Chinese, and tolerance for impure cretins was the order of the day from Beijing.

"How is the wounded officer doing?" asked Ning.

"He is healing," said Dazhu. "Fortunately he is right-handed and the bullet hit his left arm."

"And the officer who lost his gun?"

"Yun Jian. An unfortunate accident. It seems the young man was spooked by the gunfire; his distraction allowed Chen to grab his gun. Anyway he has dishonored his family and will never be promoted."

Mei entered with a plastic water bottle sweating from the refrigerator. "Thank you," said Ning, watching her sway out of the room. He turned to Dazhu: "A beautiful flower. She will make some man very happy—if she does not already," he said with a wink, to make sure Dazhu knew he was aware of the sub-chief's hobbies. Dazhu raised his glass of *báijiǔ*; Ning lifted his water bottle, then shifted in his seat as delicately as physics allowed. "Nothing tastes as good as fresh water on a hot day," he said. "You know, I have noticed recently that the carp from the river seem smaller."

Dazhu wondered if the fish were really smaller or if Ning had simply grown larger by comparison.

"And people are forbidding their children to swim," Ning continued. "It seems they are developing a rash."

Dazhu thought back to the American, Mister Dean, who also had a rash and had been in the river. "I suspect those pig farms are polluting the Li," Ning continued. "We must conduct environmental inspections. If necessary we will order the riverbanks cleared."

"Cleared?" Dazhu eyed his bottle of *báijiŭ*. "Many thousands live along the river."

Ning slapped his thigh and shifted upright in his chair. "Inspector Fang, on pain of reviewing primary-school geography, I remind you that the Li feeds into the Pearl and thence the watershed for the entire south of China. Besides our local concerns, the sanitation of the Li impacts the health of hundreds of millions of citizens from here to Hong Kong. Let them excrete what they will into the Pearl from Guangzhou; my charge is the Li above the dams."

"Very well, Secretary," said Dazhu, wishing he could toss his glass of *báijiŭ* in the fucker's fat face despite the waste of good alcohol.

Ning settled back into the chair, which strained and creaked. "That small Zhuang boy now working across the street," said Ning, nodding in the direction of the ivory shop. "What happened to his mother?"

"He is not Zhuang," said Dazhu quickly. "His parents were both Han."

"He is so dark."

"The houseboat people live in the sun," said Dazhu. "They grow as bronze as the fishermen. At any rate his mother seems to have disappeared." He reached for his pack of Zhonghuas, hoping to change the subject. "Cigarette?" Usually Dazhu smoked cheap, sweet Hongtashans but he always kept some pricey Zhonghuas on his desk to impress party officials.

"Thank you but no," said Ning. "The doctor insists they are not good for my heart. And besides, have you seen the new billboards from Beijing?"

"*The gift of cigarettes is the gift of cancer!* How true, and yet like the start of so many journeys, how very distant seems the return."

"Indeed," said Ning.

"Speaking of tobacco," said Dazhu, "We have recently intercepted trucks going into the lotus-wood mill with bales of tobacco from Yunnan province."

Ning sat up again.

"As the mill does not produce cigarettes," Dazhu continued, "I found this curious. Meanwhile, many trucks leaving the mill are laden with two-hundred-liter drums—hardly the normal containers for lumber. I don't know what to make of it, but I pass it along."

"Interesting," said Ning. "Thank you for your vigilance. Now I must be off." He downed his water and left.

Back in the parking lot, Ning felt the heat of the asphalt burning through the soles of his shoes. The potted papaya sagged like a crucified prophet. He lowered himself carefully into his Audi—the black metal roof was too hot to grab for leverage—and descended slowly until the final sudden collapse into the seat as the car listed sternly to port. He adjusted the wedgie in his underwear, cranked the AC, and fished out his cellphone.

"Mr. Hu, this is Nong Ning."

"Honorable Nong, how providential to hear from you," said Tianhua, who was himself stuck in traffic in Guangzhou. "Did you receive the gift?"

"Indeed," said Ning. "A most generous offering. It is already being carved. I am most grateful."

"The pleasure was all mine. How gratifying to do business with a collector of such exquisite taste."

"Thank you," said Ning, certain Tianhua was lying. "Mr. Hu, I understand your lotus-wood mill is receiving large shipments of unprocessed tobacco, and shipping truckloads of sealed drums. Pardon my query, which I assure you is not of an official nature but merely a function of my natural curiosity..."

"No apologies necessary, Honorable Nong. I understand completely that men of your gargantuan intellect are possessed with an equally substantial hunger for knowledge. In my business I am always looking for fresh opportunities, and I believe I have recently found one in tobacco."

Ning knit his brow. "Far be it for me to second-guess your business acumen," he said, "but is not the tobacco industry quite mature, and highly regulated? I am unclear on entry points for innovative newcomers."

"Indeed so would I hope is the mindset of the established tobacco companies," said Tianhua. "But I believe there is a huge opportunity in the new business of electronic cigarettes."

"Is that right?" said Ning casually, not letting on that he had never heard of electronic cigarettes.

"Huge," repeated Tianhua, suspecting Ning had never heard of electronic cigarettes. "It's thought that these e-cigarettes do not cause cancer. You see, a vial of liquid nicotine is vaporized into a fog that can be inhaled with no tar."

"Of course," said Ning, grateful for Tianhua's face saving explanation. "So you are making these e-cigarettes in the lotus mill?"

"Oh no," said Tianhua. "We are not equipped for manufacturing in Guangxi; we have no tool-making or injection molding, much less assembly workers. We are just processing the tobacco into liquid nicotine, and selling it to manufacturers."

"I see," said Ning casually, not wanting to seem like it was any great concern of his even though he was seething to be left in the dark. "I do not recall seeing any permits for the production or transport of this liquid nicotine in the district."

"Ahh, now I see your natural curiosity has taken a more official tone," said Tianhua. "Not to worry—at the moment I am assured that no permits are required for liquid nicotine. Besides, it is perfectly harmless. It comes from a plant!"

Chapter Twenty-Five

It was eleven on a warm Thursday night and the storefronts along the Sint Annenstraat were coming to life. T.K. understood the concept as non-metaphorical: Windows trimmed in fringe and glowing red neon framed live and barely dressed women engaged in suggestive poses on or around chairs or poles, beckoning shoppers. Some windows featured whole groups of women, standing around like one of those Dutch master paintings of merchant burghers in their guild hall, minus the tall hats. The prostitutes were also merchants, and they had a guild, but that was about as far as you could carry that metaphor. Most were eastern European; the legality of their recent immigration was imprecise, but once in a window in the red light district of Amsterdam they were hardworking taxpayers.

Sex tourists staggered out of bars and hooch parlors. T.K. parked his rented bicycle along the Oudezijds Voorburgwal canal across from the Hash Marijuana and Hemp Museum, wrapping the heavy chain lock around a signpost that warned against taking pictures of prostitutes in the windows. In a city of junkies and bicycles, strong locks were a way of life and indeed required by law. T.K. thought Amsterdam possibly had more regulations around bicycles than around sex and dope parlors. It was a good bike as rentals go—a Workcycle, from the manufacturer on the Lijnbaansgracht in Jordaan, which rented out heavy black lugged-frame Dutch bikes with front racks strong enough to hold a passenger, and they didn't scream ORANGE like most of the tourist rentals, nor were they plastered with corporate sponsorship logos like the New York bikes.

The thought of New York made T.K. shudder reflexively and check his back. No goons on his tail here. He hadn't bought a phone since the last one in New York went over the Williamsburg Bridge. He'd incinerated his credit card—the one he used to rent theCitiBike that went onto the rails—and opened a new account at a new online bank in Meg's name. His wife. Or was she his ex-wife by now? Either way he knew he could trust her, maybe more now that the hastily packed baggage of matrimony had been left at the carousel. He'd loaded up ten thousand dollars on prepaid debit cards from six different Wal-marts in New Jersey, Connecticut and Long Island—the same cards gang members use in prison to bribe guards. He'd considered paying cash for his Amsterdam ticket at the midtown Delta office but decided that would only draw more attention. Who pays cash for plane tickets? They'd probably flag his passport. Criminals knew best: In the United

Corporate States of America, Wal-Mart debit cards were much safer than dead presidents.

He'd had no luck retrieving his manuscript from Trixie's purse. His dear departed agent lived alone and had no relatives, but T.K. managed to track down Cleary, the assistant, who said she'd been through all of Trixie's stuff; no thumb drive. He had no laptop, no phone, and the only copy of his book and notes was on the thumb drive in his watch pocket. As soon he got into Amsterdam he headed for the Central Library to check email on the public computers.

Mr. Howe was still in Lower Manhattan Hospital, where the staff had started invoking HIPAA rules and refusing to talk to him. On his visits T.K. had tried to find out more from Howe about Blokov, his Russian boss in Amsterdam, but the patient just stared at the TV in his room. If Christian International Aid was really a CIA front, why would a Russian be running it?

Most of the better Amsterdam whores were Russian; they looked like actual supermodels and were less likely than the plus-size prostitutes to offer early-bird discounts. They typically worked in the VIP zone behind the thirteenth-century Oude Kerk, with its soaring wooden vaults under which Rembrandt prayed, in shops with pidgin English-Dutch names like Sex Paradijs; indeed to go by the signage in De Wallen, the proper Dutch word *seks* had gone the way of *thee* and *thou*. You had to tail off on the side streets if you wanted *seks* with Africans or Asians; the transvestites worked across the Achterburgwal canal in the so-called blue light district.

"How much?"

The Aussie was swaying, cigarette stuck to his bottom lip, hanging with four friends and staring at a tall Russian in a short window. T.K. hadn't had a drink since the disastrous dinner in New York last week, and he was amazed at how sobriety made even mildly drunk people seem so obviously wasted.

The Russian prostitute, in a thong, was skinny enough to be in magazines. Even under the red light you could see her wide pupils, and T.K. was pretty sure she was more stoned than the Aussie—most likely a junkie and possibly insane, maybe the kind who would bite your cock. Amsterdamers liked to warn tourists about the cock-biters and watch their eyes bulge, but T.K. suspected it was the same old misogyny making the rounds ever since Eve bit the apple. At any rate some of these customers probably deserved a chomp—maybe Garamond Rockwell if he ever paid for sex. *Ever?* All men pay for sex, thought T.K. It's merely a question of venue.

The Russian opened the side door and addressed the Aussie. "Fifty euros," she said in decent English. The standard price for twenty minutes.

"What's it include?" he asked.

"Blowjob and fuck, missionary," she said, reciting the basic menu with no substitutions.

"How much for doggy style?"

"Full package is one hundred euros. Everything plus extra ten minutes."

"Turn around," said the Aussie, twirling his finger. She spun and he stared.

"Nice thong, baby!" said another tourist.

T.K. was thinking about the dioramas at the American Museum of Natural History, where you could stand in the Akeley Hall of African Mammals and see wildebeests from the Serengeti Plains and gorillas on Mount Kivu and Angolan antelopes and Libyan desert oryx and chimps from the Cavalla River of Ivory Coast, all without taking a step, and he imagined in the same way, standing here in the oldest part of Amsterdam, that he was standing everywhere in the world.

This perspective was not tidy or rational—not like zooming out on Google Earth to take in the whole globe. It was more like seeing all of Google Street View all at once. There was no morphologically human way to interpret it, any more than you could imagine what it would be like to process the view from thirty thousand eyes like a dragonfly. But it felt at once surreal and super-real, like light bent through water, and T.K. arrived at the disorienting conclusion that this hyper-world in his mind on a street in De Wallen was not imagined but really existed, that the real world was playing out on a proscenium in his brain and was in fact slightly bent.

Merely a question of venue.

"Bloody fucking well then, I'm in," said the Aussie. He stubbed out his smoke, stepped through the door and nodded to his buddies, one of whom said, "See you at the Bulldog in an hour, mate." Then he was inside the window, another mammal in the diorama, until the Russian girl drew the curtain closed.

T.K. crossed over to the Dollebegijnensteeg—Alley of the Mad Beguines, named after the women's religious order that spread across northern Europe in the thirteenth century. Beguines were not nuns, probably because their families weren't rich enough to pay for ordination, but they lived in celibate monastic enclaves; many practiced mysticism and were ostracized by the Church as insane. The most famous Beguine was Marguerite Porete, author of *The Mirror of Simple Souls*, a medieval French text that described the process of achieving oneness with God through divine love. What got the attention of the Church was her suggestion that reaching the highest level of oneness obviated the need to receive sacraments or even attend Mass—a notion that the Bishop of Cambrai regarded about as favorably as teeth on his cock. The inquisitor William of Paris pronounced her a heretic. The book was burned, as was she, on a stake in Paris in 1310.

At the corner of the narrow alley, a sign on a building advised *Camera Toezicht*—"Video Surveillance." Did anybody really need to be told they were being surveilled in Amsterdam's red light district? T.K. turned down the alley and felt vaguely envious of people who lived in a time when surveillance required reading someone's book—and when writing one could get you burned at the stake.

The windows down the alley featured "exotic models," meaning Nigerians and Asians. The lane was claustrophobic—barely wide enough for two bicycles to pass—and intensified his nagging sense that he was crossing farther than ever from that warm place of detachment into the prickly zone of personal involvement. But hadn't he known it? Hadn't he set down that narrow alley when he first met Ming on the houseboat? And did he really think she was here? Based on what? The tale of a Chinese prostitute in Manhattan? The name of some Russian guy supposedly running Christian International? *Blokov.* Sounded like a Cold War spy in a Pink Panther movie. He might have thought Mrs. Howe lifted it from fiction except for the near certainty that she had no familiarity with Western spy satires.

A crowd had gathered in front of one shop so that it was impossible to pass in the alley. In the window, an Asian woman was performing advanced yoga poses in a thong. Men were cheering.

"C'mon, baby! Oh yeah, that's it!"

She was dark, maybe Thai or Vietnamese but also possibly from Guangxi. "How much?" T.K. asked through the window in Zhuang. The woman fell from her pose, stared at T.K. and opened the door.

"You speak Zhuang?" she asked him.

"My Mandarin is better, but I can get by. You're from Guangxi Region?"

"Guilin city," she said.

"I'm looking for a woman named Zeng Ming. From down the Li River."

The prostitute pressed her lips into a thin line and crossed her arms below her small breasts. "We don't have names here," she said. "I need to get back to work."

T.K. pulled out two orange fifty-euro notes. "Here's double pay. For twenty minutes."

She stared at the money for half a second.

"Please," said T.K.

Then she shut the door in his face and reappeared in the window.

T.K. buried his hands, and his banknotes, in his pockets, then turned and angled into the crowd. But as he moved past the main door of the building he noticed a small brass plate over the mail slot:

V. BLOKOV

Alleen op afspraak

"By appointment only." No phone, of course.

He leaned in and pushed a thumb against the buzzer. Nothing. He banged on the door. No answer.

In the window, the Zhuang girl had pulled out a small foam pad and launched into the Halasana "plow pose"—a shoulder stand with legs bent at the hips back to the floor.

"That's it, baby!" said an American tourist. "Christ I bet you could lick yourself!"

"Fuckin' right she could," said another guy. "Bitch is a fuckin' acrobat. C'mon baby, downward doggy style!"

T.K. shoved his way past the gawkers. He hurried to his bike, then rode down to Dam Square, turning west on Leliegracht, out of the disgusting whore and dope district, crossing the Spuistraat and its darkened bookstores, over the Singel moat and the ring waterways to Jordaan and its quiet, elm-lined canals. There, on the north quay of the Egelantiersgracht, amber lights glowed through the leaded-glass double doors of 't Smalle, his favorite bar in the city. He parked, locked, and pushed open the doors. Everything was right where he remembered it—the stained-glass medallions of unicorns and grapevines, the dim gaslight chandeliers, the paneled oak inglenooks under the windows. He sat at the bar, elbows on the brass rail, and eyed the publican.

"*Bier?*" asked the barkeep.

"Cognac, *bevallen.*"

Merely a question of venue.

Chapter Twenty-Six

You really couldn't justify a twenty-five-dollar Bloody Mary, thought Richard Cerf, even in a hotel bar in midtown Manhattan. Because when you boiled it right down, it was little more than vodka—in all its brand-conscious iterations a base-grain alcohol that Richard wouldn't wash his golf balls with—and canned tomato juice. Children were dying in Africa for lack of fifty-cent vaccinations, and New Yorkers with big watches were paying fifty times that for a cocktail. But the King Cole Lounge in the St. Regis Hotel was where the best hookers came—the really classy ones, the ones who looked like supermodels and fucked movie stars. It was in fact where Richard had met Lao, one of his regulars. Or was he one of her regulars? Either way. The variety of women at the bar on any given night was astounding, and yet they all drank those pedestrian Bloody Marys, and you had to buy them several. Expensive whores in an expensive bar—it was some kind of symbiotic relationship, he thought, like those luminescent bacteria that live on anglerfish and by their glow lure prey for the host.

Then there was the famous Maxfield Parrish mural, a vast golden canvas behind the bar picturing Old King Cole on his throne, surrounded by attendants bearing his pipe, bowl (more of an urn in this Greek-styled depiction) and of course the fiddlers three. Parrish, the great illustrator of *Arabian Nights* whose style followed no school or movement beyond his own vague neoclassical sensibilities, had spent most of his life in the Cornish Art Colony along the Connecticut River Valley that divides Vermont and New Hampshire. He died at age 95 in Plainfield, two stops up the Amtrak from T.K.'s home in Bellows Falls. Richard pulled up a saffron upholstered bar chair, ordered a thirty-dollar Scotch from the old barkeep in the brocade vest, and toasted T.K. and Maxfield Parrish.

It was only eleven o'clock—still a bit early for the ladies, so Richard didn't mind when an Asian businessman about his age sat down in the empty chair next to him and ordered a cognac. In fact, he had a vague feeling that he knew the guy. Maybe from long ago? Ad sales at the *Toledo Blade*? No. And then it hit him.

"Knock knock."

The Asian man spun around.

"Harry?" said Richard.

"Harry Hu!" said Hu Tianhua, completing the frat-house joke. "Is that Richard Cerf?"

"In the flesh, and plenty of it."

They shook hands and stared at each other. "How many years has it been?" said Tianhua.

"I'm gonna say twenty-eight," said Richard. "You look like you're doing well for yourself." Tianhua was wearing his usual Prada loafers and a Kiton Neapolitan-cut suit.

"I have a few businesses in China," he said. "And you?"

He shrugged. "Still filling up the space around the ads," he said.

"Ahh, I remember now, you edited the *Daily Trojan* senior year."

"Those were the days," said Richard. "In some ways that was the best job I ever had. We broke real news in those days. I mean, the *L.A. Times* followed us."

"And now?"

"Well now I make more money," he said, twirling his thirty-dollar Scotch. "But I have much less fun." A feeling of embarrassment washed over him and he suddenly didn't feel like volunteering the name of his magazine to his old frat brother. This caught him by surprise as he was generally quite content to point out, in a way that suggested resigned satisfaction with his disappointing career, how *Other Half* magazine brought smiles to millions of Americans every week, lessened the anxiety of the dentist's office and, as prime bathroom reading material, possibly even contributed to the nation's regular bowel movements. Fortunately his old friend let him off the hook.

"I too have some publishing interests," said Tianhua. "I own presses and we do mostly work for Western firms, but we also publish our own books in China."

"Really?" said Richard. "What kind of books?"

"All kinds," said Tianhua, sniffing his cognac. "Mostly non-fiction, current events, that sort of thing. At least what the censors will allow."

Both men laughed. Chinese censors seemed like such a trivial annoyance at the bar of the King Cole Lounge. "I have a friend who's a freelance journalist writing a book in China," said Richard. "Name of T.K. Dean."

Tianhua sat up straight and swiveled his bar chair in Richard's direction. "Is that right?"

"Heard of him?"

"Oh no," said Tianhua, lying easily; China was a big place. "What is the nature of his book?"

"It's about the abortions. On second thought, probably wouldn't pass the censors. Happy to put you in touch with him if you like."

"Please do," said Tianhua, pulling out his phone. "Can you give me his number?"

"Certainly. At the very least he's always good for a drink." Richard grabbed his phone and scrolled, then realized he had no current number for T.K. "I don't actually know how to reach him right now, but let me give you his ex-wife's number here in New York. She'll know how to find him."

"Excellent!" said Tianhua. "It's always nice to connect with the friend of a friend."

They toasted their good fortune, and exchanged numbers.

Chapter Twenty-Seven

It was long past three o'clock when T.K. paid his tab at 't Smalle and unlocked his bike. The alcohol had cleared his head of the red lights of De Wallen, and the late spring air blew the dark locks of his hair softly across his face as he pedaled over the Prinsengracht and south toward his hotel off the Westermarkt. It had rained while he was drinking, and the paving stones glistened under streetlamps. Again he was a boy in Vermont, riding through the night. But at the Anne Frank House he stopped. Her tree was gone—the *Anne Frankboom*, the giant horse chestnut in the back courtyard, which she had described in her diary, had fallen in a gale in 2010, just as experts warned it would. The hundred-and-fifty-year old tree was infested with leaf miner moth caterpillars and rotting from a fungus called Artist's Conch; Amsterdam's elms had survived the blight, but its horse chestnuts were not so lucky. Botanists estimated almost half the *Anne Frankboom* had been reduced to the tensile strength of a wet sponge. But cutting it down was too controversial, so the city spent a few hundred thousand euros shoring it up and improving the soil. In the end, it fell on a garden shed; no one was injured. New shoots were growing out of the stump, and eleven saplings had been donated to museums and parks around the United States. T.K. thought back on the ambrosia beetles that ravaged his father's sugar maples every few years, consigning limbs and whole trees to the crematorium of the sugar shack. He wanted to believe they cut the *Anne Frankboom* into firewood, but suspected it had been ground up and embalmed as compost.

"Dead or alive, dead or alive."

He thought about his hotel, then turned east onto the Leliegracht and rode back into De Wallen. He locked his bike in front of the Sex Museum on Damrak and walked back to Dollebegijnensteeg. Despite the hour, the pavements of the red light district still trembled under the march of hooligans and tourists; he figured he could loiter around the entrance to the alley until dawn and no one would notice. Sooner or later, someone had to go through Blokov's door.

The alley was so narrow that you couldn't see into the windows until you were right on top of them. But even from the corner by the canal, T.K. noticed scarlet light spilling from the Zhuang girl's window, casting the alley and a group of rowdy British tourists in a blood-red glow that made him mourn the lanterns of China. He walked down the alley, and as he got closer he realized that the yoga girl was gone; the shift had changed, and a new girl was posing. As T.K. drew closer, he could see why the window was radiating even more red than most of the red-light windows: The new woman, tall with narrow cheeks and far-apart eyes, was wearing a bright red *qípáo*—the skin-tight slit gown popularized in Shanghai during the Jazz Age. The dress was as red as the Chinese flag, and as T.K. approached he could see that it was in fact made out of a Chinese flag, the five stars of the canton curving as if in orbit around her breasts.

"Proper boss threads, me tart!" said one of the Brits, who was wearing a crimson Liverpool FC home jersey. "Be you a Scouser too?" He lifted his red shirt out from his chest—exposing his grey boxers as the shirt unfurled from his waist—and pointed at her red dress: "Look, the proper tint of communism and alcoholism!"

"Is right!" said his buddy, who wore thick round spectacles and fancied himself a connoisseur: "Now 'at bird has class."

"And I'll wager lungs of a proper size," said a third who, noticing her wide eyes, twisted his whiskered face into a squint until his head looked like a sea urchin. "Look mates, she's got one eye in Tocky and one eye in Crocky. Tell me tart, are yer lungs well jarg?"

Zeng Ming knew but a few phrases in English requisite to her new profession, none in Merseyside slang. She smiled, waved and pursed her lips at the Brits, not yet noticing T.K., who was in the shadows of the door.

"Come 'ead," said one of the louts to his friend, shoving him toward the canal. "It's almost four bells and yer proper skint. Am goin' the bog for a burst." They turned to leave as Liverpool

Red said to Ming: "If you find yerself Merseyside, look me up, lass! You'll never walk alone on Anfield Way!"

They moved back from the window as T.K. stepped from the shadows. Red light spilled across his face. "Ming?" he said into her eyes.

When she saw him, her counterfeit smile wilted and she drew her hands up around her face as if in defense against something too real. "Teddy?" She mouthed the word but could make no sound. Infrared tears in the false light streamed down her cheeks, and she saw that he was crying too.

"Ming!" he said again, then he threw open the door and landed in the window. They embraced, kissed hard and cried. She smelled of jasmine but it was cheap perfume, not the flowers of Guangxi. Still he inhaled her.

The drunken Scousers had turned to watch the commotion, then stood swaying in front of the crimson tableau.

"I told youse 'at bird was a bit of all right," said the one in glasses.

"Tellin' ye," said Red. "Am put odds 'im gettin' one fer free,"

"She's 'is judy, ya nit!"

T.K., still clutching Ming, reached a hand out and drew shut the curtain.

"Attaboy!" said Red. " 'Ave yerself some proper privvy." And with that they staggered off toward the Oudekerksplein, singing: *"Down Anfield Way the world is gay, all Kopites are to tingle; with rows and rows of crimson flags from Bootle up to Din gle!"*

"How did you find me?" Ming said through sobs, kneading his long hair and relieved to speak Mandarin.

"Later," he said. "We need to go, now."

"Where is Jintao?"

"I don't know. Let's go."

"My clothes..."

"Never mind. Just your passport. Now!"

"My passport! They have it!"

"Fuck."

Four bells rang from the tower of the Oude Kerk. The alley had emptied, and the song of the Scousers, halfway to their hostel, echoed off the stones of the old quarter: *"The toast is to eleven men who wear the scarlet jersey; their names will live forever more, along the River Mersey!"*

T.K. grabbed Ming and led her from the window to the door. But they were too late: their passage was blocked by a large, scowling man. *"Blokov!"* said Ming.

"Mr. Dean?" said Blokov in sandpaper English. "I've been expecting you." Blokov was a human olive—round, green, and hard in the center. He wore a size XXXL chartreuse track suit that was still too small; thick tufts of matted grey chest and back hair poked out from all around the collar like a wet angora scarf.

"Mr. Blokov, you're not wearing your cross," said T.K.

Blokov reflexively looked at his chest, and in that split second T.K. shoved his full weight into the giant, catching him off balance and sending him sprawling onto the cobblestones, arms pinwheeling. T.K. reached into Blokov's pocket and found what he was looking for: a Russian passport and an iPhone. The passport he stuffed into the gun pocket of his own leather jacket. The phone he clicked awake. *Settings→Phone→My Number→Memorize→Put Phone Back in Blokov's Pocket→Run.*

"This way!" said T.K., grabbing Ming's hand and sprinting up the alley toward the canal. But after two strides, the mouth of the alley darkened behind the silhouettes of three men in sack suits who weren't tourists.

"You again!" said T.K. "Fuck! This way!" he said to Ming, spinning her round and back down the Dollebegijnensteeg.

"Who are they?" said Ming, tearing open the slit on her gown up to her panties so she could run faster.

"Old friends from New York." They leaped over Blokov, who was still trying to right himself like a turtle, and kept on running across Sintannendwarsstratt, deeper into the alley. "Wait!" said Ming. "This street is blind!" T.K. skidded to a halt and turned back. The goons had already passed Blokov.

"This way!" he said, doubling back to Sintannendwarsstraat and running north to where the short street opened onto the front plaza of the Oude Kerk. From there they cut over a block to Warmoesstraat, then down a short alley that dead-ended on the back side of the sprawling Beurs van Berlage, the old commodity exchange building now used for art exhibitions. T.K. grabbed a door of the Beurs and prayed. It opened. "Hurry!" he said. "The other side opens onto Damrak." They raced through the maze of darkened hallways that finally emptied into the colonnaded main hall. High above, skylights traced in cast iron were just beginning to brighten with dawn. T.K. spun in a circle; a hive of portals led off in every direction. "This way," he guessed, leading Ming forward. In minutes they were out on the Damrak, running north to the Sex Museum and T.K.'s bike. He pounced on the bike and slipped his key in the padlock.

Ming screamed. "They're coming!"

The suits had spotted them and were now in front of the Medieval Torture Museum (formerly the Vodka Museum), which was only ten doors down from the Sex Museum. T.K. jiggled the key, but the lock wouldn't budge.

"Hurry!" said Ming. The suits were a block away.

Finally the lock sprang open and T.K. unleashed the chain. "Get on!" he said, lifting Ming onto the front bracket. He leaned into the pedals, but the bike wouldn't move. "Fuck!"

"What's wrong?" said Ming.

"The spoke lock!" The fucking spoke lock, required by law on all bikes in Amsterdam. Who except a Dutch person ever remembers the spoke lock? He leaped off the bike, holding it upright to keep Ming on the cargo bracket, dug into his pocket with one hand for the key and turned the spring lock under the seat. *Clink!* It opened just as the men loomed; T.K. swung the heavy bike chain around his head like a mace, catching one of them in the face. The man reeled and moaned as T.K. wheeled around and pedaled north up Damrak, Ming's knuckles tight around the handlebars behind her. He veered left on tiny

Karnemelksteeg, dodging a pair of early-morning tourists, then shot across Sint Jacobstraat. At Nieuwezijds Voorburgwal the whine of a small-bore engine swelled behind him. *"Fuck!"* One of the suits had found himself a scooter. "Hold on!" T.K. yelled to Ming, then raced across busy Nieuwezijds, dodging trolleys going both ways. One of the trains stopped to let off morning commuters, blocking the scooter just long enough for T.K. to weave down the Korsjespoortsteeg, past the Dominican church.

But just as they approached the bridge over the Singel, the bicycle lurched, swerved and spun on its side as Ming screamed. "My dress!" she said. "It's caught in the wheel!" The Chinese flag had wrapped around the hub and spokes of the front wheel; she was pinned underneath, between the frame and the cobblestones. T.K. flipped over the bike and tore off what remained of her gown, leaving her in nothing but a hooker's white lace bra and panties. The suits had not yet followed down the alley, but T.K. knew they would be close.

"C'mon," he said, dragging the stricken bike with the entangled red gown to the top of the bridge. He heaved it over the north side into the canal, where it sank into the murk. "Can you swim?"

"I think so," said Ming.

"Think hard."

"I can swim."

He unzipped his leather jacket, dropped it to his feet, then pulled off his t-shirt and handed it to Ming. "Put this on." Then he shrugged his jacket back on. "Give me your shoes."

She kicked off her satin pumps. He stuffed them in a small trash bin hanging from the iron balustrade of the bridge. Then he dropped his thumb drive in the bin, praying to the gods of European socialism that municipal trash collectors were on one of their regular strikes.

"Jump after me—feet first, it's only about three meters deep; try not to hit the bottom, and don't drink the water." Then he hauled himself over the rail and into the tarn. As soon as he bobbed up Ming followed, spinning out her long dark hair as she surfaced. "Under the bridge," he said, and they paddled beneath the span, where an iron tie ring driven into the quay provided purchase. They bobbed together, holding the ring. Ming wrapped her bare legs around T.K.

"You're wearing your boots and coat," she said.

"On purpose. When we start swimming, we need to stay mostly underwater; swimmers will draw police. So when we swim, my clothes will help weigh us down. Don't worry, I'll be holding you. How long can you hold your breath?"

"I don't know. Where are we swimming?"

"Practice. Now." She dunked under the water and came up twenty seconds later. "Keep trying. Longer. We wait here until we hear the scooter pass."

Tendrils of fine green seaweed, like tinted hair on a St. Patrick's Day reveler, clung to the scalp of the quay, undulating in the brackish wake. The dark water smelled like a smoked herring sandwich. A pair of mallards paddled by. Fork-tailed swifts, beaks holding bits of straw, darted in and out of a nest they were building under the span. After a few minutes the scooter whined across the bridge; when the sound ebbed, T.K. said "Let's go." He held Ming around her waist, pressing her long, nearly nude form under his own body. "If you feel the bottom with your feet, don't try to stand," he said. "Nothing but muck and bicycles down there."

"I'm cold," she said. "Where are we going?"

"My hotel, near Westermarkt. It's about half a mile. We zigzag over to the Keizersgracht canal." They swam south in the Singel one block, then turned right into the narrow Blauwburgwal cross-canal and under the bridge to the Herengracht, where they again floated south. "This is where we're most exposed," he said. "It's a major canal with a lot of traffic, okay?"

Ming nodded through shivers.

"So we need to watch out for boats underway, and stay close to the boats tied up on the quay. See that next bridge? The Leliegracht's on the other side—our next turn. It's about three hundred meters. The boat bottoms are thick with barnacles; be careful, they're sharp. And be quiet—sound flies on the water."

They paddled alongside the skiffs tied to the eastern quay of the canal. Suddenly a scooter with a large rider revved and zipped out from the Bergstraat, on the quay right above them. They ducked underwater, but when they came up, T.K. could see it was only a young woman on a small-frame Vespa with a cello strapped to her back. "Keep moving," he whispered. "We go under the bridge, then right."

The small, tree-lined Leliegracht canal was quiet and almost idyllic compared to the Herengracht, like a country stream, and for a few minutes Ming forgot how cold she was as they floated under the elms and a twittering colony of red-masked European goldfinches. Dawn was spreading; the city was awake now, and a group of schoolchildren in blue and white uniforms marched along the quay, singing the nursery rhyme of the mariner Berend Botje, first in Dutch:

> *Berend Botje ging uit varen*
> *Met zijn scheepje naar Zuidlaren,*
> *De weg was recht, de weg was krom,*
> *Nooit kwam Berend Botje weerom.*
> *Een, twee, drie, vier, vijf, zes, zeven,*
> *Waar is Berend Botje gebleven?*
> *Hij is niet hier, hij is niet daar,*
> *Hij is naar Amerika.*

And then in the English version:

> Bernie Butler went out sailin'
> In his ship to Zuidlaren.
> The way was straight, the tide was slack,
> But Bernie Butler never came back.
> One, two, three, four, five, six, seven,
> Did Bernie Butler go to heaven?
> He is not here, he is not there,
> He went to America.

"Why do they all speak English?" whispered Ming.

"Television."

"What are they singing?"

"It's about a sailor who leaves home for America and never returns."

The children's voices made her think of Jintao, and then she was cold again. Ahead under a small bridge was the last bend, into the wide Keizersgracht. "Almost there," said T.K. softly. "See that triangle on the far quay, before the next bridge?"

"Yes." A series of steps led down to a triangular stone platform that jutted into the canal.

"That's the Homomonument at Westermarkt. We get out there."

"The Homomonument?"

"It's a gay thing. Commemorates persecuted gay people. It's a perfect place to climb out."

Tourists were already gathering at the monument, laying wreaths. "People will see us," said Ming.

"No choice. Hotel is just around the corner." Just then a dull thumping sound vibrated through the water. T.K. whipped around and saw a pontoon skiff with two yellow-jacketed crewmen. "Police boat! Dive!" he said, wishing he had said something that didn't sound like the captain of a submarine in an old movie. Ming swallowed half the sky and ducked under. They pushed beneath the surface, T.K. holding her down under his weight. The black water down deep felt colder against Ming's bare skin, and she was suddenly afraid of whatever was down there; she curled up her feet, not wanting to find out what the bottom felt like. The outboard motor of the police skiff throbbed louder until it was right above them. Ming thought she could not hold her breath any longer. Then the motor grew more faint; Ming was about to pass out and kicked at T.K. He pulled her up slowly to the surface, both of them gasping air.

"Teddy!" yelled Ming. He spun around and saw a paddleboat ten feet away, making directly for them. The boat was designed for four passengers but at least six were on board, and the boat listed and swayed under the load of tourists and their cameras.

"Down!" he yelled, and they sucked air and dove again. When they came up, the paddleboat had passed, but more boats were coming as the city approached rush hour. "We need to cross the canal," said T.K. "Underwater. Are you ready?"

"*Dui,*" she said. "Let's go." They dunked under and powered west across the 30-yard canal, emerging along the quay a few yards north of the Homomonument. Minutes later they were pulling themselves onto the polished marble triangle as tourists stared slack-jawed.

"Swim club," T.K. explained to the crowd, enveloping Ming in his sodden leather jacket. "Every morning. Very refreshing. Then we go for a run. *Gezondheid!*" Then to Ming: "*Yùnxíng!* Run!"

Minutes later they arrived, panting, at his hotel. In the lobby they smiled and waved as they passed the sputtering concierge, then bolted up the stairs to his third-floor suite. In seconds they had stripped off their weeping clothes and stood together under a steaming hot shower, for the first time naked and locked in love. Their sex was brief and standing, as the muck of Amsterdam washed down the drain. "Now tell me what happened that night on the barge," said T.K., kneading her pale, smooth back with a sponge.

"When they found me in the hold they took me away," she said. "Jintao they took alone. Two days later they released me; Jintao was already back at the boat. We were met by someone from Christian International who gave me a passport with an EU visa and a plane ticket to Amsterdam. They said I would be met here by someone and that Jintao would follow. When I got to Schiphol, it was that Blokov who picked me up. He spoke no Mandarin, only Russian and English. I never heard anything about Jintao. I had to work for Blokov, they said to pay for my ticket to Amsterdam. But I didn't want to be in Amsterdam. I wanted to go home! They said that would cost money too, and...I needed to work." On saying the word *work* in the context that they both understood, she began to weep. T.K. stopped scrubbing her back, but he did not hold her.

"I don't think you've told me everything," he said.

She turned to face him. "Everything?"

"What about the miscarriage on the boat?"

She nodded. "You were there."

He squeezed the sponge hard until it was dry. "Yes, I was there. I was there when you miscarried a pig fetus."

She looked up, startled. "So you know."

"Fang Dazhu told me. They ran tests. It was a pig fetus."

At the sub-chief's name, Ming fluttered and scowled. "Yes, it's true. It wasn't a miscarriage. *It was an abortion! I* aborted a pig's baby!"

T.K. slammed his fist, still clutching the sponge, against the tile. *"Tell me the truth, goddamit!* I'm tired of people lying to me! Why did they find you with a pig fetus?"

"Because I couldn't give birth to a pig's baby!"

"I said the truth!" he yelled, shaking her under the water stream.

"That is the truth!"

"Bullshit!"

"I swear it!" Then she collapsed to the floor of the shower and bawled. *"That baby's father was the pig Fang Dazhu!"*

T.K. felt his muscles go slack. "What?"

"I was pregnant with his baby! That night on the barge, I knew if I was caught pregnant they would give me another abortion. So I pretended to miscarry the pig fetus. My plan was that we would somehow get away, me and Yong and Jintao and the new baby, maybe go to Yunnan Province or Tibet or farther. Maybe even San Francisco, which Jintao read about in that book you gave him. But after they arrested me, Dazhu took me into his office and told me that Yong was dead. Then he forced himself on me again—on his desk. I told him to stop, told him I did not want to have his children. He said he didn't care, they would abort the baby anyway. That's when I knew I could not love another of his children, especially without a husband."

"Another?"

Ming was still on the floor of the shower, curled in a fetal ball. Now she rose up to her knees as the water slid over her shoulders and breasts. "Jintao!" she sobbed. "Jintao is Dazhu's son! That pig has been taking me for years. I also think he works with those Christian International people—finding them women he has tired of. As he does nothing without the favor of money or sex, they must pay him. That must be why they are chasing you, because of what you know."

"Well when you figure out what I know, please tell me. Fuck." He pulled Ming to her feet and wrapped his arms around her small frame.

"I decided I could not have another of his babies," she went on. "I love Jintao so much, but...every time I look at him I see Dazhu leering at me."

"I'm so sorry," said T.K., trying to imagine what it meant to be the mother of a rape baby; the closest he could come was to think how his own mother felt raising the son of a drunken manic depressive. It was not hard to imagine his father forcing himself on his mother. And the truth is that no matter how hard parents try to envision their children as distinct individuals, they always see them as two halves of themselves. "What happened to the baby?"

"After I came back to the barge, I aborted it myself, when Jintao was at school."

"Yourself?"

"It's not hard to find the drugs. I thought it would be easy but the cramps were unbearable. I threw it in the river. And I didn't care."

T.K. shut off the water and wrapped a towel around Ming. "He'll never touch you again," he said. "But we don't have much time. I paid for the room with cash but they'll find us eventually." He dressed, picked up the hotel phone and punched in a long number.

"Meg, it's me."

"Teddy? Where are you? It's so early."

"Fuck, sorry about the time. I'm in Europe. Listen, did the divorce go through yet?"

"Why, having second thoughts?"

"Did we ever think it through the first time?"

"Yes. I mean—no, we never thought it through, and yes, the divorce is final."

"Thanks Meg. Listen, there's a woman in Hong Kong. A reporter. Australian. I want you to take down her number."

"Why?"

"I just want you to be connected to her."

Meg always hated the way T.K. kept his work so secret, even when he needed her help, and this time her disappointment took the form of a deflated sigh. "I know better than to ask why," she said. "By the way, some Chinese guy called looking for you. Says he wants to publish your book in China."

"You don't say," said T.K. "How'd he get your number?"

"Richard Cerf. Said they went to college together. Anyway I told him the truth, which is I had no idea where you were or how to reach you. I told him to call your agent."

"Trixie's dead," said T.K.

"What?"

"Did you give him her name?"

"Yes. I mean, she's your agent. Was that wrong?"

"It's a long story." He gave her Kathleen's Hong Kong mobile and said, "I can't stay on this line. I'll call you again in an hour." Then he hung up and flipped through Blokov's damp passport, reciting the entry stamps and visas: "*Amsterdam, Beijing, JFK, Shenzhen, Xian, Amsterdam, Kiev, Sofia, Amsterdam, Minsk, Bucharest, JFK, Lomé, Guangzhou, Ho Chi Minh, Chongqing, Amsterdam*—this guy is a regular Silk Road Svengali, with a bit of ivory smuggling thrown in."

"I'll be back in two hours," he told Ming, tossing Blokov's passport on the bed.

"Where are you going?"

"To get you some clothes and a passport. And a marriage license."

"What?"

"Well you can't get married in a wet t-shirt. Oh, I almost forgot: Will you marry me?"

"Marry...do we have time?"

He pulled her into his arms. "Trust me. I have what passes for a plan."

Outside in the Westermarkt he found one of the city's few remaining pay phones and called Blokov's mobile number. It rang twice.

"Who is this?" said the Russian.

"Mr. Blokov, I believe I have something of yours," said T.K. "Such a well-travelled man; your passport is surely important."

"I can get another one."

"Of course you can. Report it stolen. But all those visas; so expensive and time consuming to replace. Does Togo even have a consulate in the Netherlands? Just asking."

"How much do you want?"

"No money. Just the girl's passport. An even trade."

"Where shall I meet you?"

"In front of the Van Gogh Museum in one hour. Don't bother bringing your friends. I won't have your passport with me. Once I get the girl's, I'll leave yours with a hotel desk, then call you with the address."

Blokov laughed derisively. "Why should I trust you?"

"I'm American," said T.K. "And besides, you don't have much choice." Then he hung up and dialed Meg.

***

They took a taxi from Amsterdam City Hall to Schiphol; the train was too dangerous. As they settled into the squeaky leather in the back of the SUV—Ming wearing a new linen skirt suit and kilim espadrilles—

T.K. went over the documents. "Here's your marriage license, Mrs. Dean"—she took it and stretched forward to kiss him—"sorry it wasn't more romantic, or in Mandarin. But it's legal."

"I love you," she said in English. It was a phrase she had learned on the job in Amsterdam, but this time she meant it, even if she didn't really understand it. Not the words, she knew what they meant. She didn't understand why love always came burdened with so much pain, starting with childbirth itself. It was as if love couldn't exist in its independent, pure form. She could love Jintao but only while hating his father. She loved Teddy but only by losing her family. Maybe love was like a magnet that gathered up everything in its path, the treasures and the junk. When do you get to sort through the scrap heap? She also wondered if it always felt colder when you went deeper, like that water in the canal.

T.K. said, *"Wǒ yě ài nǐ.* I love you too." The phrase came with its own set of confusions for him. How to explain the seemingly random trajectory that caused his divorce to coincide so perfectly with his desire to marry Ming? Was love a zero-sum game like the food chain, where the life of a parsnip or a pig must end so that another creature may thrive? And what was driving his emotional hunger, his sudden place at the top of this food chain? Marriage would get Ming out of Amsterdam, but there was more to it; deeper concerns flooded over him, not least his crushing guilt over the death of Yong, and the lost boy Jintao.

They kissed again. He returned to the stack of papers in his lap, opening her passport. "Here's your visa. It's a K-3 non-immigrant, which means you can enter the U.S. for now, and apply later for permanent residency. The idea is to allow spouses to travel together, even though we won't be."

"What? You are not getting on the plane?"

"I'm getting on *a* plane, just not yours."

"What do you mean?" For a minute she panicked and again felt the cold, deep water of the canal.

"U.S. Immigration pre-screens at Schiphol; I'm sure my passport has been flagged by Dutch police after last night. It's safer if you travel alone. Meg will meet you at JFK; she'll be holding a sign with your name in Chinese when you come out of Immigration. She'll take you to my apartment and get you settled in. She will transfer my money to a joint account in your name. You can trust her."

"But where are you going? When will I see you?"

"I'm going to China. To get Jintao."

"But how? You can't travel there."

"Maybe I'll swim."

The taxi swung into the departure drop-off lane. T.K. told the driver to let off Ming, then circle around with him. "Here's where you get out," he said to Ming. "We shouldn't be seen together." They embraced and she slid out of the cab, crying.

"Ming," said T.K. She turned and stooped to the window. He thought about telling her that his book was gone; he'd walked back to the trash bin on the bridge but it had been emptied—no thumb drive. To make himself feel better he had stuffed Blokov's passport into the bin. *Sorry Blokov, but I lied,* he thought. *I'm American!*

He didn't tell her the book was gone. Instead he said: "Don't talk to anyone wearing a cross. I don't care if he's the pope." She smiled. She thought that when she next saw Jintao she would tell him that not all leaving is to escape something. Then Ming, like his book, was gone.

Chapter Twenty-Eight

The proper way to write "No Smoking" in Chinese requires twelve characters and can roughly be translated as: "Honorable One, please take note that you are about to enter a no-smoking zone for persons." This written emphasis on the honorific and the formal has no modern English equivalent and helps illuminate the translation gap that renders English versions of Chinese menus so obtuse. Nevertheless translations must be made, and so the freshly silk-screened sign on the door of the Yancao Lucky Essence Company of Guangxi listed, in English and simplified Chinese, the following proscriptions:

NOT ENTER WITHOUT PERMISSION

NO SMOKING

KEEP QUIET

NO PHOTOS

BEWARE OF SLIPPERY

As he stepped through the door, Nong Ning registered the paradox of a smoking ban in a liquid nicotine factory. The reception area was spotless and quiet, not at all like the dusty chaos on the other side of the factory compound where lotus trees were still dismembered by giant screeching saws, then loaded onto trucks bound for the coat-hanger factory down south. The room smelled incongruously earthy and antiseptic, as if someone had put a cigar store in a doctor's office. Soon an inner door whooshed open and Hu Tianhua burst into the room, hand extended. He was wearing blue disposable booties over his Prada penny loafers. "Honorable Nong, I am so grateful to see you." They bowed and shook hands.

"The pleasure is all mine," said Ning.

"Please, this way," said Tianhua, gesturing toward the inner door. "Oh, if you please, we must cover our shoes." He indicated a bootie dispenser on the floor. Ning struggled briefly to insert his extra-wide feet in the dispenser; he had never seen foot booties, indeed never experienced the hygienic rigor of modern tech manufacturing; the electronics factories were well south of Guangxi, and the local abortion clinics barely mandated latex gloves.

"We shall begin, as Confucius recommended, at the beginning," said Tianhua, leading his guest down a stairwell to a receiving dock where several workers were loading bales of dried tobacco leaves into carts. "We start with the finest high-mountain leaves," said Tianhua. "They are carefully dried and sorted by our own representatives in Yunnan province before being shipped directly here." Ning nodded ostentatiously out of respect for the process. "Come." The next stop, through another door, was the vast extraction room, where workers in hair nets and surgical masks stacked the brown leaves into a dozen gleaming steel fermentation vats connected by pipes.

"It looks like a brewery," said Ning.

"In fact the initial process is quite similar to beer making," said Tianhua. "The leaves are fermented in purified water; the conversion of sugar to alcohol releases the nicotine alkaloid from the leaves. But at that point it is too diluted. Follow me." He led Ning through another set of doors, into another large hall with smaller stainless steel tanks and coils of tubing. "This is the distillation room," he said, "where the fermented tobacco liquid is condensed to a pure concentrate. It comes out here"—he pulled Ning to the other end of the room, where a slow drip of clear liquid fed into a sealed glass tube. "There it is," said Tianhua, radiating pride. "The purest essence of nicotine!"

"It's brilliant!" said Ning. "A simple process of reduction."

"I have found most things, and most people, are simple when reduced to their essence," said Tianhua, wondering how many British Thermal Units it would take to reduce a man of Ning's girth to his essence, whatever that might be. "But we are not finished. You see, the purified liquid nicotine is tasteless, and also at this point *too* strong; pure nicotine is one of the deadliest toxins known to man—even a drop on your skin could kill you. So we dilute it with propylene glycol, a viscous food additive, and introduce various natural flavorings, from tobacco itself to candy flavors for younger smokers."

"It is so important to consider the next generation," said Ning.

"Come, let us get off our feet," said Tianhua, meaning let us get the morbidly obese Nong Ning off his feet before he topples and breaks something. "My office is this way."

As they walked, Ning asked, "What is slippery?"

"Slippery?" said Tianhua.

"The sign at the entrance cautioned about slippery floors. Is it possible that the nicotine concentrate could leak onto the floor?"

"Oh, I should think not!" said Tianhua. "The sign refers to the water that is used to ferment tobacco leaves. Of course we have the required spill plans and holding pools, but occasionally a stuck valve could redirect some water onto the floor. Most of the waste water is pumped directly into the river. It's perfectly natural."

"A relief," said Ning. He wanted to observe that the cadmium and arsenic dumped from Mr. Hu's metal-plating factories into the Pearl were also "natural," in that trace amounts of both heavy metals existed somewhere in nature, but he bit his tongue—distracted by a technician in a haz-mat suit, who walked stiffly over to the wine-bottle-sized vial of pure nicotine, by now nearly full, at the end of the distillation line. With his helmet and breathing apparatus, the worker reminded Ning of the spacemen in the *Star Trek* movie that filmed here a few years earlier. The technician turned a large valve-cock, stopping the drip-drip-drip of nicotine, then bent carefully and removed the vial. He set it aside on the floor and slid a new vial into place, then reopened the valve. He picked up the full vial and carried it precariously through an automatic door. The entire operation was handled in a manner that suggested it had been rehearsed to the point of protocol; every movement of the technician appeared choreographed precisely. Or maybe *choreographed* was an inadequate description: It went beyond dance and seemed more like a military exercise.

Tianhua's office was on the sawmill side of the complex and thus considerably less hygienic. A haze of wood dust covered every surface including the boss's little-used desk. The wall calendar was two years old. "Forgive the mess," said Tianhua with an expansive wave of his left arm, as if to excuse the entire room. "I am rarely here, as you know, and I have been traveling out of the country." Both men settled into stuffed chairs around a tea table; an assistant delivered a pot of fragrant green puer. "How is the ivory carving going?" asked Tianhua.

"Oh very well," said Ning. "The artist is currently engaged in the orgy scene at the whorehouse of Yuxiang. It is rendered in, shall we say, exquisite detail."

"Perfect," said Tianhua. "I shall look forward to seeing it." In fact his personal interest in orgies from Chinese literature or for that matter contemporary sexual hedonism trended to apathy and abutted outright disdain; he found the prostitutes at the hotel bars in New York an annoying distraction from his business meetings. Making money was, in the end, so much more enjoyable than ivory tusks or erections—both of which could be recreated in more reliable plastic in a tool-and-dye shop and an injection molding machine, of which he owned thousands. There was so much more, and less, to life than what was conventionally advertised as pleasurable. Reduced to its essence, it all came down to cash. "I bring fortuitous news on your dam project," he said.

"Truly?" said Ning, sipping his tea in studied nonchalance.

"I must admit that when you first told me of your plan I was skeptical, for all the reasons we both understand. Beijing is not in the business of building dams anymore, or dislocating thousands of people. Nevertheless I have identified not inconsiderable foreign interests that are likely to ally with us, and exert influence in Beijing."

This news did not surprise Ning, who understood from the beginning how a dam could benefit all manner of businesses, foreign and local. So instead of expressing gratitude he set down his teacup slowly and said, *"Us?"*

A lesser strategist than Mr. Hu might have taken offense at the question, but Tianhua recognized in Ning's caution the beginnings of a reliable partner, and thus he was not put out. "Perhaps in my enthusiasm I am getting ahead of myself," he said. "Since our lunch last spring, I have fully envisioned the two of us exploiting all opportunities together, pairing your local knowledge"—by which he meant Ning's local control over land permits, construction and migration—"and my supply-chain experience. Plus after all, we are Chinese. Our guests require, shall we say, local hosts who can make them feel most welcome."

"You make it sound as though we are opening an inn," said Ning.

Tianhua laughed. "The comparison is apt," he said, "especially given Guangxi's picturesque landscapes and deserved reputation for hospitality. But I am not proposing we engage in the laundering of bed linens." What he was in fact proposing, as Ning well understood, was the introduction in this remote outpost of an innovative type of corruption now entrenched in China's more populous regions. This new fraud did not involve blatant bribery of officials, which these days could land everyone in jail if you crossed the wrong party man; there was no quid pro quo. In fact no money changed hands directly between the interested parties. No, this more sophisticated form of corruption, which might have been predicted after Deng Xiaoping loosened the economy while maintaining tight political control over citizens, was entrepreneurial in spirit. In Western terms it could be thought of as a public-private partnership: Corporations got the access to resources and workers, and party officials profited by land sales and local investment.

For Tianhua, it was business as usual. For Ning, it was the chance to finally get what he deserved after years of serving the people.

It was win-win.

"These foreign interests—American I presume?" said Ning.

"Yes."

"What do they want the power of the Li for, precisely?"

"I'm not sure," said Tianhua truthfully. "But they desire it most ardently. The rewards could be substantial. Of course, there remains the issue of the river people."

"I am working on that," said Ning. "Fortuitously I have nature on my side. It seems the Christians have been fouling the water with their swine. The carp are smaller, and the children develop rashes when they swim. I am working with the police to quantify the damage. Many villages collect their water from the river; when citizens learn the extent of the pollution they will demand action. At that point Beijing will accede to our wishes and clear the river of settlements."

"A good plan," said Tianhua. "But I am worried about that American who was caught with the river people."

"Mr. Dean," said Ning. "He was deported for practicing journalism under a business visa. Our sub-chief escorted him to the border himself."

"I am aware," said Tianhua. "But I worry he may be more dangerous abroad than in country. You know he is writing a book about the abortions."

"Well I don't imagine his book will find a publisher in China!"

"Of course not," said Tianhua. "But things are different today. People will hear about it on the Internet, perhaps even find ways to read it. And at any rate, if the river people become some sort of international cause, Beijing may conclude it unwise to uproot them. Appearances have become so important these days. We have trading partners."

Ning sipped his tea while admitting to himself he had not considered this implication. Even his wife, who could generally be counted on to play devil's advocate, had not thought to bring it up. "But after all, we don't really know what he is writing," said Ning.

"On the contrary," said Tianhua. He removed a thumb drive from his jacket pocket. "We have his book right here, along with all his notes and contacts. It would be extremely damaging."

"His book?" said Ning. "How did you get it?"

"It seems his literary agent in New York suffered a sudden demise. This was in her possession. Our American friends can be quite resourceful."

"We should destroy it immediately," said Ning.

Tianhua laughed. "I shall pitch this in the Li five minutes from now. But don't be so naïve as to think it is the only copy."

"Of course," said Ning, regretting his comment. Although his technological acuity bordered on leaden, he did vaguely understand the concept of digital duplication. "Far better to destroy"—

—"that which is best left unstated," said Tianhua, mindful of his status as a legitimate businessman. "Mr. Dean has gone to extraordinary lengths to protect the woman whose husband was killed in that houseboat incident. She is now his wife and has surfaced in New York with American residency. As for Mr. Dean, he has disappeared but I suspect if we can find the boy, we will soon find Mr. Dean."

"The boy?"

"The woman's son, from the houseboat. Have you seen him?"

"No," he lied. Ning had no interest in protecting the boy, but a vague instinct told him it could be advantageous to know something that Hu Tianhua did not.

"Well then," said Tianhua. "Why don't we take a stroll along the river?"

Descents

The Last Part

Chapter Twenty-Nine

The immigration officer at Chek Lap Kok thumbed through T.K.'s passport and stopped at the visa for mainland China. He studied the big red PNG stamp like it was a rare butterfly, looked up at T.K., studied the visa again, then flipped to a blank page and slammed down his entry stamp. "Welcome to Hong Kong," he said.

T.K. smiled, grateful that "one country, two systems" still existed nearly two decades after the handover. He wondered how long it would take until China ended the charade and required a Mainland visa to enter Hong Kong. They would pick a summer weekend when some saucer-eared British royal was getting married and all of England was distracted. People have their priorities.

He bought an MTR ticket with cash at the machine and rode the Metro into Kowloon station. On Nathan Road he paid cash for another burner phone—different store, this time using Hong Kong dollars—and made one call.

"Kathleen? It's me."

"Teddy! Where are you?"

"Kowloon."

"Bad idea."

"I need your help."

She paused, then said: "Come over to Central. Take the train, not the boat. Meet me at the Garden Road ticket window for the Peak tram."

The smart thing would have been to not show up. Just meeting secretly with Teddy, even in public, somehow felt like cheating on George. On the other hand, wasn't George essentially cheating on her with all his business secrets? She was in the truth business, or so she liked to tell herself, and her boyfriend was undoubtedly keeping all sorts of truths from her. Sometimes George's circuitous ways left her feeling the rage of a wronged lover. But in her more expansive moments she understood why it had to be that way—work is work, fun is what you do on Saturday night. She should just blow off Teddy like a bad date. She could always claim later that she lost him in the tourist mob around the tram stop. But she couldn't do it, for the same reason that Teddy called her, and not George. Because underneath all her reluctance and regret, as she grabbed her bag and clicked shut the door of her Robinson Road flat, lurked the terrible truth that she knew why Teddy didn't call George.

An hour later the two of them were lumbering up the mountain in the funicular, squeezed between gawking tourists and wide-eyed children watching the steep tracks recede. T.K. was happy to see her, happy to hear her pronounce vowels in that lazy Australian summer-day way, and happy to ponder how eyes so ice blue could feel so warm. He looked at her like she were a gift he did not deserve. The towers of Central shrank to a pincushion beneath them as T.K. explained his rushed wedding to Ming at Amsterdam City Hall, and his search for Jintao. "Thank you for doing this," he said.

"You haven't told me what I'm doing yet."

"I need you to work your Vietnam connections so I can get the boy over the border. Assuming I can find him."

"Wait a minute. You're going into China?"

"I have to. He's there."

"You're insane. If they catch you it'll mean prison, and I hear Chinese prisons are several notches below one-star."

"I hear they don't serve *báijiǔ*," said T.K.

"Besides," Kathleen went on, "my Viet sources are in Hanoi. It's a hundred miles to the Guangxi border."

"Well your sources must have sources. Somebody's gotta know somebody along that border who's an honest smuggler. Somebody who can get him to Hanoi; I can't be seen with him anywhere near the border—too dangerous, and too many people who'll do anything for money. He needs to blend in. Once I get him across I'll lose myself in Nam, then meet him later in Hanoi and get him a visa to New York."

"And how do you plan on getting into China?"

Suddenly the tram jostled to a halt under the white columns of the little-used Barker Road flag stop. The doors swung open for just one passenger, a tall Western man in a glen plaid tropical suit and cordovan double monk straps.

"Hello, George," said Kathleen, feigning nonchalance, lips curled in a thin frown. In truth her heart was in the back of her mouth. T.K. stared past his old friend, making sure none of his new friends were also getting on.

"Kathleen! Teddy! What a small world!" said George. "I *love* riding the Peak tram," he said with theatrical expansiveness. "It does wonders for your perspective."

"Why are you following me?" T.K. said.

George made a hurt face. "Is that any way to greet a friend? Don't take it personally, T.K. For God's sake I get followed everywhere I go, so naturally I try to stay in practice with a little tailing of my own."

"And those Russian goons who've been chasing me since New York? And the Chinese guy in the Trotsky t-shirt? And Fu-Manchu on the escalator? I suppose they're all friends of yours."

George winced. "More like associates of business partners. I do apologize for all that messiness. I tried to stop it. I'm here to help you, actually. Help you stay alive. You really should go home, Theodore, and I don't mean New York to find another book agent; in fact Bellows Falls seems like a fine idea right now. This is so much bigger than you, or your book. Don't get involved. Because I'm afraid there are other players in this game who will simply view you as collateral damage."

"*Game?*" said T.K. "What are the rules of this game, George? Are there any? Because your fucking little game turns out to be sex slavery, and when you're on the receiving end of a drunken stranger's cock in an Amsterdam window, the game feels slightly rigged."

Some English-speaking tourists turned to stare. A woman hurriedly pushed her young son to the rear of the carriage.

"Well I'll grant you that," said George, eyes pinging around the carriage. "The game is rigged. These mutual assistance treaties are so complicated, and yet they gloss over so many details."

"Treaties?"

"Every country has them—agreements to assist each other in legal matters both civil and criminal. I'm no lawyer but if you ask me, what they really do is codify which unsavory activities everyone will tacitly condone, in the interest of larger cooperation. When you get right down to it, it's well on the path to one-world government, just not quite the way they imagined it down at the food co-op."

The tram slid into the terminal at Victoria Peak; the doors hissed open.

"What'll it be?" said George as they stepped out and angled away from the tourists. "The Lion's Pavilion? Or Madame Tussaud's? They have an extraordinary Xi Jinping—you'd think he was breathing—although their Obama is a bit stiff for my taste. I guess I should be careful what I say about the boss."

"Obama?" said Kathleen, who by now had shed her jaded journo visage and was visibly slack-jawed. "Or Xi?"

"Well that's a fine question and an even finer line," said George. "I suppose it doesn't really make any difference.

Obama, China, Aunt Jemima—they're all just interchangeable brands."

"And the venture capitalist," said T.K. "What's your brand? Or is that just a cover?"

"On the contrary," said George as they strolled with no apparent commitment along the path to the pavilion. "The United States government has one of the largest venture cap development funds in the world—a whole floor in the Honk Kong consulate, even more square footage than they give the NSA. And there's more in Langley."

"The CIA?"

"Of course. Information technology waits for no one; you have to go out there and find it, before it finds you. Like I said, it's a game."

"Like Christian International Aid."

George frowned. "These public-private partnerships are fraught with peril. It was supposed to work like Voice of America but I'm afraid it backfired."

"Backfired?"

"If you must know, Christian International was propped up by the CIA since day one. It was seen as a way to spread support for American ideals, and it did for some time. But because of the whole church-state thing we had to provide some cover; it had to be at least nominally run by private religious interests. And it worked fine, when actual Christians were in charge. But somewhere along the line, the Christians got thrown to the lions when the Russians moved in. It certainly wasn't under my watch, but now I'm afraid it's my job to sort it all out."

They paused to take in the panorama. Beyond the spires of Central, Victoria Harbor shimmered emerald green, its patina etched by hundreds of frothing wakes from Maersk Triple-E container ships bearing 18,000 truckloads of cargo; fishing junks; ferries; and Mediterranean yachts. On the other side of the harbor, cranes hovered over massive new towers being cloned in Kowloon. To the left, 747s floated down to the tarmac on Chek Lap Kok island. Obscured behind a veil of haze was the promise, or dread, of yet more: There beyond the New Territories sprawled the Mainland metropolis of Shenzhen, the former fishing village now twice as large as Hong Kong itself, with its own brace of mirrored-glass belfries.

"You know when Mies and his art-school buddies were inventing the skyscraper in Chicago, everyone thought it was a dangerously Marxist idea," said George. "Those dark slabs accommodating millions of faceless laborers symbolized the twilight of individualism; critics said the socialist hive had arrived—straight from Nazi Germany no less! Who could have guessed his invention would become the ultimate icon of capitalist power?"

"Mies knew," said T.K. "He was about as red as Goldwater."

"The reddest thing about him was his nose," said George. "A testament to the creative powers of alcohol, he was—churning out those landmark buildings while consuming a bottle of Scotch and ten cigars every day."

T.K. narrowed his eyes. "What was it Nietzsche said? *A little poison now and then: that makes for pleasant dreams.*"

"*And much poison at the end, for a pleasant death,*" continued George. "It always boils down to Nietzsche with us, doesn't it? I don't know if Mies read Nietzsche, but he definitely figured out you didn't get the big money designing glass cottages for house collectors," George went on. "Those he did to fuck the wives; the real money came from his corporate masters. And government contracts of course. All the same."

He turned to the city. "That new tower going up in Kowloon will be the tallest in Asia, with the highest hotel in the world. We're moving there next year—the whole consulate. We'll be a floor below the Ritz Kowloon and two floors above General Electric, which is convenient." He chuckled at his own thoughts. "The average American thinks our consulates and embassies exist to perform vaguely official duties of state, but the truth is almost everyone in those offices, myself included, works to secure overseas contracts for U.S. corporations."

George shifted his gaze down closer to the near side of the harbor, where the ferries were docking at the Central piers. "I'm sad to leave the island, and walking to the club and all. On the other hand, we'll have spectacular *views* of the island. That's what counts these days. It's all an illusion, right?"

"Like democracy in Hong Kong?" said Kathleen.

"Like democracy everywhere," countered George. "What all these hippies and libertarians and *Occupy* protesters don't understand is that democracy is like a restaurant menu. You're given this illusion of 'choice' "—he made quote marks with his fingers in the air—"but the truth is, the menu has been carefully designed to frame your choices a certain way. The customer doesn't write the menu. Never has."

"And you're the chef, George?" said T.K.

He shrugged. "I'm afraid there are too many chefs stirring the broth these days. That's the trouble: No one's in charge. Me? I'm more like the *saucier*. It's my job to keep it from curdling. Because when you boil it right down, it's all about stability. *Stable* government, much more than any particular *form* of government, is the secret sauce. It's in the best interest of society. Journalism like yours just rocks the boat. Even yours Kathleen, although I doubt Mr. Murdoch sees himself as part of the counter-culture. Me, I decided it was more important to be a good American than a good journalist."

"The only way a journalist can be a good American is by being a good journalist," said T.K.

"*Bravo!*" said George, clapping his hands. "They'll put that on your tombstone, in smudgy newsprint that washes away in the first spring rain. I admire you, T.K., always have you know. And I don't want you to get hurt."

"Too late for that, George. Your *stability* has proven very unstable for people I love."

"Love?" said George. "Theodore Kincaid Dean in love? Stop the presses! Whatever happened to objective detachment?"

"It turned into you. So maybe you should tell me what detachment feels like."

George sighed. "Before you go all morally superior on me, let me tell you what gets me up every morning." He turned to Kathleen. "Darling, what I'm about to say is totally off the record."

"As in not for publication?" said Kathleen. "I can't promise how I deal with it personally. And that's on the record."

"Fair enough." He drew a breath and gathered his thoughts. Kathleen crossed her arms and scowled. T.K. stared at him impassively.

"It's difficult to quantify with precision," George began, "but the CIA's Illicit Finance Group has estimated that Internet fraud and online corporate espionage, whether from organized crime or government channels or both, it scarcely matters, is costing the world's economies a *trillion* dollars a year, and I'm not talking Hong Kong dollars. That's more than a fourth of the entire U.S. annual budget. The direct cost is mostly borne by corporations, banks and merchants, including Main Street merchants, but it gets passed on to consumers in the form of higher prices for everything. And privacy breaches, apart from being enormously inconvenient to citizens, can even endanger lives. So this is a real problem with real victims. How to stop it? For the past few years the U.S. government, through my fund, has been leading the development of a new technology called BODG." He pronounced it as an acronym, *bodge.*

"BODG?" said Kathleen.

"Named after the Beijing Online Diplomacy Group where it was first proposed—a series of high-level multi-lateral meetings to deal with online piracy. You won't read about those meetings in Hillary Clinton's book—it's all still classified—but she was there alright, and quite animated as I recall. I was standing behind her, against the wall. Anyway, BODG grew out of earlier technology that was developed for PayPal verification. I won't bore you with the details but BODG is considerably more complex than any current Internet security code, and regarded as unbreakable. Basically it has its own brain and is constantly evolving new code. The key thing is, once it gets switched on, no one can stop it, derail it, or switch it off, which is what makes it impervious to hackers."

"So what does this have to do with Russian sex trafficking?" said T.K.

"Well you see," said George, "there's a key point to be made about BODG. It only works if the whole world is on board. Any holes in the Internet are like cracks in the dyke—after that, the deluge."

"Wait a minute," said Kathleen. "So you're saying this BODG business is like the Doomsday Machine in *Dr. Strangelove*?"

"In the sense of all-or-nothing, yes," said George. "Of course BODG isn't a chain of nuclear weapons, and this isn't the Cold War. BODG is designed to protect global commerce, to put everyone on the same footing. We'll go instantly from the chaos of no one in charge to having one massive app, if you will, in charge of everything."

"Stability," said T.K.

"If you like, yes," said George.

"You were about to tie this to Russian sex trafficking."

"Precisely. You see, as I said, BODG won't work without universal adaptation, and the Russians have been, to put it mildly, a bit prickly on the issue. They won't admit it, but everybody knows why: The Russian government is the largest kleptocracy on the planet. Putin controls the Russian mafia, which controls the multi-billion-dollar global business in pirated credit card data, mostly through TOR."

"TOR?" said Kathleen.

"The Onion Router," said George. "It's open-source software that directs Web traffic through thousands of anonymous relays and servers around the world."

"The Dark Web," said T.K.

"Precisely," said George. "It's a black hole, an alternate universe that's actually larger than the visible Internet. Completely untraceable Web traffic. It's used for lots of things, some of them good like academic research—"

"—and government surveillance," said T.K.

"And that," said George. But it's also a great place for bad guys to hide, including terrorists and card pirates, which is a form of terrorism. Since credit cards are the currency of the realm, Putin and his cronies have essentially cornered the world market in counterfeiting. I mean we used to worry about North Korea, cranking out millions of fake twenty-dollar bills on very sophisticated Swiss paper, but that all seems rather quaint now. Not surprisingly, Russia has proved somewhat reluctant to embrace technology that would shut down their racket. Of course they're under enormous international pressure to go along, and they must weigh the possibility of sanctions, but still it was deemed prudent at the highest levels to toss them a bone, as it were. That's where those mutual assistance treaties come in. China and the U.S. have tacitly agreed to look the other way when it comes to the Russian mob's low-tech crimes, including prostitution. It's a tradeoff."

"A sacrifice," said T.K.

"In a sense," said George. "It's not pretty I know, and I'm not personally proud of it, but there are the larger concerns to weigh."

Three Chinese teenagers, girls in black and white school uniforms, approached shyly with a small camera. "Please," said one. "You take our picture?"

"Of course," said Kathleen. The girls giggled, handed over the camera and posed in front of the view of Hong Kong. "Smile!" said Kathleen. They giggled again, and she snapped the photo.

"Now one with you," said the lead girl, corralling her two friends next to Kathleen, T.K. and George.

"Count me out," said George firmly but with staged humor. "I'm not very photogenic." He stepped away behind the camera.

"The same goes for me," said T.K. The girl with the camera frowned but finally snapped Kathleen with her friends. They bowed and skipped down the path, warbling about the funny Westerners who didn't want their picture taken.

"Well, enough sightseeing for one day," said George. "Shall we head down?" As he led them back toward the tram station, an elderly British couple intervened and held up a camera. "Excuse me sir," the man said to George, emboldened by the relative success of the Chinese girls. "Would you mind just snapping us?"

"Not at all," said George distractedly, taking their camera.

While George framed the picture of the couple with Hong Kong in the background—"Smile!"—T.K. pulled Kathleen back slightly by the elbow and whispered: "Darling, shall we dance?"

"What?" she said.

"When we get in the tram, let me lead," he replied, locking eyes with her. "Watch your elbow." She nodded and, picture taken, they caught up with George and entered the Peak station just as the tram was boarding.

"Let's ride in the rear carriage," said T.K. "I get the willies in front going down."

"As you wish," said George, leading the way through the back doors and indicating a wooden bench. "Smart not to ride in front I suppose," he said. "You know these funiculars have no internal brakes; the only stopping mechanism is a giant drum in the winding house up top. If the cable were to snap, the car would plummet down the mountain—straight into the Bank of America Tower on Connaught Road, I imagine."

"The bank would win," said T.K.

"Another case of too big to fail," said George.

Kathleen shuddered.

"Don't worry dear, it could never happen," he said. "The cable is nearly two inches thick and can hold a hundred and thirty-nine tons. As for human error—it's all computerized now; the conductor is just there to make the passengers feel safer."

"No one's in charge," said T.K. "George, let the tourists take a load off; we'll stand." George nodded; they took a spot in the aft door well. At Barker Road, the tram stopped and the doors swung open. T.K. wasn't sure exactly who would step on, but he expected bad news. Indeed, through the forward doors stepped Fu-Manchu—still wearing his beige silk suit and winkle-pickers. He smiled and tipped his straw fedora at T.K. as the doors closed.

"I gather a friend of yours has joined us," said George.

"Or yours?" said T.K. "Mr. Wang, the Christian without a cross. I've met a few of his ilk lately; they seem to be proselytizing around the world."

"Missionaries will do that," said George.

T.K. pressed his thumb into Kathleen's elbow. The carriage aisle was packed with tourists. As the tram began its steepest descent into the May Road station, T.K. glanced around furtively for the flag stop button. Unless there happened to be a passenger embarking at May Road—and no one ever got on at May Road descending, you could just walk down to the Mid-levels escalator—the tram wouldn't stop there. He saw the green button, behind a pear-shaped American woman in cargo shorts and a shiny t-shirt that said I SURVIVED THE PEAK TRAM. He tried reaching behind her but there was no way to circumnavigate her equator without inappropriate touching.

Mr. Wang was threading his way through the crowd, smiling, apologizing in several languages—"Excuse me, *pardonez moi madame, duìbùqǐ.*" George's eyes were pinballs, ricocheting around the carriage as it groaned down the mountain. The tourists kept up their chatter but T.K. could hear no words; the only sound to his ears was the collective hissing of a hundred digital cameras as the passengers snapped away out the windows, and the tense murmur, more a feeling than a sound, of the funicular cable straining beneath the floor. He checked his watch: ten past four. Chairman Mao was waving.

Just as the tram descended into the May Road station, T.K. felt the cable tighten and slowly haul the carriage to a stop. The tram gods were just: There on the platform was a wizened old Chinese woman, stooped over a cane, waiting for her ride down to Central. T.K. let out a deep breath and leaned into Kathleen's elbow, directing her subtly toward the doors. As they swung open, she made a move to disembark but he held her back tightly, smiling at George. Mr. Wang was still excusing himself through the scrum and had almost reached them. The old woman with the cane slowly climbed the steps into the front carriage; T.K. watched from the window. Finally she was aboard. Mr. Wang was an arm's length away and reaching into his jacket pocket. In the split second before the doors closed, T.K. turned to George and said, "So this is what it boils down to." Then he pushed Kathleen forward and they hopped off just as the doors closed. George tried to follow but it was too late. He stood behind the glass, fuming, as Mr. Wang slipped in next to him and stared at T.K., who was waving from the platform.

"Let's move," he said to Kathleen. "Wang is sure to get off at McDonnell Road and give chase, maybe up the tracks. We'll take the Green Trail down to Magazine Gap Road. Then we can lose him in the Botanic Gardens."

"Then what?" said Kathleen.

"Then we split up. I'm sorry to get you involved in this, but so far you don't know my plans so you're of no use to the bad guys, whoever the fuck they are. Let's keep it that way."

She stopped and grabbed his arm. "No! Now it's my turn to lead. You need a contact in Hanoi. I'll find someone."

He shook his head. "If you do that you'll be finished here," he said.

The low afternoon sun filtered through her blond hair and cast diffused shadows across her worried face. "I'm finished here anyway," she said. "You can't write anything in Hong Kong anymore. I can do more from Australia."

T.K. set his jaw defiantly. "You don't deserve this kind of trouble."

"And the boy?" she said. "What does he deserve?"

T.K. stared off at the skyline, then into her eyes. He took her hands. "We need to keep moving."

They ran down the Green Trail toward Mid-levels, but neither had spent much time in this exclusive quarter of the island, with its gated luxury condo complexes and terraced golf courses. And neither realized that before it hooked around to Magazine Gap Road, the Green Trail re-encountered the funicular track.

Mr. Wang saw them first. He was sprinting up the tracks, taking the narrow concrete steps two at a time, when they crossed paths. In seconds Wang attacked with practiced skill, drawing T.K. into a crouch before cinching his right arm around his throat and trapping him in a neck lock. "Struggle only makes it worse," said Mr. Wang calmly. "Now tell me where to find the boy—the one you call *Donald Duk*."

"Teddy, don't move!" said Kathleen. "He can snap your neck—I took judo."

"So did I," said T.K. as he scraped his boot heel down Mr. Wang's calf and slammed it onto his foot. Mr. Wang screamed and let go, staggering across the tracks. But as he regained his balance he flipped open an ivory-handled stiletto and again came at T.K. On the path next to the tracks, Kathleen frantically searched for a weapon—a stick, a brick, anything. All she could find was a smooth black rock; in desperation she hurled it at Mr. Wang. He flinched and ducked out of the path—but in that instant of distraction he lost his footing while crossing the tracks. At that location the tramway dips from its steep descent through a small valley, requiring a series of sheaves to hold the cable down at ground level. While attempting to regain his balance Mr. Wang set his right foot down directly on top of the moving cable, which rapidly drew his foot under a spinning sheave, slicing off the pointed toe of his loafer, and his own toes as well. In his agonized wail, he dropped the knife, which was, in truth, now rendered obsolete as Mr. Wang was in no position to give further chase.

T.K. frowned. "My mother always told me not to play on the tracks."

Chapter Thirty

Contrary to its iconic skyline, vast portions of Hong Kong are in fact rural and even wild, with mountain trails, nature reserves and, in the far northwestern corner of the New Territories, rice paddies. The paddies are losing ground to new housing developments with names like Palm Springs and Fairview Park, but if you take a taxi up the San Tim Highway not quite to where it meets Shenzhen at the Futian checkpoint, then branch onto Palm Springs Boulevard and head north into Wai Po, you come to a place where the paddies tail off into Shenzhen Bay. From here it is less than three miles across the water to the Hongshulin Seashore Ecological Park, a deeply forested land's end of Mainland China that, unlike the nearby urban crossings, is infrequently patrolled. Sharks are rare in the shallow passage, and a strong swimmer can make the crossing in under three hours.

It was two o'clock in the morning. The moon was just past full and high in the sky, flashing chrome daggers across the sea and over the rice stalks, which whispered on a breeze. On the edge of the paddy road, a pack of feral dogs snarled over a pile of duck bones from the nearby night market. Kathleen scanned the far China shore with binoculars, seeing and saying nothing. T.K. made a final inventory of his waterproof kayaking backpack, stuffed with vacuum sealed bags holding his passport (bearing a new Vietnamese visa from the consulate in Hong Kong); a new burner phone and portable charger; ten thousand Chinese yuan; eighty-thousand Vietnamese dong; lightweight clothes of dark cloth that would be hard to see at night and wouldn't get dirty too fast; a hand towel; a disposable razor; a bar of hotel soap; and a pair of espadrilles.

"Did you get the pills?" he said.

Kathleen lowered the binocs and dug into her handbag. "I had to tell my doctor I was having panic attacks, which is not too far off the truth. The pharmacist called them *forget pills*. I hope you don't take these with booze." She handed over a vial of fifteen white Rohypnols.

"Not for me," he said. T.K. twisted open the lid, shook the pills into his palm and examined them in the moonlight.

"La Roche, fast dissolving. White."

"Sorry, they didn't have candy-striped."

"No, it's perfect. They started adding blue dye in the U.S. when this shit became the date rape drug of choice. Makes your martini turn blue, kind of gives away the game. They also made them harder to dissolve. But the old white ones are still being sold overseas."

"Got a hot date in China?"

T.K. transferred the pills into a small waterproof earplug case. "Whoever has Jintao isn't likely to hand him over by asking politely."

"So chemical warfare."

"You never know. Plus I might have a panic attack." He handed back the empty drugstore vial. "Looks like you've got one refill left."

"Pop quiz," said Kathleen, raising her binocs to scan the shore again.

T.K. sighed and recited his lines. "Contact is An Thanh, a trader in the village of Cốc Mán, across the border from Nongchao. He speaks French. Mention his name in the public market and anyone will know where to find him."

"Let's go over the crossing."

"I buy a Xiaomi GPS smartphone in Nongchao, then take the Yan Bian Highway five clicks southbound. Just past the village of Kugong, bear right off the highway onto a branch road; past the first settlement on both sides of the road, stay left at the fork to coordinates twenty-two degrees 34.13 north, hundred-and-six degrees 40.83 east."

"Forty-point-eight *four*," she corrected.

"Eight four," he said. "It's a fucking fraction."

She glared at him.

"Eight *four*," he repeated. "Strike due north on that longitude a hundred and forty meters over paddies to the Guichin Boundary River. There's no fence; a short swim and good morning Vietnam."

"Province?"

"Cao Bằng. Follow a saddle north between two mountains; that's the path down to Cốc Mán, Cao Bằng Province, about two clicks."

"Perfect."

"I attribute my good memory to alcohol," he said, swigging from a small flask of cognac that he tucked back into his waterproof bag.

"How you can drink so much and not get stupid amazes me," she said.

"The secret is in remembering the stupidity next time."

"For fuck's sake Teddy, this isn't a Raymond Chandler novel. You can't actually drink constantly and expect to function."

"He did."

"Philip Marlowe? He was a fucking fictional character."

"Chandler. I'm talking about the writer."

"Did he ever swim across Shenzhen Bay?"

"He worked in Hollywood."

She ignored him and continued. "An Thanh will be waiting for you in Cốc Mán. He'll take Jintao to Hanoi; you'll be on your own. Meet them at the U.S. Embassy at noon exactly two days after you hand him over; wait across the street from the side entrance on Ngō Five Láng Ha. Assuming his mother is now an American resident, he won't need refugee status; I hope to Christ he has his Chinese Resident Identity Card."

"Knowing Jintao, he's memorized his ID number," said T.K.

"Because that's what you would do?"

"Meaning what exactly?"

"I'm sorry. Look, I know you love this kid. I just hope you're doing the right thing—for him and for you. Chinese nationals can't fart without showing their ID; how do you expect a *wàiguórén* with a PNG passport to get around?"

"You don't need papers to sleep outside, or take local buses," he said. "You worry about your man in Cốc Mán. I'll worry about me and the boy." He caught himself and regretted the phrase; T.K. Dean *never* worried, he was merely concerned. Yet his slip-up presented an entirely new concern—the concern, but not quite a *worry*, that he had crossed from concern to worry on this mission, which if he were honest he would have to admit *scared* him for a second. Whatever. Because if *worry* was a word that slowed him down, *whatever* was the one that always pulled him forward. *Whatever*—and with that he stripped to his boxers and smeared Vaseline across his arms and legs, which he had shaved earlier that day. "Can you get my back?" he said, handing her the jar. When she finished, he belted on the backpack and slipped on goggles. Kathleen held a pair of flippers in her right hand, and when she offered them to him, her eyes were red.

"These would disqualify you in competition," he said, slipping them on his feet. "I'd hug you but I'm covered in grease. Actually I'd hug you and tell you how much I love you, but I'm wearing flippers and goggles, and covered in grease."

With that the dam broke. She threw her arms around him and wept. "I love you too," she said. "Oh fuck, what am I saying? I love that you love her."

He held her for as long as he dared. "I need to make land before daylight," he said finally, nodding at the far shore. He pulled himself away, cinched up his belt and waded into the blackness beyond the rice. She waved one last time, and he disappeared into the swell.

But for one painful jellyfish sting and the tang of salt in his mouth, the swim may as well have been a granite quarry in Vermont. For T.K. long-distance swimming had nothing to do with either distance or location. The way to keep going was to not think about where you were, or how far you had to go. And the way to do that was to focus on the moment—every stroke, just another...stroke. He played music in his mind on these swims—always the early Mozart symphonies, not because they were all that great but because their cadence was so simple and predictable and swimmable, as you would expect from symphonies written by a twelve-year-old, and in his mind T.K. was twelve like Mozart and swimming in New England again and his parents were still alive, before the horrible accident in the sugar shack, and before the terrible day in the sugar bush when he found his father's body. What could be more bitter than sugar, or sweeter than sugar converted to alcohol? God, he loved chemistry!

In truth of course T.K. was no longer twelve years old nor particularly sober, and the swim enervated him. What kept him steady on course was the magnetic pull of home—and he understood, like countless travelers by night in sight of a lee shore, that he was coming home. And when his arms no longer paddled freely and the shallow seabed wrapped around his fingers, he clawed himself up out of the wake, coughing and heaving on the beach, buried his head in the damp sand, and wept. God, he loved this country!

Chapter Thirty-One

The men and women came, more than three hundred of them, from all over the district. They worked in the "informal" sector and wouldn't be missed for a few days by a boss or a party leader who did not owe allegiance to Nong Ning. They came from the back-alley print shops that cranked out Little Red Books to sell in Beijing's "antique" markets; from the stone bridges where they poled Japanese tourists in bamboo rafts along the river; from the taxi stands where they loitered on wobbly scooters with no brakes, seizing on guileless Americans who could be convinced to pay fifty yuan for the short ride down to the river; from the dusty trailheads up to the karst peaks, where they hawked paper fans and bottled water to Western hikers whose expensive boots, breathable jackets and GPS-enabled smartphones were made in China; and from the backyard smelters where women labored over glowing cast-iron pots, melting down recycled plastic water bottles from North America (where unlike China the tap water was actually drinkable). This bronze-skinned army of underground service workers poured out of transport trucks and filed into the courtyard of Nong Ning's house.

Ning stood under the eaves admiring the procession and tasting the irony. If the Chinese formal economy existed largely to export gadgets and gear to the West, the informal sector was something of an import business—catering to rich Western visitors with their Chinese gadgets and gear in tow, bringing coal to Newcastle. But there could only be so many tourists, he reasoned, especially as the country's air grew increasingly foul, and thus only so many jobs accommodating their hairy asses. No, the future for all these workers was in the factories, Ning decided. And was he not in an increasingly excellent position to make that decision? What good fortune—no, what good *planning*, he allowed himself.

"Honorable husband!"

Ju was scowling in the doorway. "Is this our home, or Tiananmen Square? What accounts for summoning this rabble?"

Ning turned and waddled back into the house. "Dear wife," he said with studied patience, "these good people were scarcely induced. Rather they are angry citizens determined to march on Party headquarters. They demand an end to the profane husbandry of swine along their sacred river. I merely offered them the chance to air their grievances here before moving on to town, so their message may be...crafted appropriately."

"And how much are you paying them for their wrath?"

Ning scoffed and waved a fat arm. "Can one put a price on fair health? Have you not seen the stilted fish, the rashes on the children? That river is sick."

She glared.

"People are so busy these days," he continued. "A hundred and twenty-five yuan per day each."

"This will come to no good," she said. "Have you considered that the pigs themselves do not appear sick? Something else is fouling the river."

"Their shit stinks."

"It always has."

"There are more of them."

"More shit is no different than less shit."

"Is that Confucius?"

"With respect, honorable husband, you would do well to honor the traditions. I cannot burn incense enough for both of us at the feet of the Buddha. If you will not visit the temple, at least see that you—"

"—release a creature into the wild, I know I know! I promise I shall drop another goldfish in the Li, assuming that besmirched watercourse can still be considered wild! Meanwhile I must attend to my angry mob before the absence of leadership truly enrages them." With that he navigated his undulant frame through the door and into the glare, dust and din of the courtyard.

***

When you got right down to it, the concrete floor in the distillation room of the Yancao Lucky Essence Company was really quite slippery. So when a local Zhuang worker named Huang Zhigao slipped in his hazmat suit, it was understandable and should not in any way have brought dishonor upon his family. And Zhigao tried heroically to hold on to the full liter of pure liquid nicotine as his legs cartwheeled in front him—actually landing on his elbows, both of which shattered like glass, as unfortunately did the flask of nicotine, which spun from his grasp as he contorted in agony from the bone slivers shredding the cartilage in his arms. His pain spasms caused the jagged tip of his left ulna, now protruding through the skin of his elbow, to tear his hazmat suit, allowing the pure nicotine to ooze inside and pool around his bloody arm.

The factory's emergency management plan had anticipated the scenario of spilled liquid nicotine; the distillation room featured a prominently mounted gate valve that, when activated by a worker, would seal the floor drains and contain the spill. Unfortunately the plan did not consider that the room's only worker would be incapacitated on the floor and soon dead from massive exposure to nicotine. By the time other workers started missing their colleague and rushed into the room, Zhigao's corpse was in rigor mortis and the nicotine was in the Li River, swirling downstream toward the pig farms.

Chapter Thirty-Two

It was the smell.

It was the smell that first hit T.K. Dean, even through his helmet, racing down a dark country road on a scooter he'd bought from a bodge shop near the bus station in Guilin. It smelled of damp and matted forest floor, the smell of Vermont, and even as the machine whined around dark karst peaks and toward the Li, he was on his bicycle in the sugar bush and it was November—yes, November, that was when he would pedal silently over the scarlet leaves that had dropped to the ground and knotted into a thick carpet, leaves decomposing into the hummus below which was itself the acidic fossilization from eons of fallen leaves.

It smelled like death.

The smell intensified as he approached the place on the river where the pig farmers stayed until it didn't smell like rotting leaves anymore but more like rotting, dead everything, as if the history of the world could be smelled. And he was still on his bicycle in the sugar bush because it was still a smell he remembered—the smell of recent death as he wheeled over the knoll to where the old trees stood, where his father had gone out yesterday afternoon looking for limb dieback and never came home for dinner and was still gone in the morning.

Time to focus. One more bend and then the river. T.K. parked his scooter in the clearing downstream from the barges. Beyond the lychee trees, their branches slumped under the strain of coral-pink fruit, kerosene lanterns glowed amber in the cabins of the houseboats. He downed a swig of *báijiǔ* from his cognac flask—the cognac itself having been finished before Dongguan three days ago—then doubled over and vomited. He staggered to the river bank and bent to splash water on his face, then heaved again at the revolting sight.

The Li was awash in dead pigs.

T.K. switched on his penlight and trained it over the water. Except he could see no water. As far as his beam could pierce the murk, there was nothing but bloated, putrid carcasses—a swelling mass of bellies, hooves and upturned snouts, stiff and dull and boiling with worms. *"Oh my fucking God."*

He turned and ran up the path to the houseboats. Outside the first barge, a three-wheeled cargo moto held a tall pallet of water bottles. He lunged up the gangplank and banged on the cabin door.

"Dean *xiānshēng!*" The old man, bone thin with folds of loose skin that draped over his greasy polo collar, bowed before T.K., then threw his arms around him, weeping.

"What happened?" said T.K.

The old man shook his head. "We don't know. Two days ago, the pigs started dying. It's something in the water. Five people also died before we stopped drinking from the river. All the pigs are dead. Soon we will run out of food and drinking water. Praise God the lychee nuts are ripe, but we dare not eat the lotus buds from the riverbank."

Behind him his wife, short and withered, nervously fingered the crucifix around her neck. "We are so scared," she said. "What is happening?"

"I don't know," said T.K. "Where is Jintao?"

"The boy of Yong and Ming?"

T.K. nodded.

"Not here, nor far," said the old man. "He has been seen in town."

"Dean *xiānshēng*," said his wife, "even before the pigs died, people were gathering in town to protest our river farms. Now the noise is louder, and they are shouting anti-Christian slogans. Last night someone cut a barge loose; fortunately the swine clogging the river prevented it from drifting. There are rumors of a dam to be built on the Li that would flood this whole valley." She paused and glanced around the cramped cabin. A tiny coal fire glowed in the stove, under a dented copper teapot. "First they drove us here because we are Christians, and now they are trying to push us further. We are at land's end. Where shall we go?"

"They don't care about your religion," said T.K. "You could be Muslims or Kaifeng Jews for all they care. They just want the power of the river. For what I don't know, except to make money."

"Who are *they?*" asked the old man.

"Foreign and Chinese business interests, I'm sure," said T.K., "no doubt allied with local officials who control land permits. My guess is they know Beijing will resist wholesale evacuation of the valley so they're trying to manufacture an environmental crisis, and blame you. If it gives Beijing some cover to repress Christians who have too many children, all the better."

"May the Lord help us," said the woman, clutching her crucifix.

T.K. scoffed. "Why not point a loaded gun to your head, then ask God to save your life as you pull the trigger?"

"Only God has the power," said the woman.

"You have the power," said T.K. "Beijing can't just ignore you. Organize your own protest—march into town, demand an investigation of the poisoned river, spread the word on Sina Weibo. Do you have friends in town?"

"Some."

"Organize them on your side; get them to join in demanding accountability, and press them to engage their neighbors. A dam will impact the whole region, not just the river communities. Threaten to refuse factory jobs. Meanwhile find someone with electricity and a freezer; take a pig's liver and freeze it, so it can be tested later. You must be able to prove your farming practices did not cause this poison. You should also organize an immediate cleanup of the river. Get these pigs out of the water and buried far from shore; find someone in town with an earth mover who can do it quickly. Once you have done all this, then you can pray that God will honor your efforts. But you can't just sit here on your boats, surrounded by stinking gore, and pray for God to fix everything."

"He's right," said the old man to his wife.

"Look," said T.K. "I will help you, in part because you can help me."

"How?"

"Your protest should divert the police long enough for me to find Jintao. We must begin tomorrow morning."

"There is no time to waste," said the old man. "Let us go and gather the people."

The pair descended the gangplank and started down the row of barges. They had walked but a few yards when a dark figure emerged from the shadows and focused a bright flashlight in T.K.'s eyes.

"Mr. Dean," said a voice behind the light.

It was Sub-chief Fang Dazhu.

"So the American cowboy has returned!" said Dazhu. "May I see your passport please?"

***

T.K. stared at the spinning Lazy Susan and tried to guess where the bacon would land. In front of the pig Fang Dazhu? How appropriate! The massive swine Nong Ning? *Perfect!* But no, it stopped in front of himself.

"Mr. Dean, you have not sampled the *làròu*," said Ning, pointing his greasy chopsticks at the bacon platter. "Did the sight of all those rotting swine kill your appetite for cold home-cured bacon?"

Fang Dazhu laughed, then jabbed his chopsticks into the pink fleshy mass, scooping a pile onto T.K.'s plate. "You know they don't cure bacon like this in Beijing; I believe its taste owes to the particular diet of pigs raised along the Li." He studied T.K.'s impassive face, searching vainly for clues. "Don't worry cowboy, these pigs were butchered weeks ago."

T.K. locked eyes with Dazhu, glanced at Ning, then downed a mouthful of slippery cold bacon. He was hungry—there had been only rice in the jail cell overnight, with no *báijiǔ*—and the Lazy Susan had few offerings. The river crisis had ruined lunch business at the Longzhou Restaurant, which specialized in local cuisine, most of it plucked from the Li. Unavailable were the famous river snails stuffed with chilies and mint, the traditional sourfish soup, the sweet lotus seed pudding, anything with fresh pork. Even the classic *zhè ěrgēn* salad was missing in action, although the crunchy water roots actually came from inland rice paddies and not the river; no one wanted to eat anything associated with water. T.K. watched the wheel of fortune spin around and around: rice tofu, rice noodles with pickled beans, spicy lamb...rice tofu, rice noodles with pickled beans, spicy lamb...rice tofu, rice noodles with...

"More tea, Mr. Dean?"

T.K. snapped out of his trance and tapped two fingers on the table, the universal Chinese sign for more tea. Ning tipped the pot over his cup, but only a dribble followed. *"Waitress!"* he yelled. "More tea!"

"Also some *báijiǔ*, please," added T.K.

"Never mind that," said Ning to the waitress, laughing. "I remind you that you are in custody, Mr. Dean. Travelling in China without proper documents is a serious offense, even for our own citizens. We are an orderly country, and you have demonstrated a troubling lack of respect for order, and for our laws."

"A nation of laws—now that's progress," said T.K.

Outside the restaurant rose a din from the street—first a murmur, building slowly like a distant wave, then cresting at the corner of Gua Hua Street as a clamor of voices and a beating of boots on pavement, the kind of sound that bodes poorly for indecision in its path and makes you wish you were on a horse above it all, getting away.

"It sounds like Parliament is in session out there," said T.K.

"The people are expressing their right to be heard," said Ning. "It seems the river folk have fouled our precious waterway, which is against the law."

As the sound of the rabble grew closer, Dazhu shifted nervously in his chair. T.K. reached across to the Lazy Susan with his chopsticks and scooped a portion of rice noodles onto his plate, noticing Dazhu's 05 Chinese Police Revolver holstered on his right hip. It was standard issue, the world's only nine-millimeter six-shooter, as opposed to the standard clip-loading twelve-round model used in the West. Chinese cops never used to carry guns. What for? Citizens have no guns to point at them, and the Party bosses in Zhongnanhai were never too comfortable with anyone, even police, packing heat; arming the Red Army was a necessary evil. But then mobs of Uighurs started attacking government offices in Xinjiang Region, which got Beijing thinking about giving guns to police. Then came several high-profile cases of knife-wielding maniacs; cops were seen on TV clumsily subduing them with batons and fire extinguishers. When Beijing finally decided to weaponize the police, leaders commissioned a Barney Fife model that would be simple to use and, holding only six bullets, cause the least amount of mayhem, as well as be able to fire both rubber and real bullets. Zhongnanhai ordered twice as many rubber bullets as lead. Of course, guns that are easy for cops to use are also easy for citizens to use—which is how a policeman was wounded with Officer Yun Jian's gun down by the barge, and how Chen Yong died.

"Which Chinese law calls for taking criminal suspects out to lunch?" T.K. asked Ning while noting that Dazhu's revolver was buckled into the holster and had no quick-release latch. He wondered if the bastard was packing rubber or lead.

"It's not every day we are graced by the presence of a renowned Western author," said Ning. "Perhaps you will regale us with some of your literary exploits—starting with the events in Amsterdam last month."

"A book talk?" he said. "Ask my agent."

"Alas I understand she is indisposed," said Ning.

"Where is the boy?"

"Jintao? A good worker although his head is so often in the clouds, or in a book—is there a difference? I think maybe he takes after you."

"He's not in school?"

"He is old enough to learn a trade."

"And I assume by that you mean a factory job."

"On the contrary," said Ning, "the boy has demonstrated an aptitude for the arts. His master says he will one day be a top ivory carver."

T.K. set down his chopsticks and stared at Ning.

"I have always found it a paradox," Ning continued, caressing his chopsticks. "Ivory is so brittle, so hard, yet those called to interpret its form are as a rule most tender." He impaled a cube of tofu on a chopstick and snapped it onto his tongue like a frog to a fly. "The artistic sensitivity is a puzzle, don't you think?" he asked, smacking his lips and jabbing his chopsticks in the direction of T.K. An errant fleck of tofu landed on the table. "But then as an artist yourself perhaps you understand. Are you tender, Mr. Dean, or brittle?"

"In what season?" said T.K.

"Season?"

"In the spring when the sap runs, the maple shoots are soft. Over the summer they harden, and by fall they are brittle as kindling."

"And in the winter they die!" said Ning.

"No," said T.K. "Only the leaves die. The branches go dormant until the rising sap wakes them in spring. That's the sugar. Adrenaline for a tree."

"So you think of yourself as a tree?"

"When I think of trees I think of myself."

The noise outside had grown and now the crowd was passing directly in front of the restaurant. It was odd, thought Ning. There was an urgency in the trembling step of the marchers and yet at the same time a faint but noticeable anxiety, like the pall before a rain that warns too late of the deluge. These did not seem like the protesters he had organized in his courtyard.

Ning turned to Dazhu and said, "What is going on?"

The waitress returned with a large pot of smoky puer tea.

"Those are river folk," said the officer.

Ning dropped his chopsticks. "What are they doing?"

T.K. reached for the teapot.

"I shall investigate," said Dazhu, rising. But before he could get on his feet, T.K. hurled the teapot straight into his lumpy face. The heavy porcelain urn exploded across Dazhu's forehead. It shattered the bridge of his nose and released cascades of scalding White Dragon Whiskers green puer (2005 harvest, buds only) down his pockmarked cheeks, soon to be blooming with second-degree blisters. Whether his shrieks of agony ensued more from the ruined facial bones or from the searing burns could be argued, but neither Ning, for whom the violence had triggered a transient ischemic stroke, nor T.K., who was out the door and lost in the crowd before Dazhu could un-holster his revolver, was in a place to debate.

Chapter Thirty-Three

"*Jintao! Pay attention!*"

Yishan cracked his switch on the workbench next to Jintao, startling the youngster. Jintao worked hard and always tried to concentrate, but there was so much on his mind, and drilling the ivory buttons was getting boring. He wished he could start carving figures in larger pieces, but the buttons were popular and Jintao was fast. Soon, thought the boy, he would ask the master if he could try something more difficult, but not yet. Yesterday while daydreaming he had slipped with the drill and cut his finger, which was bad enough—but unfortunately the button shattered, earning him a crack of the switch on his shoulder. Yishan was careful never to hit the apprentices on their hands.

Jintao hated the master's switch, but there were worse jobs in China for a twelve-year-old. At least Yishan let him borrow books from his collection, mostly art books about the history of ivory carving. His favorite was a large picture book about a relief sculpture called the Barberini Ivory that was carved in Constantinople in the sixth century. It was so valuable that even rich people couldn't own it; it had to be kept behind glass in a famous museum in France. The Barberini was a flat panel about a foot wide and tall—it must have been carved from a huge elephant tusk—divided into five rectangles. The large center frame depicted a triumphal emperor, probably Justinian, on horseback. The unknown artist was so masterful that the horse seemed to be leaping right out of the frame. Behind the emperor was a barbarian who looked sort of like a Chinese peasant, thought Jintao; he was stooping in deference to the ruler, who must have just conquered his land. Above was the figure of Christ surrounded by the sun, moon and a star, which made Jintao sad because it reminded him of his father, who was always praying to Jesus and all it got him was dead. Maybe he was with Jesus up in the stars now.

The book said the Barberini artist was suggesting that Christ ruled the cosmos, and the emperor ruled on Earth. Jintao thought it would be better to rule on Earth because the cosmos seemed cold and had no shattering malt toffee sticks. At any rate his favorite part of the Barberini Ivory was the bottom panel, which depicted a procession of exotic bare-chested barbarians in feathered headdresses, offering tribute to the emperor. They marched with a tiger and a small elephant, and one of them carried a massive ivory tusk over his shoulder. Jintao thought he would love to go to Africa and see elephants someday.

In a dusty glass case next to his workbench the master kept a small personal collection of scrimshaw, which he told Jintao was sort of like ivory but carved from whale and walrus teeth. Yishan said the pieces were created by men who went to sea in ships to catch the whales, from a place called New England more than a hundred years ago. Jintao knew that was where Mr. Dean was from, and whenever he looked at the scrimshaw he thought of Mr. Dean and wondered whatever happened to him and if he was drunk. At sea these sailors would pass the time by drinking, and by carving pictures of whales and ships into whale teeth. Yishan also had a book with pictures of scrimshaw owned by a famous American named *Kěnnídí*. The book was in English and Jintao couldn't read much of it, but Yishan told him that this man *Kěnnídí* was not himself a whaler but in fact a U.S. president from long ago—from the time of Mao and the great famine, which you weren't allowed to talk about. Sometimes Yishan let the boy hold the heavy pieces of scrimshaw, and Jintao loved to run his fingers over the etched designs of sailing ships, slanted into the wind before a rolling sea and bound for distant lands. In his mind he recited Psalm 107, which his mother had taught him:

They that go down to the sea in ships, that do business in great waters;

These see the works of the Lord, and his wonders in the deep.

For he commandeth, and raiseth the stormy wind, which lifteth up the waves thereof.

They mount up to the heaven, they go down again to the depths: their soul is melted because of trouble.

They reel to and fro, and stagger like a drunken man, and are at their wit's end.

Jintao wondered if his mother had journeyed on a ship like their barge to get wherever she was, and if she was at her wit's end. He wondered if she was in the cosmos.

Then they cry unto the Lord in their trouble, and he bringeth them out of their distresses.

The door to the shop flew open. The noise of the street crowd rushed in like kindled fire, and the silhouette of a tall man blocked the bright sun. *"Where is he?"*

At the strange Westerner's demand, the apprentices dropped their tools and swiveled on their stools. Jintao had to look twice to believe it. "Mr. Dean!"

When T.K. saw the boy he rushed into the narrow studio. "Jintao!"

Yishan leaned over the baby elephant tusk he was carving for Nong Ning and threw up his hands. "Please, you can't come in here!" he sputtered, thrusting out the pig whiskers on his chin and hoping vainly to maintain authority over his business. T.K. shoved him roughly aside; the old artist pinwheeled backward and collapsed into the scrimshaw case, sending whale teeth tumbling over his head. A male sperm whale can reach a length of more than sixty feet and weigh more than fifty tons; its cone-shaped teeth are partially hollow but still weigh more than two pounds each. So when a nineteenth-century sperm whale tooth (engraved with a scene of said whale battling a giant squid) landed squarely on Yishan's age-creased forehead, it knocked him out cold.

Jintao ran to T.K. and buried his head in his chest. "Where is my mother?"

"She's safe. She's fine. Let's go."

"Shame on you, Mr. Dean."

T.K. spun around to the voice at the door. Fang Dazhu was so inherently grotesque that his bloodied, shattered brow and blistered face barely registered as a depreciation. And yet he was visibly unhappy. "You left the table before finishing your tea."

"It spilled," said T.K. in Zhuang, loosening his hold on Jintao. Dazhu was pointing his 05 Chinese Police Revolver, which was not loaded with rubber bullets, between T.K.'s eyes. Jintao, sensing this was about something bigger than his own problems and stirred by the new information about his mother, dashed for the rear door. Dazhu pivoted and fired high, shattering a fluorescent shop light which rained white phosphor dust onto Jintao's head.

"Jintao! Stop!" said T.K.

"Excellent advice, Mr. Dean," said Dazhu. "Because if either of you move I shall be compelled to shoot you both."

T.K. narrowed his eyes at Dazhu. He could smell the *báijiǔ* on his breath, and exuding from his pores, as the officer moved closer. He looked at the barrel of the gun and smelled whiskey on his father's breath, in the sugar bush. "You would shoot your own son?" said T.K.

Jintao's jaw went slack and he felt dizzy. "Son?" he said.

Dazhu laughed. "I already have my one child." He drew back the hammer on his revolver.

"Easy with your weapon, Officer Fang."

Nong Ning, recovered from his transient ischemic stroke (which he did not even realize he'd had) but heaving in short breath, pushed himself arduously through the door. "We want them alive." Dazhu scowled but shifted the barrel of his gun from Jintao back to T.K.

Jintao was scared. His master was out cold on the floor; Mr. Dean was staring at a gun held by an angry policeman with a melted face who could not possibly be his father, couldn't be true; and the important fat man, Mr. Nong, who always came into the shop to look after his ivory, what did he want? *Where is my mother?* Before anyone could react he bolted out the back door and into the rancid perfume of the Xiu Shui alley. Beyond the gate, in the main road, hundreds of river folk were jamming the street and pushing toward the center of town; others were joining the march.

Lunch in the shop was always hurried and today had been no different. The workers and Yishan had gathered on the floor around a common rice pot with their smooth ivory chopsticks and shoveled down a few mouthfuls along with steamed radish greens and chicken feet prepared by Yishan's wife. There was a pot of rare Jun Shan yellow tea, which was the master's favorite. And then Yishan would crack his switch against the floor, point to the Confucian wall banner *("It does not matter how slowly you go so long as you do not stop!")* and it was back to work; Yishan's wife would clean up later. But later hadn't come yet, and the ivory chopstick that fell from the lap of a journeyman carver from Shanghai named Min Lisan was still in the middle of the floor. Dazhu was already having a hard time seeing through the caked blood around his eyes, and the fractures on the bridge of his nose had impaired his balance. So when he stepped on the chopstick and it rolled under his shoe, it might as well have been a log floating down the Androscoggin River, except Dazhu was no lumberjack and they weren't in New England.

As he reeled backwards, his revolver flew from his hand and spun across the floor, releasing the cocked hammer and sending a nine-millimeter bullet into a hundred-liter air compressor, which exploded and blew out the clerestory windows on the north side. The carvers scrambled for cover under their workbenches. T.K. lunged for the door but Dazhu was up in seconds, blocking him. As the pair locked and struggled—Ning cowering in a corner—T.K. grabbed the closest weapon he could find, which happened to be the baby elephant tusk, still being sculpted in the orgy scene from *The Carnal Prayer Mat*.

As blunt instruments go, baby elephant tusks are not very blunt; the young animals have not had time to smooth the points of their ivory by rubbing on trees. So when T.K. thrust the ivory into Dazhu's abdomen it pierced clothing, flesh, spleen and stomach as smoothly as a lance, and came straight out the back. Dazhu staggered back wordlessly and collapsed on top of the rice pot, which was still half full. The gore-flecked tip of the tusk, protruding from his lower back, sank into the still warm rice. Ning gasped and wondered, first, if Dazhu would survive, and second, if the ivory could be saved. Maybe the other way around. He instinctively shot a glance at Yishan, hoping the artist's demeanor could foretell the fate of his masterful carving. But Yishan, who had come to after the explosion, was still shaking the daze out of his head.

Exsanguination is the technical term for bleeding to death, and although it figures in the medical lexicon it more typically applies to hog butchering. The goal is to quickly and cleanly cut the jugular veins and carotid arteries to induce rapid blood loss and brain death of the pig within ten seconds. Abdominal stab wounds are far less efficient, in pigs or humans, and the extra time required to drain blood from the gut is thought to cause considerable anxiety. Fortunately for Fang Dazhu, his alcohol-ravaged liver impeded clotting, and within twenty seconds he had lost half his blood into the rice pot. His long-suffering wife was a widow in thirty.

Chapter Thirty-Four

Traffic Control Officer Yun Jian heard the shot and then the explosion. He was beat-walking outside the ivory shop, having been pulled off traffic duty to monitor the march as it threaded through town. Soon the marchers would meet up with the straw crowd whipped up by Nong Ning—the ones who believed the river people were fouling the water with their pigs. That could spell more trouble than either side had bargained for. The pig farmers were repellent, he thought—even worse than Japanese, or his father. On the plus side lots of them, especially those Christians, were at least Han Chinese and not filthy Zhuang like the sub-chief who probably never bathed. Anyway, the march was certainly more exciting than speed traps. Still it made him nervous—not because he had no gun to assert authority (Dazhu had confiscated his revolver after the accident at the barge, and he was secretly happy not to have it) but because he felt a vague insecurity that authority itself had arrived at some brink and that the old authority of police and Party and his father was rapidly fading before some powerful new force that he didn't understand but which he suspected had something to do with computers and smartphones and didn't take orders from the Ministry of Security. What made computers any different from books, which had existed in China since the Tang Dynasty? What kind of power could flow from a bunch of silicon chips? His brother worked at an electronics factory in Dongguan where they made the printed circuit boards for Samsung phones, and he never spoke of any esoteric forces.

Jian shrugged off his concerns and pushed warily through the front door of the ivory shop. Inside, through the smoke and debris of the blast, was the dead sub-chief, skewered and served on a bed of sticky rice and coagulated blood. The workers were still hiding under their benches. Yishan, groggy and nursing a bruise on his forehead the color of an aubergine, could only point to the rear door, which had just slid shut.

"Get them!" said Ning, bent over in a corner, panting and heaving.

Jian hurried across the shop floor and out the back. Down the alley, running toward the street, was a tall man and a small boy who looked like his head had been dusted in flour. *"Stop!"* he yelled.

The running man clutched the boy by the collar, halted and turned around slowly.

Could it be? thought Jian. Yes—it was the homosexual Westerner with the earring! In his hand was an 05 Chinese Police Revolver. And the boy was the one who lived on the barge, the son of the dead man who'd grabbed his revolver. His head filled with the explosion of firecrackers, and images flashed of the terrible night on the river, and he knew his future had arrived.

"No, you stop," said T.K. raising the gun to Jian's head. They were not eight yards apart; he recognized the cop from his speeding arrest last winter. *"You again?"*

"You again!" said Jian.

"Where is your gun?" said T.K.

"I have none," said Jian.

The street beyond the alley was now empty: the protest had moved on toward the government offices yet it seemed, even from a distance, louder.

Theodore Kincaid Dean was *concerned* about the recent turn of events. Yes, he was concerned that he had impaled a state security officer with an elephant tusk—an officer who happened to be Jintao's biological father—severely complicating his already tenuous status in China. He wouldn't kill another cop (before leaving the shop he had removed the remaining four rounds in Dazhu's revolver and re-loaded with the sub-chief's rubber bullets) but he was willing to inflict a few kinetic-impact contusions if necessary. What concerned him possibly more was the tenor of the crowd in the streets; he knew the Christian pig farmers too well; they would take up their cause with religious fervor, but they would take their cues from Jesus; they were followers, and nobody on the river was a leader even by default, much less by design. Even bad leaders can be better than chaos, he thought, and so it was in this context that he mourned, marginally, the death of Fang Dazhu. Because right now he felt strongly that the local police would be far more dangerous and unpredictable without Fang than with him. And then there was that fat Party man, Nong Ning: what the fuck was he up to?

"Ever been to Vietnam?" said T.K.

Yun Jian shook his head no. Those Vietnamese were such curs.

"Well you're going now," said T.K. "Where's your patrol car?"

"At the station. Across the street."

T.K. waved the gun in the direction of the street. "Let's go."

***

Sun Ju was so anxious that she nearly spilled hot aster tea over her husband. Ning lay panting on the settee, barely waving a paper fan before his face. His generic prickliness in the afternoon heat had been compounded by the day's events, and he felt feverish. As he fanned himself, flaps of blubber like raw squid dangled from his arm and oscillated back and forth, generating more breeze than the fan itself.

"This will cool your inner heat," Ju said gently, passing the medicinal cup. Something needed to be said, she was sure, but what? *I told you so?* Shaming was unlikely to end well, and would not change anything. Surely Ning's own personal shame was greater than any guilt she could pile on. Better to let him stew, and rest. So instead she simply said, "I'm so sorry."

"Sorry?" said Ning. "Sorry for what? My inner heat? It is nothing but the gears in my brain turning. Dear wife, know that I shall be cooler tomorrow, and our fortunes vastly improved!"

Ju flinched instinctively. "But today you might have died...like Fang Dazhu!"

"He is no great loss, although the manner of his demise would grieve an ivory connoisseur."

"I respectfully disagree, honorable husband. You know I carried no charitable feelings toward that awful man, but he brought discipline to the police, and discipline is what we need right now. The people are angry and divided; more than ten thousand have gathered so far. Can you not hear the din even as you lie here? The town is standing at the precipice."

Ning snorted and lobbed his empty teacup to the foot of the settee. "Has it ever occurred to you dear wife that the view from the precipice is always magnificent?"

"I fear tonight's darkness," she said.

"Bùyì!" said Ning. "I'll not hear a word of it! Land disputes, pollution, these concerns have inspired so many protests and are in fact the two chief causes of unrest in our country, but to what end? Another day, another irate mob."

"Still," said Ju, "this is the first time we have witnessed irate mobs protesting land grabs and pollution at once. Together these issues press down with great weight—perhaps more weight than even Beijing can bear."

"On the contrary," said Ning, "the combination of factors works brilliantly in our favor."

"Forgive me honorable husband. I am not clever like yourself."

"I shall merely call off my protesters, then take credit with Beijing for diffusing a potentially dangerous situation. By tomorrow my status in the Party will have risen tenfold. Now what would your beloved Confucius say to that?"

"He would say *Be not ashamed of mistakes and thus make them crimes.*"

"Speaking of crimes, we must find that American who wears the earring."

***

Yun Jian drove the Ford patrol car. The smell of body odor and cigarettes sickened T.K., sitting next to Jian with the gun. Jintao was in back. As they swung onto Pantao Road, T.K. glanced at the Family Planning Clinic, thought of Ming and nearly puked. That would be a nice way to cap his Guangxi crime spree: puke in a police car. He took a warm swig of *báijiǔ*, which calmed his stomach and forced some presence of mind. That's what the booze gave him, presence of mind, yet he had to admit it was his own sober presence of mind that caused him to retrieve Dazhu's hip flask off his gored body in the first place. Could there be mindfulness without alcohol? In death perhaps, but then Dazhu wasn't saying anything. He pushed the thought out of his mind. "Take the Jimacun Road," said T.K., waving the revolver forward.

Two turns, then out the west gate and the road started to wrap around karst peaks. Beyond the third curve, a camouflage Shaanxi Baoji Wolf 4x4 armored personnel carrier was parked in the middle of the road, red lights flashing. A People's Liberation Army gunner at the roof turret was sighting his 12.7-millimeter cannon right down the center stripe. Yun Jian stopped his cruiser and backed into a side street.

"Not good," he said to T.K. "Either they are looking for you, or stopping marchers, or both."

"You're a cop," said T.K. "Go through it."

Jian laughed and pointed at the menacing green personnel carrier. "PLA doesn't take orders from traffic cops. That Wolf holds six troops armed with Bullpups, plus the gunner, and a commandant who has heard every bullshit story from here to Tibet. Not to be fucked with."

He was right and T.K. knew it. He also knew that unlike Chinese cops, PLA infantry knew how to use their weapons.

"Every road out of town will be same," said Jian.

Right again, thought T.K. "Fuck."

"*The caves,*" said Jintao from the back seat. Jian and T.K. turned to him. "We can use the caves. At least, I think that would work. But I don't think I know the way."

"I do," said Jian. "The boy is right. I can show you the way out. We need a lantern, some food and water."

T.K. stared at Jian, wondering whether to trust him, wondering what choice he had. He pulled some blood-stained banknotes from his jacket—all the money he had found on

Dazhu—and handed a wad of yuan to Jintao. "Get out at that shop on the left, buy a lantern and some kerosene. Then cross over to the food stand and get some rice noodles and dumplings and as many water bottles as you can carry. Don't speak to anyone on the street. We'll wait here. Do you have your identity card?"

"Yes."

"Good boy."

Yun Jian drove the trio to the tomb site where T.K. had entered the caves with Ming. "You know about this?" said T.K.

"I am the only cop in Guangxi who knows about this." Then he thrust open the door and led the way.

At the underground pool by the graves of Ming's babies, T.K. paused. "Wait," he said. Jian stopped and turned. Bats carved parabolas above, casting abstract shadows from the lantern across the blue water of the pool. T.K. looked into the small piles of stones and the two crosses. Life is short for everyone, he thought. When you boiled it right down, his life or Ming's or Fang Dazhu's wasn't that much longer than a baby's, or for that matter a fetus. It was all just a medley, wasn't it? Never a complete song. It began in a dark place and ended in one, and just kept going. And in that moment he understood that everyone was in the cave and there was no exit, and he had no concerns.

"Did you know them?" Jintao was looking at the graves.

"I did not," said T.K. "But I do now."

"You don't need to point that gun at me," said Yun Jian. "It could go off. It scares me. You have the lantern; how far can I go without you?"

"I don't know. How good are your eyes?"

"There is no light in the caves. A gazelle could not see."

T.K. held up the lantern and stared into Jian's eyes. He always thought he could read a liar by his eyes, until the day he found out Meg had been lying to him about her lovers for two and a half years. Looking straight into his eyes and lying. He'd never guessed. About that one thing he'd never been *concerned*. But Jian looked just vulnerable enough to be telling the truth. T.K. laughed. "Rubber bullets," he said, and he stuffed the gun into his jacket pocket. From his other pocket he pulled a handful of nine-millimeter shells.

"Real bullets," he said, and he tossed them into the pool.

They walked, and crawled, for hours through the caves until finally they came to a large amphitheater, its ceiling so high that the lantern could not illuminate it. They could only make out the tips of stalactites oozing blue-green calcium. Unseen fruit bats shrieked high above. Jian stopped and looked around at the edges of the light. He pulled out a pack of Hongtashans. "I used to hide from my father in here. Cigarette?"

"I don't smoke. Where do you hide from him now?"

"He died," said Jian.

"Fathers always do," said T.K. "Where do you hide from him now?"

Jian's eyes narrowed. "I can't."

"I know."

"What about *my* father?" said Jintao. "How could that policeman be my father? I don't even know him."

"Lots of people don't know their fathers," said T.K. "It's better you don't."

Yun Jian's jaw slackened. "Fang Dazhu was the boy's father? Not the man on the barge?" That would make the boy half filthy Zhuang.

"Chen Yong was my father!" said Jintao. "My father is dead!"

"Your father is dead, Jintao. But your mother is alive and waiting for you in New York." He tipped the lantern. "We're getting low on kerosene. Let's go."

After another twenty minutes of sliding through a narrow gore in the rock, a vague perception of grey light began to infiltrate the crevice. It grew brighter until finally a brilliant gash of late afternoon sun appeared, as if through gilded clouds in a Baroque painting. "This is it," said Jian. "The exit on the other side of the sound and light show. Now what?"

"Now you flag down a vehicle for us," said T.K. "Commandeer a car. Official police business."

"No good," said Jian. "They will expand the roadblocks. Widen the net. You need to stay on the paddy trails. You need a moto. You need to ride by night."

Chapter Thirty-Five

Cai Shenfu, a tailor with a small shop in the center of town, twisted the throttle of his 1969 Vespa Sprint Veloce and leaned into a curve. He loved riding home to his rice-farming village, found the speed and fresh air exhilarating after twelve hours behind a sewing machine. His father was a tailor and had taught him how to fix sewing machines, which were not all that different from scooters, he thought. So when the clutch failed on his Vespa, he figured out how he could make a new clutch plate out of a coffee can. Okay, he got some advice from a friend who worked at the scooter shop, but he did the job himself. He also added some custom chrome trim and wing badges, along with a sweet two-tone yellow-and-black paint job. He had to make a lot of shirts to pay for the paint job, but it was worth it to have such a unique bike that attracted many women. He hoped someday to meet a wife on his scooter, and ride her around town every evening. When you sit at a sewing machine all day, you have time to dream. Besides, it was a small dream. Even a poor tailor deserves a scooter and a nice wife, right?

He was thinking about the wife that wasn't when he came around the bend and saw a policeman standing in the middle of the road with his arm extended in the universal *halt* pose. *What the fuck is this?* He pulled over and shut off the scooter.

"Does your headlamp work?" said Yun Jian.

"Certainly," said Shenfu. He switched it on.

"I need your machine. Police business."

"What? You want to take my scooter? How will I get home?"

"Where are you going?"

"Jimacun. I live there."

"Wait here," said Jian. He moved back to the center of the road. In a moment a black Great Wall Motors diesel SUV hummed like a bee around the bend. When it pulled to a stop, a middle-aged man in a polo shirt and wraparound shades rolled down the tinted electric window. A blast of frigid air escaped.

"Good afternoon," said Jian.

The man nodded stiffly.

"Police business. You must give this man a ride to Jimacun."

The driver grimaced and nodded without speaking or even looking at Cai Shenfu. Yun Jian waved at the tailor. "Get in," he said. Shenfu climbed into the passenger seat and the SUV sped off.

After a few minutes Jian flagged down a maroon Hongqi sedan going the other way, back towards town, and got in, without saying goodbye to T.K. and Jintao.

T.K. examined the bright yellow scooter with contempt. It looked like a bumblebee. "My lucky day," he said. "A fucking bodge job."

"What does that mean?" said Jintao. "Will it run?"

"Anybody's guess. For a while, maybe." He moved the bike off the road, out of sight behind a mulberry tree, and the pair waited an hour for darkness to fall. Soon they were off, spinning through the narrow lanes between rice paddies, southwest toward the border. Their remaining cash amounted to four hundred eighty-two and a half yuan, about eighty dollars, that T.K. had extracted from Fang Dazhu's wallet. They'd need all of that for fuel and the smartphone that would guide them to the GPS points on the frontier; there was no money for food or bottled water, but they could find fruit along the way. No time to eat anyway. Besides, thought T.K., most people in the world live in a constant state of low-level hunger. He considered that the concept of readily available food is a recent Western development and actually quite foreign to all life on earth. And if the natural condition of life is hunger, what is the ability to stuff something in your mouth at the first hint of famish but unnatural? To stay hungry is to stay engaged. To stay hungry is to be alive.

And so they lived. By day they huddled in temple shrines along paddies and streams, taking turns sleeping after rehearsing the GPS coordinates of the escape route; T.K. wanted to make sure Jintao had memorized the way. He wrote out the directions in Chinese, simplified and traditional, as well as in English and

French and made Jintao recite them again and again until he had memorized the instructions. "That night on the barge," said T.K. "I promised you we would read together again."

At night they rode on, avoiding larger towns with traffic lights and cops. On the scooter Jintao linked his arms tightly around T.K. and pressed his head into his back. They bought fuel from roadside vendors who stored gas in plastic 7-Up bottles. Luckily Cai Shenfu had kept a bottle of oil under the seat, to mix with the gas. Without oil the tiny two-stroke piston would seize up after a few hours. Occasionally they found papayas and custard apples and mulberries in trees along the trails and streams. And at dawn after the third night they reached the edge of Nongchao and the frontier. The karst peaks down here by Vietnam were smoother, worn down and round like giant river rocks, and the slopes were terraced in tea plantations, with the better leaves growing at higher elevations. T.K. pulled off the road and into the cover of some waist-high tea bushes. The bright leaves were glazed in morning dew that bent tiny rainbows from the low sun. It was going to be a hot day, thought T.K. A faded sign painted on the side of a tea-drying barn said *"Visitez Vietnam 4 km."*

Courage, thought T.K. in French. *Courage*.

He handed the cash to Jintao. "Walk into town and get a Xiaomi smartphone," he told the boy. "Buy a hundred megs of data; should be plenty. Make sure it's activated and the battery's charged, then turn it off and come back. Any leftover money, buy food. Don't talk to anyone on the street, and stay away from the border checkpoint; that's where the trucks will be lined up. They'll be looking for us at all the crossings. Got it?"

"*Dui!*" said the boy.

"Jintao!" said T.K.

Jintao stopped and turned back.

"Recite those map coordinates while you walk."

He smiled and saluted, then said in English: "Yes *sir*!"

"And Jintao...Turn off the phone."

He watched the boy skip down the road into town. *Sir,* he thought. He called me *sir.* T.K. had always called his own dad "sir." *Own dad?* He wasn't Jintao's dad! He felt like a dad. He tried on *Dad* for size, and decided he liked it. He liked it better than *Sir.*

Jintao had enough money for the phone, a handful of pork-stuffed fried tofu balls (the pigs down here were safe) and, for dessert, two shattering malt toffee sticks—one for him and one for Mr. Dean. Being twelve years old, he ate his shattering malt toffee stick first, as he strolled back out of town. He could see the trucks idling at the border. The idea of an official customs checkpoint fascinated him. He had only ever heard of people smuggling things across the border—elephant tusks for ivory, pangolin scales for women's health, bear bile for hangovers, heroin for drug addicts. He never imagined some people could cross the border legally, under the eye of authorities. Certainly not him and Mr. Dean. He was thinking about all this activity at the border and how they were going to cross when he forgot to turn off the phone.

***

Nong Ning was feeling much better today. Despite the searing heat, which by mid-morning was radiating in dreamlike waves off the rice paddies, he felt fresh and rejuvenated, as if he had spent a week at the Longshen Hot Springs where Japanese tourists dipped in pools and let thousands of tiny doctor fish suck on their skin. In truth his calm was the contentment of the oblivious, for it is a fact that those who worry are those who know more and thus have more to worry about. Ning made it a lifelong habit not to know any more than he needed to know. It was his own form of meditation, not that he put much stock in conventional Buddhist traditions of mindfulness. In fact he didn't know enough about Buddhism, which he associated with the nagging of Sun Ju, to know when he was being mindful, even when he clearly was. Could one be mindlessly mindful? He was not mindful enough to know.

A perfect example: He had not the slightest clue how the American could be tracked from his electronic devices, other than a vague understanding that satellites were involved. He was content to believe that it took an American to find an American and that the American George Chambers, the furtive business associate of Hu Tianhua, knew very well how it all worked. This Chambers fellow—a curious sort. Ning felt certain he was a spy and should be handled like a hot wok. Not that it made any difference to him. He assumed all businessmen were on some level in bed with their governments, which after all made business possible. How else could it be?

At any rate when the inept traffic officer Yun Jian resurfaced and admitted, after a beating and some chili oil in his eyes (for Ning was a traditionalist who believed in the old-school, low-tech methods), that the American and the boy were bound for Vietnam on a scooter, Nong Ning drove himself and a state security officer from Nanning down to the border immediately, taking up rooms in the Good Citizen Villa in Shuolong. The hotel, on a muddy bend along the Guichin Boundary River, was a dump with clogged toilets and mosquitoes in the rooms; it's a wonder every guest didn't check out with malaria. But the food was surprisingly good, and it was the nearest large frontier town west of Nanning; likely Mr. Dean would try to cross somewhere near here. The security officer, a slate-faced man in his thirties named Duan Kanghu who scowled and had greasy hair, said that the American named Chambers was trying to locate Mr. Dean electronically. It had something to do with triangulation and involved U.S. military technology developed to locate Osama bin Laden, using servers that had stored previous information about Mr. Dean's movements; with the existing data any new device in his possession, even a laptop with Wi-Fi, could be identified and then tracked—but it did require the suspect to be in possession of a device that was turned on, at least for a few minutes.

They assumed Mr. Dean would buy a phone at or near the border, and they assumed he would have the boy make the actual purchase. Jintao would need to show his Resident Identity Card, which the server bots would detect when it was scanned; there was no need to stake out every mobile shop along the Guangxi-Cao Bằng border. It wasn't rocket science, explained the security officer Duan Kanghu. Actually it sort of was.

***

Sun Ju was deeply concerned. She did not share her husband's bliss in the face of the unknown. And there was so much unknown! The death of Fang Dazhu frightened her; so did the long-haired American (she saw his image on the news after his arrest) who killed him. Why were the pigs dying? Surely not from their own shit. Shit was undeniably bad and could make you sick, but not that sick that fast, she thought. And the lotus buds, and the small fish? The Christian rabble in town had been calmed when Ning called off his hired protesters—he made sure the news cameras from Beijing captured him "leading" the masses away from the town square—but how long would that last? Anyone in China who could afford it was buying property overseas, and sending their children to study in America. Even President Xi can read English! Was the "real Revolution," as Ning called it, nigh? Of course no one would say so in public. No one believed in the current system, but everyone believed that everyone else believed. When people stopped believing in other people's beliefs, who knew what could happen?

Sun Ju no longer knew what she believed, except she believed that both Confucius and Siddhartha, who lived at the same time, were real men, not gods, and as such achieved liberation that any human could attain. The paths to liberation were many and on this day, in her husband's absence, Ju was on a path across the rice paddies to the Water Temple beyond the city gates. Her intention was to burn a joss stick at the feet of the Buddha. Along the way she encountered a small boy with a pus-engorged stye in one eye and a large green cricket tied to a red thread he had unraveled from his sock. The bug was perched on his forearm. One end of the thread was wrapped around his index finger, and when the cricked jumped off his arm, the thread tightened like a dog leash and jerked the insect backwards, to the delight of the child.

Ju pulled a ten-yuan note from her scarf and handed it to the boy. "Will you sell me your cricket?" she said.

The boy beamed and untied the thread from his finger, handing her the bug and the leash. He crammed the banknote in a dirty pocket and skipped off down the paddy trail toward the village sticky bun shop. Ju carefully wrapped the cricket in her scarf.

At the temple she bought a joss stick from the keeper, lit the end and set the smoking bundle beneath the wooden icon of Siddhartha. She kneeled, bowed, and unwrapped her scarf on the dusty stone floor. The cricket hopped across the Buddha's toes, trailing the red thread.

***

"Jintao! You left the phone on!"

Jintao—cheeks swelled with two pork-stuffed fried tofu balls—choked, then flinched reflexively, as if expecting the crack of a cane. *"Duìbuqǐ!* I'm so sorry! I...was walking and eating and I was so hungry and..."

"Never mind," said T.K. "Let's go." He straddled the Vespa, jumped on the kickstart and twisted the throttle. The motor sputtered and protested, then let out a guilty roar. It was never clear if a hard-starting Vespa was the fault of a dirty idle circuit or just the fault of being Italian. At home he would clean out the carb and curse the Italians, taking care of both possibilities; today he could only pray. Jintao climbed on and they spun off down the Yan Bian Highway.

T.K. saw the black Audi S6 in his mirror about three clicks south of Nongchao. It was gaining fast: no laws of fluid mechanics could favor a three-port 1969 Sprint Veloce over a twenty-first century German saloon car with a V8 twin turbo power plant, even one technically made by Volkswagen. If only he could get to the turnoff, then he could swing onto paddy trails that with luck would take them down to the boundary river in the general area of the coordinate. Fuck, what if the river was fenced everywhere except the exact longitude Kathleen had given? *One-oh-six and forty-something east, right?* The Chinese would never be so arbitrary. But the Vinks? Who the fuck knew? *"Those bastards were some crazy,"* his dad used to say. "I mean stone-cold whacked. Pretty much anyone who got outta there alive learnt how to shoot first and ask questions later—and a body what says different is a fuckin' liar with a capital *F*. A course the Frogs didn't shoot at all; they ran asshole to starboard when they saw 'em comin'—*beaucoup dinky dau*, they called 'em. 'Taint no Canuck neither—'at's genuine Froggie for loony-tunes."

T.K. twisted a handful of throttle and bowed low over the headset. "Lean in!" he told Jintao above the scream of the engine. The boy buried his head in the small of T.K.'s back and locked arms around his waist. Kugong...Kugong...*where the fuck was Kugong?* There it was—just ahead, a cluster of dusty grey tile roofs, and beyond it the fork toward the river. The Audi was less than a thousand feet back; in his mirror T.K. could make out the four-ring logo on the grille, which gaped like a shark's mouth. He was back on his bicycle in Vermont, escaping the bad guys, but now he could feel the heat of the wok under him, felt like he was circling the rim. He let up on the throttle and then pulled it wide open, hoping to squeeze a few more drops of vapor from the carb. But instead of gaining, the bike whined and stalled, then jolted forward, then paused and jumped again.

"Fuck!" He knew it.

The clutch on a classic Vespa is a series of thin steel plates sandwiched between cork plates inside a cylinder, all of it held tightly together by springs and set into motion by the engine crankshaft. The pressure of the cork against the metal keeps the whole thing spinning and the rear axle turning—until the rider engages the clutch lever, which compresses the springs and pulls the steel plates away from the cork, releasing the axle. As technology goes it's fairly simple—the operative principle is friction—but a lot can go wrong when metal starts spinning and rubbing.

Clutches eventually fail, because all metal under tensile and cyclic stress is subject to fatigue. Some metals, like the forged steel used to make woks and clutch plates, can withstand extreme amounts of heat and stress before suffering fatigue. Others can't, like the cheap tin-plated steel used to make coffee cans. Which is why the Piaggio Motor Company of Pontedera, Italy never made clutch plates out of coffee cans. T.K. felt the scooter, which at that moment represented his life, spinning more slowly, down to the bottom of the red hot wok.

He downshifted for torque. The turnoff was dead ahead; he could see rice beyond, and a few trails into the paddies. *C'mon...c'mon you motherfucker!* He slid into the turnoff, past the settlement, left at the fork. Nothing but rice now. The clutch was slipping badly. He took the first trail, which disappeared down a far slope that he figured must drop down to the river. The bike was heaving and lunging; Jintao squeezed tight and tried to keep his head from whipping back and forth as the scooter heaved. The Audi skidded to a halt at the trail head. Duan Kanghu hopped out of the passenger seat, revolver drawn, and climbed on top of the car. Nong Ning clambered slowly from behind the wheel and stood by the road, squinting. The Vespa moaned and clanked, then seized. It was over.

"We're bailing!" said T.K. as he slid the moto onto its side. "Get into the rice, stay low!" Jintao dove into the shallow water. T.K. ducked behind the leg cowl of the fallen bike and pulled out Dazhu's pistol. He drew a bead on the largest target he could find, which happened to be Nong Ning's chest. He fired—direct hit—but the rubber bullet bounced harmlessly off the commissioner's impenetrable layer of blubber. The fat man kept walking, like Godzilla in the face of miniature mortar rounds. Still, the shot impressed Kanghu, who didn't realize T.K. had a gun and didn't know the bullets were rubber. He crab-crawled hastily off the car like Jackie in Dallas, then took cover behind the hood. Ning hit the dirt as Kanghu opened fire.

T.K. took out the Xiaomi and checked his coordinates. *East one-oh-six, forty-one point three. Fucking close enough! The river's gotta be due north maybe two hundred meters. Please God no fence.* "Jintao, move down the hill! Stay in the paddies."

"Dui!" The boy sloshed forward as T.K. exchanged fire with the cop, who had a poor line of sight from the road and was starting down the trail. "I'm right behind you," he said to Jintao, and soon the pair were scudding like water rats through the rice toward the river. When they got to the hillside the paddies ended and the trail descended through woods. T.K. could see the glint of the river between trees.

"Let's go!" he said. "Run!" Jintao practically cartwheeled down the path as T.K. followed behind, glancing back for signs of Kanghu, who had lost sight of them. They paused at the bank, catching their breath. T.K. pointed to the far shore. *"Vietnam."* No fence on either side. No guards. He scanned the terraced hills beyond. "There's the saddle. The other side is Cốc Mán. Let's go."

His father always called Vietnam hell on earth; now he was desperately trying to get there. But as they stepped into the swirling grey water, Jintao cried. "I can't swim!"

T.K.'s jaw dropped. Kanghu appeared at the top of the hill and was starting down the slope. "Hold on to my waist," he told Jintao, and they slid into the cold water.

The current was swift and even though Jintao was small, his thrashing slowed them down. T.K. struggled to move forward. The river, placid and narrow from above, now loomed wide and dangerous. Then came the bullets. "Hold your breath!" said T.K. "We're going under!" They sank below just as Kanghu dropped his gun and dove in.

As it turned out, Kanghu was a very good swimmer. He caught up to T.K. and Jintao in the middle of the river, then pulled the boy away. T.K. turned mid-stroke, sliced deep under the surface and paddled under Kanghu, launching himself straight up into the cop's crotch. Kanghu screamed but held on tight to Jintao, who was coughing up water. "I'll drown him!" said Kanghu as T.K. surfaced. The three of them were drifting swiftly downstream toward a small falls over a boulder. "Back off or I drown him!" He placed a hand on top of Jintao's head and pushed him under.

"Stop!" said T.K. "Okay! *Stop!*"

Just then Kanghu and Jintao slid over the falls and disappeared in the froth. T.K. reached out for a half-submerged tree stump and hung above the swirl. The stump had fallen over from the Vietnam side; in moments T.K. was standing on the far shore, looking for the pair.

Two minutes later Kanghu and Jintao surfaced downstream, on the China side. Ning was waiting with Kanghu's revolver. For a minute they all just stared at each other across the water.

"We could shoot him now," said Kanghu.

"He's in Vietnam," said Ning.

"Hot pursuit," said Kanghu.

"Let him go!" T.K. shouted. "Let the boy cross and I'll swim back."

Ning laughed. "But Mr. Dean, you don't have a visa."

"I'll reapply at the consulate."

Ning laughed louder. "Okay, Mr. Dean. You swim back across and the boy can go."

"The boy can't swim. I need to come across and bring him over. Then I come back."

Ning laughed again. "Kanghu! Escort the boy across the river."

The security officer scowled.

Jintao stared at the tea plantations of Vietnam. He understood this as a bad time to daydream, but he couldn't help thinking about his mother, somewhere on the other side of that water. Then Kanghu grabbed him and waded back into the stream. On the other side, Theodore Kincaid Dean, concerned, started for the China shore.

He arrived in China before Kanghu and Jintao landed in Vietnam. "Welcome to the People's Republic, Mr. Dean," said Ning, who was holding Kanghu's gun. "Where is Inspector Fang's revolver?"

"In the river."

"I am grateful for the Central Party's wisdom in issuing rubber bullets."

"I'm grateful for your fat ass," said T.K. "I really didn't want to kill another one of you bastards."

Ning's laughter was pierced by the gurgles and cries of Jintao. Across the river, at the edge of the Vietnam shore, Kanghu was holding Jintao's head underwater. All you could see was the boy's long hair, matted and tangled like Medusa's, and his flailing arms.

"What the fuck!" said T.K. "You fucking bastard, I'll kill you!" He sprinted for the water.

"Stop!" said Ning, aiming the gun first T.K. and then Jintao. "Move and I'll kill both of you!"

"You fuckers! He's just a boy! You're drowning a boy!" He prayed Jintao could hold his breath longer...just a little longer.

Ning shifted his weight; his gout burned the soles of his feet from all the walking and standing, and his underwear was miserably twisted up his butt crack. He actually wished he could just go for a swim in the river. His cheek muscles twitched. "Let him go!"

Kanghu sneered. "What?"

"Set the boy free!" said Ning.

The cop pulled Jintao's head from the water but held him tight.

"Do you not speak Mandarin?" said Ning. *"Ràng nánhái qù!"*

"No." Methodically, as if in a trance, Kanghu forced Jintao's head under the water again.

Ning lifted the revolver to a point between Kanghu's eyes. *"Ràng nánhái qù! Xiànzài!"*

"You would shoot a national security officer?" Kanghu yelled as he struggled to hold Jintao under the water. "I have grave doubts."

"You are in Vietnam," said Ning. "Perhaps you are defecting."

Kanghu shook his head no. Jintao's arms had stopped flailing.

"You would drown the son of Inspector Fang?" said T.K.

"What?" said Kanghu.

"It is true," said Ning. "Drown the boy and bring dishonor to your family and your career."

Kanghu lifted the boy from the water and tossed him onto the bank like a netted fish. Jintao's face was blue but he coughed and drew a panting breath.

"Run!" said T.K. from across the water. "Run, Jintao! You know the way!"

Jintao retched up a plume of foul water, sighted a path through the woods and, still drooling river scum, sprinted toward the saddle between the mountains. In no time he was gone.

CHAPTER THIRTY-SIX

The execution was at dawn, but the metal door clanged open a good hour before first light spilled through the high, narrow window. The cell was clean, just large enough for a bamboo bed frame and a squat toilet, with a few square feet to move between them. The concrete block walls had been skimmed in a coat of ochre clay; a bare compact fluorescent, hanging from a short cord, had burned all night. Above it, rain fell like pebbles on the metal roof. A fly, wrongly incarcerated, circled the toilet hole in the floor. Rainfall and the drone of the fly—there was nothing else to hear. Shit was the only smell, and weight the only feeling.

"Hello Teddy."

George Chambers stepped into the cell. A guard's polished boot flashed in the jamb, and the door thudded shut. "May I sit down?"

T.K., in a clean white disposable prison jumpsuit, was on the edge of the thin tick mattress, back straight, feet on the concrete floor, eyes fixed on the opposite wall. His head was shaved. He motioned to George without eye contact, and his old friend sat down next to him and removed his straw fedora. "Where's Jintao?" said T.K. flatly.

"He's at the U.S. embassy in Hanoi," said George, eyes scanning the corners of the cell. "He's safe. Arrangements are being made to reunite him with his mother in New York. Meg has been a huge help getting them situated."

T.K. took a deep breath. *Meg.* She came through in the end. After all the lies and deceit and infidelity, what remained was the Meg he thought he knew. She was there all along. Or maybe it was like a constantly repeating tape loop that returned to the beginning when Meg was a good person, and inevitably the tape would play back the part where she lies and cheats. Not that it mattered now.

"Teddy I'm sorry. We've done everything we can."

"True that."

George frowned, regretting his own choice of words. "Unfortunately it came to light that Inspector Dazhu had slipped on a chopstick before you impaled him, which somewhat complicated the self-defense claim. And we worked hard on the foreign journalist angle. The Secretary of State flew to Beijing. With Jimmy Carter. When he realized you had the same literary agent, it was a no-brainer. But when you boil it right down, killing a defenseless police inspector in front of witnesses leaves very little room to negotiate. I mean fuck, you'd get the death penalty in half of America. I'm afraid we've run out of arguments. And time."

T.K. laughed. "*Arguments?* There were no arguments in that trial. There was a sentence, which they could have read on the first day and saved a lot of time."

"Justice is rather hurried in this country," said George.

"Reminds me of an old Yiddish story," said T.K. "A child is killed in a village. They blame an old Jew, say he was bit by a bat and has rabies, he's crazy. They lock him up and he asks to see a Jewish doctor. The doctor comes in with a flask and says, 'Can you swallow this wine?' "

" 'Of course I can,' he says, and he downs half the bottle.

" 'If you can swallow then you don't have rabies,' says the rabbi.

" 'They won't believe me,' says the old Jew.

" 'Just swallow and you will be saved.'

"So he goes into the kangaroo court and the judge says, 'Since you are a man of faith I will give Yahweh the chance to save you. I have written *guilty* and *innocent* on two pieces of paper. If you pick the right paper, you will go free by the grace of Yahweh.'

"Of course the old Jew knew the Christian judge had written *guilty* on both pieces of paper. So he grabbed one piece, crumpled it up and swallowed it. The courtroom exploded. 'Now how will we know what you have chosen?'

"The old Jew said, 'Just look at the remaining paper and you will know I swallowed the opposite.' "

George grinned and shifted on the mattress. "I'm glad you haven't lost your gallows humor."

"*Fusillade* humor," said T.K. "I am to be shot at dawn."

George checked his Rolex. "You have about forty-five minutes."

"I always thought it was a cliché. *Shot at dawn*. Didn't know it really happens."

"In China at least. Something to do with all that *fēngshui* twaddle. New beginning for the spirits, whatever."

"Spirits! I need a drink."

George withdrew a brass flask from his jacket pocket and twisted off the cap. *"A little poison now and then: that makes for pleasant dreams."*

"And much poison at the end, for a pleasant death," said T.K. "I knew I could count on you. You're a good friend, George."

"I merely know what friends are for."

T.K. tipped the flask of *báijiŭ* to his lips and gulped as from a mountain stream. "Thank you, George," he said. In seconds the bliss rose like boiling maple syrup to his brain, then sent spasms of joy down his arms and through his legs to his toes. He smiled, closed his eyes and swayed.

"George. Next time you're in the club, ask Yiqian to check his cellar for an Eighty-two Pétrus. Then order it for me. Drink it with Kathleen."

"I'll do that, Teddy. I'll do that."

T.K. took another long swig. "Leave some for me," said George, intercepting the flask and sipping.

"I have something for you to give Ming," said T.K. He retrieved the flask, then turned away from George and rummaged through the small stash of belongings the guards had let him keep. "It's my watch," he said. "The Chairman." In his hand was the Mao watch. "I know she would want it."

"I'll make sure she gets it," said George.

"Go ahead, put it on," said T.K. "I'd like for you to wear it, for now."

"I'm afraid I've already got a watch," said George, glancing at his Rolex.

"Then put in on your other wrist. That way you won't waste time looking at the wrong wrist."

George laughed and strapped on the watch. T.K. handed him the flask. He raised it in a toast and drank.

"Why do you care so much about a dam?"

George gazed up at the light bulb. "Clean power," he said, taking another swig. "The world so desperately needs it."

"*Clean power?* When did you start hugging trees? Sorry George, it smells dirty to me."

George sighed. "Bitcoin mining."

"Bitcoin *mining?* What, like digging for bitcoins? I thought it was virtual currency."

"It is virtual, but it still has to come from somewhere. Bitcoin is created—*mined,* if you will—by solving complex math problems that require massive computational power. It's all about the algorithms."

"What the fuck sense does that make?"

"Frankly none at all to you and me, or most people. It gives me a headache just thinking about it. That's why it's such a good business. At any given time there are maybe ten thousand developers around the world creating bitcoin algorithms, but nobody else in the world is paying the least attention." He paused to catch up with his eyes, still darting around the cell. "Do you see where I'm headed?"

"It's a vacuum."

"Precisely. A vacuum just waiting for capital, and sound management. But to scale it requires gigawatts of electricity—enough to power an African nation. Half the power goes to the supercomputers, the other half to cooling them down."

"The dam."

"The dam! The most economical way to cool a bitcoin mine is with cold water—water that's also being used to make the power. Right now the biggest mines are in Iceland, but they're running out of glaciers and they also retain this quaint idea that corporations and foreign governments can't lobby their legislators. We had hoped the last recession and all the bank failures up there would take care of that, but the Icelanders hold on to their dim Enlightenment fantasies of democracy."

"Which brings us to China."

"Which brings us to China. The Li is fed from high mountain springs and is surprisingly cold."

"You'll recall I swam in it."

"So you did."

"I'm guessing it's about more than cold water."

"There are colder rivers in the world. But the Chinese truly understand the importance of public and private partnerships.

Currency is too vital to be left to a bunch of open-source codeboys and Edward Snowden wannabes. Next thing you know the Russians are stealing everything. The only way to make it secure is with web tracking technology being developed by DARPA for the military. People think quantum physics is some academic circle jerk; they have no idea. We've got Structured Query Language apps based on subatomic mechanics that would blow your mind. Did you know the military can forecast the weather anywhere in the world six weeks in advance, with pinpoint accuracy? We've got search engines that make Google look like a player piano. We can track names and places all across the Dark Web, even the Deep Web. That's how we found you and Jintao so fast."

George stopped himself, exhaled and went on. "I knew a lot, but I didn't know you'd killed a police officer. I wouldn't have helped find you if I'd thought it would come to this."

T.K. shook his head in disbelief, while believing everything. "If the U.S. government cared so much about controlling currency, why didn't they nationalize the credit card industry?"

George felt relieved T.K. had changed the subject from his own capture. "A regrettable lack of foresight, and one that will not be repeated as we move into virtual currency."

"Sounds like a libertarian's worst nightmare."

"Remember when Rand Paul dropped out of the presidential race?"

"*Personal reasons,* he said."

"You could call it that. Some important people got through to his wife. Made it clear that a presidential campaign would be very bad for her husband's health. Same with Elizabeth Warren."

"She has a wife?"

George rolled his eyes. "She's off the menu."

"The menu?"

"The official choices. The menu. Democracy works fine as long as nobody tries to order off the menu."

"If voting changed anything, they'd make it illegal."

"Emma Goldman," said George. "The anarchists are usually right."

The tumbling rain on the roof tailed off, and the cell grew uncomfortably quiet. "Supposed to clear up later," George said.

Teddy smiled. "Where's the server?"

"The server?"

"When you located me in Nongchao. I mean, I was pretty careful to hide my cyber tracks until Jintao left the phone on. Had to be a server somewhere, right?"

George chuckled. "Teddy, you're the server."

***

The door slid open and a stone-faced guard appeared.

"He's drunk," said George, now wearing his hat, in broken Mandarin. "You'll have to prop him up." The guard looked suspiciously at T.K., who was slumped on the mattress, eyes rolling.

George stood and buried his hands in the pockets of his suit jacket. His own eyes had stopped rotating around the room, his gaze fixed on the floor. A single tear ran down his left cheek. "Goodbye old friend."

In the courtyard of the prison, five soldiers with QBZ Bullpups stood in a line facing a bank of hay bales. The cracked pavement was studded with potholes, now filled with rainwater. The dawn sky was dull grey. Two guards dragged the prisoner around the puddles to a spot in front of the hay, then flopped him into a molded plastic lawn chair. His hands were bound behind his back with a zip-tie. A guard stepped forward and fit a black hood over his slumping head, tightening a cinch around his collar. He was blind drunk and blindfolded, and in the darkness and haze of his final minutes, sound carried like over water. He vaguely heard rifles being shouldered. The commandant barked an order. He could feel his watch ticking on his wrist. Chairman Mao was smiling and waving. It was 6:18.

***

T.K. Dean checked his Rolex and noted the time: 6:18. He was in his Mercedes S-Class, or rather George's, not three miles from the prison when he heard the guns go off. He tried not to think about his best friend, tried not to imagine the string against his neck and the hood that must have smelled like rotting leaves, and he was back in the sugar bush in November on his bicycle, looking for his father at dawn. Up over the last knoll to the big old tree, the one that was so huge and so full of sap that it could take four taps every spring. And finally it took his father, swinging stiffly from a rope on a low branch.

When you boiled it right down, it was pretty easy. The plastic earplug case with the Rohypnols made a passable suppository—as in, not terribly painful passing either way. In fact he was about to take the pills himself when George walked in. Slipping them into the flask after taking his own swig was the only option, right? After that, swapping clothes and grabbing George's Rolex and diplomatic passport was simple. The hardest part was shaving poor George's head; his own razor had been confiscated of course, but he knew George always carried a Swiss pocket knife since their dig days at Psalmodi. It wasn't the ideal shaving tool and he had to lubricate his friend's skull with fecal water from the toilet hole, but George was in no condition to mind the dozen or so nicks and cuts, and the risk of infection was, in the global topography of George's current problems, localized. When it was over he looked close enough like Prisoner Dean to satisfy a Chinese firing squad. The Dimmer Twins. We all look alike to them, right? There was a reason T.K. never went to journalism school, and this was it: they didn't teach the basics.

T.K. had popped the fuse for the car's built-in nav system, which could almost certainly be tracked. As he drove south by southwest, he opened George's passport and checked the photo, then glanced at himself in the rearview mirror. *Close enough,* he thought. Close enough for the Vinks at the frontier post. *Close only counts in horseshoes and government work!* That was his father, annoyed whenever Teddy did something not quite good enough. Well wasn't that perfect? Wasn't he doing government work, in fact on official business for the government of the United States? *Close enough.*

The dull sky broke open and the road rose high toward the blue horizon. In the distance stubborn fog blanketed the valley of the Guichin Boundary River. Beyond, in the amber wash of first light, the green terraced tea plantations of Vietnam rose like Aztec temples, and T.K. Dean had no concerns. He thought of Ming, and everything was bright.

Epilogue

"Like a spring torrent after a long, cold winter, the United States has moved with crescendo strength during recent years to provide assistance for population and family planning throughout the developing world."
—Reimert Ravenholt, director of USAID Office of Population, 1973

After his escape, T.K. was *concerned* that he could be charged in America with contributing to the death of a U.S. consular officer—albeit in a tragic case of mistaken identity. Fortunately the Chinese government, always anxious to save face, said they could not verify the whereabouts of George Chambers. His car was found abandoned in Hanoi; surely his disappearance was an issue for Vietnamese authorities. To complete the face saving story, China reported that T.K. had been pardoned at the last minute and released at

the Vietnam border. The paperwork documenting this pardon
was, of course, in order and signed by Nong Ning.

T.K., Jintao and Ming reunited in New York. After a few
weeks getting settled, the newlyweds left Jintao with Meg
and took off for a honeymoon in Amsterdam (Ming's idea,
something about closure), where they rented bicycles and drank
beer, which didn't count. The first stop on the first day was the
Central Library, where T.K. retrieved his book and notes from
the server where he had uploaded them months earlier. Then
they went to the police and, with Ming's testimony, had Vasily
Blokov arrested on charges of human trafficking.

The book was published to acclaim and became a bestseller
in the U.S. and Europe. The only negative review appeared
in *Crown* magazine, where Garamond Rockwell labelled the
author "a hackeyed Orwellian wannabe with barely passing
grades from the Hemingway school of hard-drinking foreign
correspondence." The book spurred international outrage over
Chinese birth control, but no one in China could read it.

Until Richard Cerf remembered he had his old frat brother
Hu Tianhua's mobile number. With the help of Kathleen,
who had moved home to Australia, T.K. was able to hack into
Tianhua's emails. There they learned how Tianhua had bribed
a water quality laboratory to conceal evidence that the Li River
contamination was caused by a toxic nicotine spill from his
factory—supported by lab tests of a frozen pig's liver saved
by the river people. That could have landed the businessman
in front of a Chinese firing squad on corruption charges.

Presented with this evidence, Tianhua, always the pragmatist, was able to see how publishing the book in China could be very good for his personal health. And so it was done. Beijing was outraged and cancelled all his state publishing contracts, but the book business was a tiny drop in Tianhua's ocean of interests, and compared to execution its loss was a small price to pay.

In appreciation for his quick-witted handling of the citizen protest in town and for preventing more serious violence, Nong Ning was promoted to district party commissioner. Two weeks later he suffered a fatal heart attack while trying to hoist himself out of his Audi in the parking lot of the ivory carving workshop. It was a hot day, and his silk underwear had been bothering him. His widow Sun Ju renounced all material possessions, including her husband's priceless ivory collection, and joined the Bikkhuni order of Buddhist nuns.

The wife of the sub-chief Fang Dazhu was so elated at her husband's death (she had been planning to stab him with her scissors during his next haircut) and so grateful for his pension that she secured a resident visa for Macau, where she opened a beauty spa in a former Portuguese military barracks that had been converted into a boutique hotel.

Traffic Control Officer Yun Jian resigned from the police force and became a sightseeing guide, leading groups of Japanese tourists through the caves of Guangxi. The Japanese were good tippers by Asian standards. They weren't so bad after all, he decided.

The dam was never built.

Jintao excelled at a Manhattan charter high school. His favorite subject was chemistry.

The Mandarin version of T.K.'s book caused a sensation in China, but by then the country had stopped the practice of forced abortions. Chinese women were having fewer babies anyway. Maybe because so many people had moved to the cities and didn't need kids to tend a farm; maybe it was something in the air, or the water.

About the author

Max Alexander is the author of *Bright Lights, No City*, a memoir about starting a business in Africa with his brother, which the *Wall Street Journal* called one of the funniest business books ever written. His memoir of moving from New York to Maine, *Man Bites Log,* was rated one of the best nature books of the year by *USA Today*. He also co-wrote *Call Me American* with Somali immigrant Abdi Nor Iftin; that book, based on a one-hour segment of *This American Life*, was praised in the *New York Times* and the *New Yorker*. Alexander, a former senior editor of *People* magazine and executive editor of *Variety*, lives in Rome. In 2020 he was a contestant on *MasterChef Italia* and was named "the most famous American in Italy" by the Milan newspaper *Corriere della Sera*. *The Bodge Job* is his first novel.